Malcolm Richards crafts s... edge of your seat. He is the... mystery novels, including the TT Blake Hollow series, the award-nominated Devil's Cove trilogy, and the Emily Swanson series. Many of his books are set in Cornwall, where he was born and raised.

Before becoming a full-time writer, he worked for several years in the special education sector, teaching and supporting children with complex needs. After living in London for two decades, he has now settled in the Somerset countryside with his partner and their pets.

Visit the author's website: www.malcolmrichardsauthor.com

BOOKS BY MALCOLM RICHARDS

PI BLAKE HOLLOW BOOK TWO

Malcolm Richards

DOWN IN THE BLOOD

StormHouse

First published in 2021 by Storm House Books

ISBN 978-1-914452-11-6

www.stormhousebooks.com

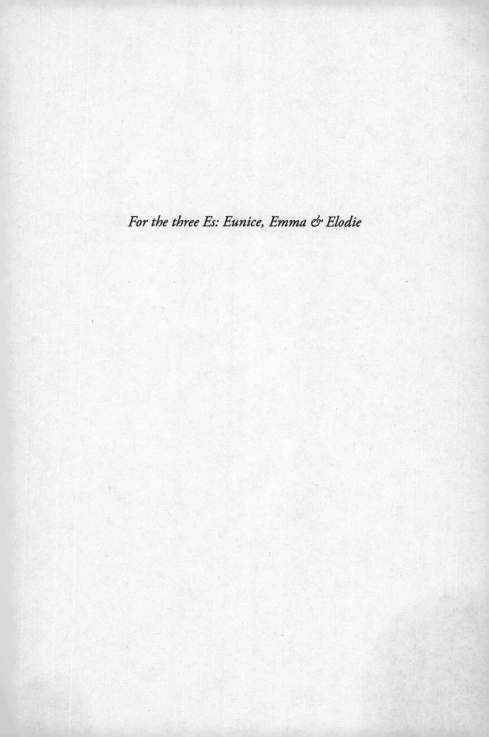

For the three Es: Eunice, Emma & Elodie

1

Blake Hollow stood in front of the bay windows, watching thick clouds heavy with rain roll in from the English Channel. Three floors below to her right, the Prince of Wales Pier was cold and lonely looking, its rows of Cornish flags and colourful bunting flapping above empty benches and Victorian lamp posts. The grey-green water of Falmouth inner harbour was restless, swelling and frothing, toying with the fishing boats and visiting yachts moored on its surface.

A storm was coming. Blake felt its approach in the jagged scar over her right shoulder and the deep ache in the joint within. A year ago, her entire arm had been rendered useless when the blade of a butcher's knife had snapped her collarbone and sliced through her brachial plexus. After months of intense physiotherapy, she had regained much of her arm's movement and feeling. The numbness that remained in her thumb and index finger, and the ache in her shoulder were a constant burden, but she gladly accepted them in exchange for stopping a psychopath in his tracks.

Blake turned away from the window to stare at her office.

She had just enough room for a desk, a filing cabinet, and a coat stand in the corner. The door to the left led to a cramped kitchenette and the door to the right, a broom cupboard containing a toilet. The centre door in the far wall had a smoked glass window with the words 'Hollow Investigations' stencilled across the middle.

She had been renting the office for a year and had only got around to decorating it three months ago. The Magnolia paint did little to disguise the dilapidation. The crack that ran from the centre of the ceiling down to the corner had grown exponentially, and since winter had returned, spots of mildew were slowly multiplying on the windowsill. Which was more than her client list.

Returning to Cornwall was always going to be a challenge. Even though there was less competition, the pool of people requiring the services of a private investigator was a drop of water compared to Manchester. She had taken on a few jobs for a criminal defence lawyer who occasionally needed help uncovering case-related evidence, and she had a semi-regular insurance fraud investigation gig. Together they covered the bills but not much more. Any other money was earned from walk-ins off the street, people looking to find missing loved ones or to expose cheating lovers. It wasn't much of a living, and the positive reputation that Blake had earned in Manchester was apparently nontransferable. As for preventing a serial killer from taking more lives right here on local soil, well, that had earned her mild acclaim. The Cornish were a tough lot to please, but Blake understood why—she was one of them.

Turning back to the window, she pressed her forehead against the glass and peered down at the swelling seawater below, then shifted her gaze across the harbour towards rolling green hills and the isolated village of Flushing, which was best reached by ferry. The ache in her shoulder intensified as the first specks of rain spattered the windowpane.

A loud buzz shattered the silence. Blake flinched. She had been meaning to replace the intercom tone to something less traumatic. One day she might even get around to it. Crossing the room, she pressed the speaker button.

"Hello?" Her voice was husky from hours of silence.

A male voice, deep and uncertain, crackled through the speaker. "I'm looking for Blake Hollow? I'm not sure if I pressed the right number."

"You did. Come on up. Third floor, first door on your right."

Blake hit the door release button, then hurried over to her desk and sat down. She felt a surge of excitement, as she always did on the occasions when synchronicity occurred. She made a mental note to complain about a lack of work more often.

Her desk was immaculately tidy. As the dull thud of the man's feet on the stairs reached Blake's ears, she rifled through her desk drawer, removed a bunch of papers, and spread them out in front of her. A busy desk gave the impression of being in demand.

The footsteps grew louder. A tall shadow appeared at the frosted glass, followed by a soft knocking. Blake got up and opened the door.

The man was six feet tall and looked to be in his early thirties. His hair was dark, his eyes the colour of cherry wood and filled with such sadness that Blake found herself taking a slow step back. Despite the grief emanating from the man, his crisp pale blue shirt and navy chinos were crease-free and professionally tailored.

He stood for a moment, a frown rippling his brow. "Blake Hollow?" he asked.

Blake forced a smile, even though she hadn't felt like smiling for a long time. "Let me guess, you were expecting a man?"

"I apologise. It was the name."

"I get that a lot."

She stepped to one side, then shook his hand as he introduced himself.

"Campbell Green. I was hoping to talk to you about—well, it's about my fiancée."

Blake invited him to sit down. It was possible this was another case of a cheating spouse, but she didn't think so. The sadness in his eyes suggested something much worse. She slipped into her own chair and placed her hands on the armrests. The rain outside grew heavier.

"What can I do for you, Mr Green?" she asked.

"Please, call me Campbell." His eyes were flooded with sudden pain, and he turned his head for a moment to stare out the window. He swallowed once, then twice. "I'm sorry. This is difficult for me."

"Take your time. Can I get you something to drink?"

Campbell Green shook his head. The fingers of his right hand twisted the silver band on his left index finger back and forth.

"Two months ago was my wedding day," he began. "My fiancée, Kerenza, we were meant to be getting married at Saltwater House, her family home in Frenchman's Creek. It's a grand old building. Or it used to be. It's been in the Trezise family for generations. Have you heard of them?"

"I don't think so. Should I have?"

Green stared blankly at her. "I suppose not. Anyway, the

guests were all there, the string quartet was playing, and we were all waiting for the bride to make her grand entrance. Ten minutes passed. Then twenty. Some of the guests started to whisper. Kerenza's family seemed unbothered. But I was getting nervous, convincing myself that she had succumbed to last-minute jitters. To be honest, I think her family was hoping that she had.

"They had never approved of our relationship. The only reason we were getting married at all was because Kerenza had threatened to estrange herself from them if they continued to make things difficult. Her father reluctantly conceded. He even offered to pay for the wedding on the conditions that we married on the family grounds and I agreed to a prenuptial contract stating that I would get nothing from Kerenza's share of the family fortune if she were to die first, or if we were ever to divorce."

Blake arched an eyebrow. "And you signed the contract?"

"Yes, I did. I loved her," Green said. He paused, taking a moment to temper his grief. "Originally, the ceremony was to take place inside the house, with the reception to be held in the old ballroom, but a week before the wedding Kerenza's father decided that we were to have an outdoor wedding with a marquee on the lawn. Kerenza was upset and accused him of changing the plans out of spite. There was some truth in that, but I believe his decision had more to do with the state the house had fallen into."

Blake had more questions, but she waited for her visitor to continue.

"Kerenza was thirty-three years old and still lived at home. Her bedroom was at the rear of the house on the second floor and overlooked the lawn. Anyway, the music was coming to a crescendo and my nerves were completely shot, so I was about to send someone to look for her. But then there she was, dressed in her wedding gown and looking like something out of a fairy tale. Except she was up on her balcony instead of down on the lawn, where we were all waiting. Where *I* was waiting.

"Everyone went quiet. I remember thinking: what the hell is she doing? And then suddenly, she hitched up her wedding dress and climbed onto the balcony balustrade. She stood there for a moment, fighting for balance, as people gasped and someone, I can't remember who, started running towards the house. I was completely paralysed. I couldn't even breathe. And then . . . Kerenza jumped." Campbell's voice cracked. Tears spilled down his face. "She jumped and she didn't even look at me."

Blake remained silent, feeling his pain and horror.

"They say she was killed instantly. Snapped her neck in two when she hit the steps. Everyone was screaming, running to her. But I didn't. I just stood there, not believing my eyes. I mean, would you?"

"I'm so sorry for your loss." Blake slid a box of tissues towards him. He took one and dabbed his eyes. "I'm sorry to ask, but do you know why she did it?"

"No, I don't. And I don't understand because until that day she seemed perfectly happy. There were no signs of depression or anxiety. Nothing seemed to be bothering her. I mean, there was tension with her father, but it wasn't enough to make her do *that*."

"Why didn't he want her to marry you?"

"Because he hired me to manage his accounts, not to fall in love with his daughter. And he wasn't keen on having his lineage soiled by someone of lesser breeding."

"What about the rest of Kerenza's family? Do they have any idea why she took her own life?"

"You're asking the wrong person."

Blake frowned.

"They won't talk to me," Campbell explained. "It's like they think it's my fault Kerenza is gone." He leaned forward, deadly serious. "That's why I'm here. Because one of them must know something, and I want you to find out what it is. That family had a hold on Kerenza. Their claws sunk right into her flesh. She told me that as much as she loved them, she couldn't wait to get away from that house. She said she couldn't breathe in there. So you see, it doesn't make sense. What she did doesn't add up."

Blake was quiet as she contemplated Campbell Green's tragic story. It truly was awful yet intriguing enough to have her curiosity well and truly piqued. But was it a case she should take on?

Across the desk, Campbell sensed her hesitation. "I know it's an unusual request. I know I'm asking a lot, but Kerenza and I, we had a whole life planned together. Our wedding was meant to be day one. We were talking about having children within the next few years, maybe travelling first. She wanted to see Cambodia, Thailand, go to all the places her father had never allowed her to go. Does that sound like someone who would jump off a balcony in front of the people who loved her, without a care of what it would do to them? To me?"

The truth was that many people who took their own lives worked hard at the pretence of living a happy, normal existence. Pretending to make plans. Pretending everything was fine. Until they couldn't take it anymore. But it did strike Blake as odd that the one person who should have known Kerenza was in trouble hadn't noticed what was really going on beneath the surface.

"Mr Green," she said.

Campbell held up his hands. "Please. Before you turn me down, let me tell you what that family did to me. After Kerenza's body was released by the coroner, they took her back to Salt-water House and buried her in the family plot. But they didn't tell me. They buried the woman I loved and refused to let me say goodbye to her. Now they won't even let me past the gates. What kind of monsters are these people?"

Pity swelled in Blake's throat. And now she was more intrigued than ever. Saltwater House. It sounded old and grand. A family burial plot on the grounds insinuated wealth and a rich history, neither of which came without controversy and questionable choices.

"If the Trezise family members are as hostile and close-knit as you say, what makes you think they'll allow a stranger like me into their home to rifle through their drawers and their deepest, darkest secrets?"

"Oh, I don't. But that's what you're good at, isn't it? Digging up people's secrets whether they want you to or not?"

"You make what I do sound sleazy."

"That wasn't my intention. Anyway, that family isn't as close-knit as they sound. Some of them positively hate each other. Maybe that's how you do it: talk to the right one and find a way in."

"Have you contacted the police?" Blake asked.

"For what? To complain they won't let me trespass on their property? To accuse them of killing Kerenza when we all saw her jump?"

"What about Kerenza's friends outside of the family? Have you talked to them?"

"She didn't have any, or at least none she ever mentioned or invited to the wedding."

"But she must have gone to school. What about university friends?"

"I know she studied Art History at Oxford years ago," Campbell said. "But she had to drop out early to help care for her younger siblings after their mother died. She never talked to me about those days, and she certainly never mentioned any friends from that time. Before that she was home-schooled."

"What about a career?"

"The Trezise family are Old Money, Ms Hollow. They don't need careers." Lines creased Campbell's brow as he clasped his hands together. "The thing about Kerenza is that she lived an incredibly sheltered life, rarely leaving Saltwater House. When we met and fell in love, it was like watching a butterfly emerge from its chrysalis. I'm not saying I set Kerenza free, because God knows I didn't. But she saw an opportunity to create her own path away from her family, where she could be anything she wanted to be. All she had to do was take my hand and walk out of Saltwater House together. But she didn't. Something or someone stopped her." Campbell reached out a hand then withdrew it. "Please Ms Hollow. Not knowing is destroying me. Could you at least try?"

Blake fixed her gaze on her desk. Of course she could try, but that didn't mean she would find anything. Cases like this, when there was little evidence and a multitude of hurdles, were always the most intriguing. But they were also the easiest to fail. And Blake hated failing. It wasn't good for her reputation or her pride. Yet turning down the opportunity of money right now seemed just as foolish as saying yes.

She looked up again and saw the desperation in Campbell Green's pleading eyes.

"I have two conditions," she said, watching relief wash over her new client. "First, that you have a clear understanding that I may not find the answers you're looking for, especially if the family is unwilling to cooperate. Second, I will be paid in full, regardless of the outcome. Time is money with or without answers."

"Of course. Even just a hint at why Kerenza did what she did will be worth every penny."

"Then I'll do my best to help you. But first, you need to help me."

Campbell leaned forward, nodding emphatically. "Whatever you need."

"Good. Then tell me everything you know about the Trezise family, starting with Kerenza. And don't leave out any detail, no matter how insignificant it may seem."

As Campbell Green talked and Blake took notes, the rainfall became more urgent. In the distance, thunder rolled across the sky, drawing ever closer.

2

HELFORD RIVER WAS a large estuary running into the English Channel that lay between the western tip of Falmouth Bay and the eastern edge of the Lizard Peninsula. A popular tourist destination, the river was known for its scenic beauty, marine ecology, and conservation programmes. With its shoreline stretching across thirty miles there was much to explore, including its seven creeks, the most famous being Frenchman's Creek, popularised by Daphne du Maurier's eponymous novel.

It was beside this creek that Saltwater House stood, where Kerenza Trezise had jumped to her death on her wedding day.

With a few hours of daylight left, Blake had decided to pay a visit to the Trezise family home. It was premature to be conducting a field trip; usually she would begin by immersing herself in research, in this case getting to know the various family members and their individual histories. But the circumstances of Kerenza's death had piqued her curiosity.

A young woman taking her own life was tragic enough, but to do it in front of her entire family, including the man she was about to marry? It felt vindictive. Or delusional. After all, no one really knew if victims of suicide lost their sense of reality before deciding to end it all, or if their minds were never clearer. Blake supposed it was a question one could only truly answer by doing.

Saltwater House was a forty-five-minute drive from Blake's office in Falmouth, along rain-soaked country roads flanked by wild hedgerows and fallow fields, and through villages of old stone cottages with Cornish palms standing in water-logged gardens. As the windscreen wipers sliced through the rain, Blake thought about Campbell Green's sad story. She knew intimately the pain of losing someone close, and the anguish of spending years wondering if you could have done anything to prevent it. What she didn't yet know was if she could supply the answers Campbell was so desperate to hear.

All she knew about Kerenza Trezise so far was that she had been thirty-five years old, born into wealth, and except for briefly studying History of Art at Oxford University, had lived a highly sheltered life at Saltwater House until the day she died. Campbell and Kerenza hadn't even lived together, which was unusual in modern Western culture, and which made Blake wonder if the pair had even slept together.

As for the other family members, Campbell had provided a brief overview. Griffin Trezise, sixty-seven, was Kerenza's father and the head of the family. According to Campbell, he was the epitome of the fervent patriarch, emotionally unavailable to his children, yet keeping a tight rein on their affairs from the confines of his study. Kerenza's mother, Olivia Trezise, had died twenty years ago from pneumonia. Also deceased was the second eldest of the children, Aidan Trezise, who had been killed in a boating accident three years ago while holidaying in Portugal. According to Campbell, he had been estranged from the family at the time due to a bitter fight with his father for reasons unknown.

Next was Abigail Trezise, thirty-two, who was cold and aloof, preferring the company of plants to that of her family. A keen botanist, she spent much of her time in the orangery at Saltwater House.

Finally, came the youngest of the siblings, twins Jack and Tegen Trezise, seventeen. The offspring of Griffin Trezise's short-lived second marriage, Jack was angry and volatile, while Tegen was kind-natured if overly naive. Their mother, Genevieve Trezise, had died during childbirth.

The road narrowed into a single lane that coiled through the rolling landscape, surprisingly flat in places, the sky huge and thunderous above. Then it narrowed again, until it was just a thin boot lace of ancient tarmac filled with cracks and potholes, bordered by tall trees with bare branches that knotted together. There were no more towns or villages, and no more vehicles.

Blake drove in silence, the rain growing heavier as she thought about the Trezise family. She had always imagined the wealthy to be constantly globe-trotting and living lives of hedonistic luxury, while hosting the occasional charity fund-raiser to balance the moral books. But from what Campbell had described, the Trezises rarely left Saltwater House and did their utmost to stay out of the limelight. Perhaps they had seen their fair share of tragedy without unduly inviting in more.

The lane suddenly twisted. The trees on Blake's right parted to reveal an expanse of water in the near distance. Helford River. Then the lane was passing a meadow of wild grass before diving into a thick wood of towering pine trees. Blake slowed the car to a halt.

The way forward was blocked by tall, imposing gates fashioned from wrought iron bars with spear-like tips. Switching off the engine, Blake unbuckled her seatbelt and pulled on her raincoat, flipping the hood over her head. Her boots splashed in rain puddles as she climbed out and peered at the gates, noting the peeling black paintwork. Beyond, the track continued before curving to the right and vanishing behind the stone wall perimeter that snaked through the woodland on both sides.

Blake stepped closer, her gaze fixed on a marble plaque attached to the left gate pillar. It was scratched and weathered, but she could just make out the name etched into the stone: Saltwater House.

Beneath the plaque was a buzzer. She pressed it then stepped back and shivered in the cold, wondering why anyone would choose to live somewhere so remote. The intercom speaker crackled, and she heard the voice of a middle-aged sounding woman with a heavy Cornish accent. "Yes? What do you want?"

Spotting the small security camera perched on top of the pillar, Blake put on her best smile. "Good afternoon. My name is Blake Hollow. I would very much like to talk to the head of the household, Griffin Trezise."

"Mr Trezise isn't expecting anyone. We don't get visitors out here. Certainly not ones in cars like that."

Blake ignored the insult as she removed her wallet from her jeans pocket, flipped it open, and held up her ID card to the camera. The woman on the intercom had to be the family's housekeeper, Violet Bodily. Campbell had warned Blake about her. Fiercely loyal and wary of strangers, she would be a tough nut to crack.

"I'm a private investigator," she said, still smiling politely. "I'd like to talk to Mr Trezise about his daughter, Kerenza. It's important."

"A private investigator? Is this some sort of joke?"

"I can assure you it's not."

"Who hired you?"

Campbell had been right. Trying to get past Violet Bodily was like trying to get past MI5. "I'm afraid I can't tell you that. Perhaps if you could fetch Mr Trezise I can ask —"

"Fetch?" The woman's voice jumped half an octave. "I'm not a dog, Miss Hollow, and I certainly don't do tricks, not even for so-called private investigators."

"That wasn't what —"

"Mr Trezise is a busy man who is still grieving the loss of his daughter. He's not going to talk to the likes of you about private family business, no matter who hired you. So, please leave."

The intercom speaker crackled once, then was silent. Blake stood with the rain drumming on her coat. She was unsurprised by the reception but impressed by the woman's ferocity. At least she now knew that the Trezise family did not suffer fools gladly, especially with the formidable Violet Bodily guarding them. Fortunately, Blake could be just as formidable when it came to patience and persistence.

She glanced up at the security camera then returned to her car, giving it a gentle pat before climbing inside and starting the engine. She slowly reversed back down the lane with her eyes glued to the rear-view mirror. Rounding the bend, and satisfied she was no longer in the camera's view, she manoeuvred the car off the track and parked at the edge of the tree line. Just because she had been denied entry to Saltwater House didn't mean she couldn't take a closer look. Besides, she hated a wasted journey.

The woodland floor squelched beneath her feet as she crept between the trees. Thunder rumbled directly overhead. Reaching the perimeter wall, Blake walked alongside it, heading away from the gates and security camera before slowing to a halt. The wall was six feet tall and constructed of fieldstone. Despite the rain, the individual stones made it climbable.

Getting a foothold, Blake hoisted herself up and peered over the top. Clusters of pine trees blocked her view. Jumping back down, she moved further along, then pulled herself up again, only to find yet more trees. The Trezise family clearly valued their privacy. Short of vaulting over the wall and trespassing, she needed to find another way to get past those wrought iron gates.

More thunder rolled across the sky. The wind changed direction, slapping her face with rain. She was about to jump down and return to her car when she detected sudden movement ahead of her and to the right.

A teenage girl, no older than sixteen or seventeen, was wandering through the trees. She wore no coat, only a sleeveless white dress that was now sodden and soiled at the hem. Her long hair was plastered to her face and back, but she appeared untroubled by the cold and barely flinched at another crack of thunder. In her left hand, she held what looked like a black pouch made of leather. In her right was a long wooden staff. As she walked, her lips noiselessly moving, she tucked the staff under her arm, dipped her right hand into the pouch, and scattered its contents in the air.

Blake watched bursts of red dust plume like fireworks before getting swept away by the wind and rain.

From somewhere in the near distance, a woman's voice began to call.

"Tegen! It's pouring down! Where are you?"

The teenager froze, her hand clutching a fist of the mysterious powder. She turned a half circle, away from Blake, and heaved her shoulders up and down.

The voice called again. "Tegen, come back inside! You're going to catch your death!"

The young woman stamped her foot and threw more red dust in the air. Then she was on the move, stomping through the trees. Suddenly she stopped dead, the wooden staff hovering inches from the ground. Her shoulders tensed and her head tipped up, like a hare catching the scent of a fox. Slowly, she peered back over her shoulder and stared at the perimeter wall.

Blake had already dropped down into a crouch and was pressing her back against the stonework. She held her breath and listened for approaching footsteps. But all she heard was Tegen Trezise humming a strange and mysterious tune that got lost in the rain as she returned to Saltwater House.

3

IT WAS STILL RAINING when Blake arrived at her mother's home, a detached three-bedroom house that stood within half an acre of land a few miles outside of Wheal Marow. Parking on the driveway, she entered the house and was greeted by warmth and rich cooking smells. Her mother Mary was in the kitchen, preparing a side salad. In her early sixties, she shared Blake's dark hair and eyes. But that was where the similarities ended. While Blake spent much of her time quietly watching the world and struggling with cynicism, Mary liked to talk and always look on the bright side.

"Goodness, bird," she said, noticing Blake in the doorway. "What on earth have you been up to? You're drenched!"

"Working on a new case."

Mary set down the chopping knife and tossed the salad into a bowl. "A new case? That's wonderful. What's this one about?"

"You know I can't tell you that," Blake said, brushing wet hair from her forehead.

"Let me get you a towel."

"It's all right, I'll get it."

"You stay right there. I don't want you dripping over my carpets any more than you already have."

Mary brushed past Blake and exited the kitchen. Blake made a beeline for one of the cupboards, pulled out a half-full bottle of Rioja and filled a wine glass. She took a sip, swirled it around her mouth and swallowed, then removed the lid of the Dutch Oven on the stove. Lamb casserole. It smelled good, but it made her heart skip a beat. Replacing the lid, she carried her wine glass out of the kitchen and into the dining room, where her gaze froze on the three place mats and sets of cutlery on the table.

"Are you drinking on an empty stomach again?" Her mother came up beside her and handed her a towel. "You better not be turning into your cousin Kenver."

The towel hung limply in Blake's hand as she slowly turned to face her mother. "You didn't tell me we were having a guest."

Mary avoided her gaze. "Must have slipped my mind. I need to check on the casserole."

Blake watched Mary hurry back to the kitchen, then followed her, wine sloshing inside the glass, the towel hanging loosely in her hand.

"By the way, I thought I might have a few of the girls around for a game of cards on Thursday," Mary said, removing the lid from the Dutch oven and stirring its contents. "You don't mind, do you?"

"I'll be visiting Faith Penrose," Blake said. "Like I do every other Thursday. Anyway, who —"

"How is she? I haven't seen much of her lately, bless her. She still not going out much?"

"No, and I don't blame her, especially when half the town can't seem to separate her from her psycho-killer ex-husband."

"Don't talk like that, Blake. People know she's not at fault."

"Oh, really? Then how come whenever she does go out people are whispering behind her back? And why does everyone in town avoid her like the plague? When was the last time *you* went to visit her?"

Mary shrugged. "I've been busy. Besides, it wouldn't be right for me to go. Not when . . ."

A creeping dread crawled over Blake's shoulders. "Wait a minute. Who exactly is coming to dinner?"

Mary didn't answer. She replaced the lid of the Dutch oven and wiped her hands on a towel.

"No, Mum," Blake said, aware that her voice had risen in volume. "Don't tell me you've invited who I think you've invited."

Mary had turned her back and was anxiously preparing a salad. "Dry your hair. You're dripping everywhere."

"And you're deflecting. You've invited him, haven't you?"

Mary moved over to the counter but still wouldn't turn around. "I thought it would be a good idea for the three of us to sit down and have a chat about things."

"Fuck!"

"Don't use that kind of language. You know I don't like it."

"You know what I don't like? You deciding what's good for me without any sort of discussion. I'm almost forty for crying out loud."

"That's because I knew what would happen if I told you."

"Well it's still going to happen, so I guess your little scheme didn't work. Jesus Christ!" Blake slammed down her wine glass and began furiously drying her hair with the towel. "What is there to talk about, anyway? I told Ed exactly what I thought about him a year ago. I made it perfectly clear back then where we both stand, which is as far away from each other as possible."

"A year is a long time, Blake. Things change. People change."

"Do you know what doesn't change? The damage that's already been done. The lives that have been lost."

Across the room, Mary's gaze dropped to the floor. "Please, bird. Your father wants to make amends."

Blake threw the towel over the back of a chair then swept up her wine glass, sending bloody droplets splashing through the air. "I knew you'd been talking to Ed. I knew it! How long has it been going on?"

"He's still my husband. I have a right to talk to him. He's still your father, too."

"Biologically speaking, maybe. But after what he did, Ed Hollow is no father of mine."

"He made a mistake a long time ago. A terrible mistake that —"

Blake felt the rage climbing her throat, trying to prise her jaw open so it could come exploding out. "Mistake? He fucked my best friend when we were eighteen. He got her pregnant, and then her psychopath of a father killed her for it. Ed lied to you, Mum. To us both, for years. I spent half of my life thinking I'd done something wrong, something so bad that it made him stop loving me, when all along it was his guilt and his shame that was destroying our relationship. Ed Hollow is nothing but a coward and a liar. Demelza died because of him. Why would I want to speak to him ever again? More to the point, why would you?"

Her heart was beating uncontrollably. The room was unbearably hot. She watched her mother twist her fingers into knots and shake her head from side to side.

"Because I still love him!" Mary cried. "Because forty years of marriage can't just disappear overnight. I'm not excusing what he did or the lies he told. But Demelza's father didn't kill her because of Ed. He murdered her because he was a madman. He killed all those other poor girls, and he almost killed you."

"That's beside the point."

"Please, Blake. Your father made a mistake. He's spent the last twenty years living with all that shame and all that guilt eating him up inside. I know he lied to us, and I know you may never forgive him, but don't you think we could at least listen to what he has to say?"

They were both silent, the casserole bubbling like an erupting volcano.

Blake struggled to meet her mother's imploring gaze. She stared into her wine glass and watched tiny ripples pool on the surface as she tried to steady her trembling hand.

The cheery chime of the doorbell sounded through the house. Blake looked up. Her heart was thrashing against her ribcage now, making her feel sick.

"No," she said. "I don't want to listen to anything he has to say. Not ever."

She drained the glass, then stalked across the kitchen to dump it in the sink and swipe the wine bottle from the counter.

"Blake, please," her mother said. "Stay."

The doorbell rang again.

Blake made for the back door.

"I'm going to Kenver's," she said. "Enjoy your little reunion."

Her mother called after her, and then Blake was outside, the rain hammering on the concrete patio. She weaved her way between the pots of plants and dying flowers, then around the side of the house.

Her father was standing on the doorstep, still waiting to be let in. Tall, in his late sixties, and with a shock of white hair, Ed

Hollow still struck an imposing figure despite the weight he'd lost.

He turned to Blake as she slid to a halt.

They stared at each other, both soaked to the skin. Blake seethed and gasped, struggling for breath, her eyes boring into his.

He stepped towards her, a look of self-pity on his face.

"Don't!" Blake yelled. "Don't you come near me."

She stalked past his white van, the bright red logo of *Hollow Construction* shimmering in the twilight, fighting the sudden urge to pick up a rock and smash it through the driver's window. Instead, she reached her car, climbed inside, and dumped the bottle of wine on the passenger seat. Ed was staring at her through the windscreen like a wounded puppy. Blake grabbed her seatbelt. It locked as she angrily pulled it across her body. She swore, pulling it harder still. The strap locked again.

Now the front door was opening and Mary was stepping out. She and Ed stared at each other, then at Blake.

"Fuck!" She slammed a hand against the steering wheel, then leaned back into the seat and shut her eyes. She sucked in a deep breath and let it out. She knew she was acting like a teenager but she didn't care. She hadn't spoken to her father in a year, and she certainly wasn't going to start tonight; she was afraid of what she might say or do if she was left alone in a room with him. Sucking in another deep breath, she expelled it and tried the seatbelt again, this time using less force. It slipped across her body with ease.

Starting the car engine, Blake pulled out of the drive and away from her parents. She sped along the country lane, rain lashing the windscreen, darkness falling on all sides. Hurt and anger churned her stomach as she headed towards Wheal Marow.

Was this how Kerenza Trezise had felt in her last moments? Or had she simply felt exhausted by life?

The road turned. Blake eased her foot off the accelerator pedal. She wondered what the last words to enter Kerenza's mind had been before throwing herself off the balcony, towards inescapable death.

4

By the time Blake arrived at Kenver Quick's two-bedroom Victorian terraced cottage on the outskirts of town, the rain had begun to ease. Her clothes were still wet and her towel-dried hair was still damp. She hammered impatiently on the door, which Kenver soon opened. He was twenty-nine years old, tall and slim, and heavily tattooed, with a nest of dark hair and large black eyes that always made him look mournful, even when he was perfectly happy. He stared at Blake and arched his eyebrows.

"What the hell happened to you?" he said.

Blake scowled. She held up the bottle of wine that she had snatched from her mother's kitchen. "Are you drinking right now?"

"It's nice to see you too. It's been a while. And for the record, now that I'm fully employed again, I'd like to stay that way. I'm staying off the booze for a while."

He opened the door wider and stepped back. Blake followed him inside. Feeling guilty, she bent over to leave the bottle of wine next to the welcome mat.

"You want coffee?" Kenver called over his shoulder as he disappeared through a door on the left.

Blake shrugged off her wet coat and hung it up. The cottage was overwhelmingly hot. Kenver hated the cold, always had done. Blake had once told him that he reminded her of a shivering Gothic greyhound, which hadn't gone down well. She followed him into the living room, with its kitchenette in the corner that was separated from the rest of the room by a breakfast bar. The tatty furniture had changed since she had last visited, replaced by new and expensive-looking sofas, arty prints on the walls, and a television that was far too large for a cottage of this size.

"It's looking good in here," Blake said, following him to the kitchenette. "I'm glad things are turning around for you. How's the job?"

"Great actually. I never thought I'd be working for a pharmaceutical company, but it pays well and the work is interesting enough."

"I never really understood your love for numbers. To be honest, I still don't understand what data analysis is."

"It's not unlike what you do. Solving puzzles, but with numbers instead of people."

"I think I'll stick with people. I always hated maths." She peeled off her pullover, and as she waited for him to make the coffee, she studied the sleeves of tattoos on his bare arms. There were more if she wasn't mistaken, and he'd removed the piercing in his septum. Ed would be pleased about that. He always said cousin Kenver looked like a pig with that ring sprouting from his nostrils. Blake tried to shake her father from her mind, but a dark cloud of anger had already rolled in.

With the coffee made, they sat down on the sofa.

"Have you eaten?" Kenver asked.

"Not since lunchtime."

"Auntie Mary won't be impressed. I have leftovers if you want them."

"You cook now?"

"No, it's Chinese takeaway."

"Speaking of your Aunt Mary, we just had a big falling out."

"That explains your mood. What was it about this time?"

Blake furrowed her brow. "What do you think?"

"Oh."

"She invited Ed to dinner, but deliberately didn't tell me. She says he wants to talk to us and make amends. She said that if she told me about it I wouldn't come."

"That sounds like a series of bad choices."

"Tell me about it."

"And how did it go with Uncle Ed?"

"It didn't. I left as he arrived." Blake picked up her coffee mug, took a sip and screwed up her face. "Is this decaf?"

"It certainly is. I like to sleep at night."

She returned the mug to the table. It was already hot enough in this sweltering room.

"Do you think your mum is missing him?" Kenver asked.

"Oh, I know she is. Worse still, I think she's ready to forgive and forget all the terrible things he's done. She's going to take him back, isn't she?"

Kenver studied her for a moment, his sad, dark eyes peering deep into hers. "You really need to get your own place, Blake. You've been back in Cornwall for a year now and you've regained the use of your arm. Besides, living at home with your mum is making you regress into a moody teenager."

"I'm so glad I came here for moral support."

"But you know I'm right, don't you?"

"You're also preaching to the choir. Besides, I've been busy recovering, building the new business, and work hasn't exactly been consistent. But I finally have a new case that will pay for a rental deposit somewhere."

"In Wheal Marow?"

"God, no. Probably Falmouth. The office is there, and it's a nice town buzzing with interesting people."

"And far away enough not to bump into dear old Uncle Ed."

Kenver's eyes wandered over to the living room door and the hallway beyond. There was a thirst there, Blake thought, and instantly regretted bringing wine into the house.

"What's this new case about?"

"I'm not sure yet. Have you ever heard of the Trezise family?"

"Should I have?"

"The eldest daughter took her own life on her wedding day. I've been hired to investigate why. You didn't hear about her death in the news a few months ago?"

"A few months ago I was still getting sober."

Blake thought about her visit to Saltwater House earlier that day, about the strange young woman performing the even stranger ritual among the trees. When she looked up again, Kenver was staring at her.

"What?" she asked.

"You're looking tired."

"Again, thanks for the moral support."

"Anyway, I'm glad you have a new case. It'll be a nice distraction from everything you've been through the last year."

"I suppose."

"Still no date for the trial?"

Blake grimaced. She knew cases such as murder took a while to get to court. They were complicated. Both sides needed time to gather evidence and witness statements, to put together a watertight case to defend or prosecute the accused. But for the victims' families it was a long, agonising wait to see justice served, and every passing day only served to fuel their anxiety, anguish, and pain. Dennis Stott had slaughtered seventeen young women, including his own daughter. Seventeen women with seventeen families whose lives had been irreparably destroyed. Blake had escaped becoming his eighteenth victim, with her own life barely intact.

She wrapped her arms around her waist. "I'm definitely not looking forward to seeing Stott's face again—what's left of it, anyway—but I'll do whatever it takes to help lock him away until the day he dies."

"And Uncle Ed?" Kenver asked, quietly. "Do you think you'll ever talk to him again?"

Blake sucked in a deep breath and let it out. If she didn't, it would haunt her for the rest of her life. She could already feel the guilt eating its way through her like woodworm through timber, even though she believed she had nothing to feel guilty for. Her father had cheated on her mother by sleeping with Blake's best friend, inadvertently causing her death. It didn't matter that everyone else believed Dennis Stott would have murdered his daughter regardless of her unborn child. If Blake did speak to her father again, there would be an expectation to forgive him. And she knew that she would, even if it was the last thing she wanted to do. Because that's what you did, wasn't it? You forgave and you forgot. Otherwise all the anger and all the hurt devoured your insides, until there was nothing left but bitterness and regret.

Blake shook her head. "All I know is that I'm still angry. And I'm busy. I don't need Ed Hollow distracting me from my new case."

"You really think Auntie Mary is going to take him back?"

"She's an adult. She can do whatever she likes, regardless of how I feel about it."

Blake thought about returning home to her mother's house. Kenver was right: the longer she stayed there, the more she was turning into a moody teenager. She was far from happy about it.

"Can I stay the night?" she asked.

"Actually, I have someone coming over soon," Kenver said, avoiding her gaze.

"I didn't know you were seeing someone. Who is it?"

"It's not a date. Not the romantic kind, anyway."

"Oh. You mean, like a hook up, or whatever you kids call it today?"

"Yes, that. And I can already see the judgement in your eyes."

"Well, you're misreading it because it's envy. Do you know how long it's been since I've shared a bed with anyone?" Ignoring the disgusted look on her cousin's face, she grabbed her pullover from the arm of the sofa and stood up. "Well, have fun."

Kenver reached up and gripped her softly by the arm. "For God's sake, sit down. I'll cancel, okay? You can stay here tonight. But do yourself a favour and find your own place. You can't live with Auntie Mary forever. You're almost forty."

Blake sat down again. "Kick a woman while she's down, why don't you?"

5

BLAKE WOKE up around seven to find the rain had stopped and her back was stiff and sore. She hadn't slept on a sofa since her university years, and these days her body much preferred the luxury of an adult-sized bed. But it wasn't just the discomfort that had kept her from sleeping. Her mind had churned constantly, flitting between her family troubles and the new case. Now, she was tired and in need of coffee. At least she wasn't hungover.

Leaving a thank you note on Kenver's coffee table, she freshened up in the bathroom, left the cottage, and made the short walk into town, where the Honeybee Café was already open for business. As she approached, the door suddenly opened. Blake caught her breath as a familiar face stood in her way.

Detective Constable Rory Angove was in his late thirties and was of average height, with a slim yet muscular build that wore his navy suit and white shirt well. His hair was dark, as were his almond-shaped eyes, while his small, protruding ears gave him an almost elven appearance. He was carrying a bag of pastries in one hand and a cardboard holder in the other that contained two cups of coffee.

Neither of them talked for a moment. Then Rory cleared his throat and forced a polite smile to his lips.

"Hello, Blake," he said. "Bit of an early start for you, isn't it?"

Blake resisted running a hand through her tangled hair, but she was acutely aware that she was still wearing yesterday's clothes.

"Got a busy day," she mumbled.

"Right. Yeah, me too."

They both remained unmoving. Blake nodded at the bag of pastries. "DS Turner still got you fetching breakfast, has he?"

Rory stiffened. "Sometimes I get lunch, too. How's your mother? Still living at home with her?"

Touché, Blake thought.

The last time she'd seen Rory Angove, they'd argued about what they meant to each other. Friends since childhood, the two had become romantically entangled as teenagers. Until the day Demelza Stott disappeared and Blake had left Cornwall for a new life in Manchester. There had been occasional sexual encounters during their twenties and thirties, whenever Blake had returned to visit her parents and needed to blow off steam. But for Rory, Blake was the one that got away. And now that she was back, he wanted them to be more than just drunken sleepovers.

For Blake, Rory was her teenage sweetheart and always would be. But they were adults now, and their lives had gone in different directions. Even though Blake was back in Wheal Marow and their paths were crossing once again, she knew she would never see Rory as more than an old friend. She'd told him so the last time they'd slept together. And now here they were, exchanging barely disguised insults and unable to look each other in the eye.

"Anyway, must be going," Rory said. "I wouldn't want Turner's coffee to get cold. Tell your mum I said hello."

He shuffled past Blake, who watched him leave then stalked miserably inside the café. Seating herself at a corner table, she ordered a black coffee from Elsie, the silver haired waitress, and surveyed the room. There were a few other early-morning patrons here; a couple of construction workers eating a full English breakfast, their high-visibility jackets reflecting the overhead strip lights, and two elderly couples sitting together and drinking mugs of tea in silence.

Blake sipped her coffee and grimaced. It was impossible to find good coffee in Wheal Marow. She thought about Takk, the Icelandic-inspired coffeehouse that she used to frequent back in Manchester. It had been one of her favourite places to sit and do research when she'd grown tired of her office and needed a fresh space in which to think. It had also been free from the sad-eyed lamentations of old boyfriends. But the coffeehouse was a distant memory now. Times had changed, and so had her life. Even though it had been her own decision to move back to Cornwall, she was still struggling to adapt.

Removing her laptop from her bag, she set it on the table and powered it up. She scanned the walls looking for signs of a Wi-Fi password. When she couldn't find one, she caught Elsie's attention and waved her over.

"Yes, darlin'?" Elsie said. "You want something to eat with that coffee? What can I get you?"

"Actually, I was after your Wi-Fi password."

"No breakfast? It's the most important meal of the day, you know."

"So I've heard." Blake smiled politely. "The Wi-Fi password?"

Elsie wrinkled her brow. "Oh, don't have one of those. This isn't fancy Manchester, you know."

"No, it's not. But it is the twenty-first century, Elsie. Most eating establishments have Wi-Fi these days."

"You've got a phone there, haven't you? Don't need Wi-Fi for that."

Blake closed her laptop and scowled. If she could get a reliable phone signal in Wheal Marow, she could access the internet by tethering her mobile to her laptop and using it as a hotspot. But Cornwall still had a shocking lack of mobile phone coverage, as well as county-wide problems with connectivity. Inside the Honeybee Café, Blake's phone signal was non-committal at best.

She stared at the wall clock. Wheal Marow Library would be open in an hour. She knew they had Wi-Fi there. Or she could drive over to her office in Falmouth, which seemed the most sensible idea. Or she could return to her mother's house, who she still needed to talk to about last night.

As if reading her mind, Elsie said, "How's Mary doing? She all right, is she?"

"She's just fine, thank you."

"You still staying with her?"

"For now."

Elsie shook her head. "You know, a woman your age should be in her own place by now, with a nice husband and a couple of kids."

"I did have my own place. A very nice place in fact. Until I gave it up and moved down here."

"Still, you must've got lonely. I don't get you modern women these days. There's nothing wrong with having a family, you know."

"And there's nothing wrong with being happy and single, which is exactly how I like it."

Elsie shifted on her feet. "If you say so."

Blake bit down on her lower lip, preventing the words that were trying to force their way out. She returned her laptop to its bag and sipped more coffee. When she looked up again, Elsie was still hovering.

"Your father was in last week," the waitress said. "He sat at this very table."

"Is that so?"

"He looked as miserable as sin, he did. Like all the worries in the world were weighing down on his shoulders."

Blake bit down harder. Her father had a lot to be sorry about these days, but she still wasn't going to take Elsie's bait. Much to the waitress's disappointment.

"Anyway, when your mother turned up, his face lit up like the sun. They were in here chatting for a good hour. Laughing and joking together. So, are they getting back together or what? Because it would be a shame to let their marriage go down the drain after all these years, wouldn't it?"

"Well, I suppose whatever they decide, it's nobody else's business but their own. Now, is there anything else I can help you with today, Elsie? Because you have customers waiting."

Elsie glanced over her shoulder at the mother and two children dressed in school uniforms who had just entered the café.

"You have a lovely day now," she told Blake. "And make sure you eat something. Put some meat on those bones."

Blake watched the waitress weave between the tables, heading towards the family. Then she swore under her breath and returned her gaze to the wall clock.

6

BUILT IN THE GEORGIAN ERA, Wheal Marow Library was an impressive looking building that had kept much of its character despite its gradual slide into dilapidation thanks to a lack of restoration funds. It had been open exactly two minutes when Blake entered, greeted the librarian Margaret Pascoe, and headed upstairs to the reference room. It was a high-ceilinged space with intricately designed cornices that were yellowed and cracked. Four large mahogany tables stood in the centre, while rows of shelves holding non-fiction books and reference manuals stood to the right. Blake had the room to herself. She sat down at a table, placed her laptop in front of her and powered it up. Next, she removed her notebook and turned to a clean page. She cracked her knuckles, which was a bad habit she was still trying to break, then opened a search browser on the computer. She began.

Twenty minutes later, Blake leaned back on her chair and frowned. She had scanned every social media and professional network site she could think of, yet she had not found a single profile. Who didn't have a digital footprint these days? It was highly unusual, especially when there were two seventeen-year-olds in the household. Even Mary had a Facebook account, and she hated modern technology.

Puzzled, Blake leaned forward again and began searching the news sites. Soon, she came upon two articles reporting the death of Kerenza Trezise. Words like 'tragic' and 'shocking' jumped off the screen, with each story quick to point out that the coroner's report was still pending, which meant there was still no explanation for the woman's suicide. Blake made a note to find out about the report, then scrolled through the rest of the search results, until one of interest made her sit up.

The article was dated two years ago and featured in the 'What's On' section of a local Truro news site. 'Local Talent on Display in New Art Gallery' was the headline. Former London gallerist Emanuel Arquette was opening Stonecrop Gallery in Truro, and his first exhibition would be a showcase of local artists, both established and new-to-the-scene. Halfway down the list of exhibiting artists was Kerenza Trezise.

Blake scribbled in her notebook. Campbell had mentioned Kerenza's interest in the history of art, but he hadn't told Blake that she'd been an artist herself. Below the list of names were two images of work to be shown, one of which was titled 'The Red Serpent'. The artist: Kerenza Trezise. Blake clicked on the image to enlarge it.

The painting was of a landscape at night, with a black, starless sky. Filling the lower half of the canvas was a giant red snake, its fat, writhing body coiling around dead trees as it slithered from a forest and into a meadow. A single yellow eye, cold and lifeless, stared at Blake. A forked tongue flicked from fanged jaws. Riding on top of its body were three naked women with wild dark hair, each carrying a long wooden staff in one hand, while the fingers of the other formed strange symbols.

Blake arched an eyebrow then bookmarked the article and made another quick search, this time for more of Kerenza's artwork. But there was nothing else.

She drummed her fingers on the table, confounded by how little she had found. While she understood the need for privacy in a time when there was no longer any, it was as if the Trezise family had made it their mission to keep their lives off-line and behind the wrought iron gates of Saltwater House. In Blake's opinion, there were two types of people who went to such extremes. Those in the public eye who were determined to protect their final shreds of a private life. And those with something to hide.

The Trezise family came from Old Money, which explained the huge house and grounds. But where had that money come from? And how much of a fortune had they amassed to afford the privilege of not having a single career between them?

Blake hopped onto the British Newspaper Archive website, the online home for millions of scanned historical newspapers collected by the British Library. Logging in, she entered 'Saltwater House' into the search bar, then narrowed the results to the past twenty years.

The first article of interest was from three years ago and was a small report on the death of Aidan Trezise, who had been twenty-nine at the time of the boating accident and was to be buried in the family plot at Saltwater House once his body had been returned from Portugal.

Another tragic story followed, detailing the death of Genevieve Trezise, Griffin's second wife and mother to Jack and Tegen. During labour, the twins' heads had become locked in their mother's pelvic brim, a rare complication that prevented them from entering the birth canal. An emergency Caesarean section was performed, barely saving both children from asphyxiation. Their mother had not been so lucky. She had bled to death minutes later from a massive haemorrhage caused by the trauma.

"Christ," Blake whispered, wondering how it felt for the twins to know exactly why their mother had died. She moved onto the next article and found yet more tragedy.

Olivia Trezise, the older siblings' mother, had vanished twenty years ago during a particularly cruel winter. A search party found her four days later, naked and lying face down in a field just six miles from Saltwater House. The cause of death was exposure to the elements, with no signs of foul play. Olivia's nakedness was attributed to paradoxical undressing, a common manifestation seen in the late stages of hypothermia, in which the sufferer becomes disoriented and mentally confused.

The article insinuated that Olivia had a long history of mental illness, and hinted at a stay at St Lawrence's, a mental hospital in Bodmin that had since closed. Quite how the newspaper had known this when the family was so fiercely private was another mystery. Either way, the story didn't match the one Campbell had been told. Blake wasn't surprised. Pneumonia had less of a stigma attached to it. But if there was a history of mental illness within the family, was it possible that Kerenza had been suffering too?

Blake's phone vibrated loudly on the table. She glanced up at the 'No mobile phones' sign pinned to the noticeboard on her left, then down at the screen. Her mother was calling.

Guilt began to spread through her chest. She snatched the phone up and hovered her thumb over the answer button. Then she withdrew it, letting the voicemail service take her mother's call.

Slipping the phone back inside her pocket, she returned her attention to the laptop screen and the search results for Saltwater House.

How old was it? And who built it?

The British Newspaper Archive contained scanned articles from all the way back to the 1700s. Blake ran her fingers over the keyboard, casting a wider net. It wasn't long before she stumbled upon a story published in 1801 in Cornwall's very first newspaper, The Royal Cornwall Gazette. As she scanned the story, her eyes grew wide.

"Holy shit," she said, a little too loudly. Campbell Green had been right about Old Money, and now Blake knew exactly where it had come from.

Picking up her pen, she began to write furiously in her notebook.

7

THE CORNISH PRESS was a small local newspaper that had been in circulation for more than a hundred years. Reporting on the likes of farming news, summer fêtes, and school sports days, it was the kind of gentle read that rarely bothered with salacious headlines and made its money from selling advertising space to local businesses. With a staff of just four, Blake was always surprised to find the office space in such disarray, with cluttered desks and stacks of papers on the floor. But that was writers for you, she supposed. She was currently perched on the edge of Judy Moon's desk and had just finished telling her about Salt-water House.

Judy, who had been friends with Blake since school, stared in shock.

"Slavery?" she said. "No wonder the Trezise family like to keep to themselves."

Blake nodded. "I know. And they're not the only wealthy family in Cornwall to have made their fortune from the slave trade. It doesn't matter how much we try to deny it, the truth is this country owes a lot to the trade. Whole industries were

created around it—sugar, tobacco, cotton, import and export—
and profits were invested back into home grown businesses on
British soil, creating thousands of jobs for regular workers. Did
you know one of the main reasons cities like London got so
wealthy was because of all the banks and insurers selling services
to slave merchants? It's horrifying, and yet here we are still bene-
fiting from it years later without even realising."

They were both quiet, shifting uncomfortably.

"So the Trezise family got their money from sugar?"

Blake nodded.

Born in Cornwall, William Trezise owned a sugar plantation
in British Jamaica in the late eighteenth century. He would
purchase Black African slaves, work them to death, then buy
more. Meanwhile the sugar plantation was making a literal
killing from the export of sugar back to Britain. Not satisfied
with the fortune he was already making, Trezise set up his own
slave transportation company based in Bristol that was overseen
by his adult children and provided him with an abundance of
slaves at a fraction of the cost. While the British slave trade was
abolished in 1807, the ownership of slaves continued in the
British-occupied Caribbean colonies. But mounting opposition
and the loss of one of his two highly profitable businesses
granted Trezise with some foresight. The construction of Saltwater House began in Cornwall. And in 1838, when every
surviving slave was finally emancipated—without compensation
—William, who was then an elderly man, sold the plantation
and returned to Cornwall, where he lived out his final days in
the decadence of Saltwater House.

Upon his death, his substantial fortunes were passed on to
his children. And on that money went, slowly diminishing over
the years, but nevertheless providing a life of luxury for Trezise's

descendants, every penny of it stained with the blood of count-less slaves, all beaten, tortured, and worked to death for a spoonful of sugar in a cup of imported tea.

Judy stared at the mug in her hands, then set it down on the desk. "How much money do they have?"

"No idea. Campbell Green was hired to manage their accounts after his predecessor got sick and died, but so far, the subject hasn't come up. Anyway, I think we can assume that the Trezise family likes to keep the origin of their wealth a closely guarded secret, especially in today's climate."

"Do you think it has anything to do with Kerenza's death?"

"Unlikely, but until I know more nothing is ruled out." Blake glanced around the room, her gaze landing on Judy's colleague, Rod, who was writing up his latest article.

"Hey Rod, did you cover the Kerenza Trezise suicide?" she called.

The journalist shot a glare back at her.

"Trying to work here," he said.

"Then answer the question and I'll leave you alone."

Judy slapped Blake's knee and failed to suppress a smile.

Rod heaved his shoulders. "We did a brief mention, that's it. There weren't enough details at the time to write anymore."

"What about the coroner's report? Has it come out yet?"

"No idea. Why don't you ask your Detective Constable friend?"

Blake shot Rod a glare then glanced at Judy, who said, "He has a point."

"I'm not talking to Rory Angove about anything."

"Why not? Have you two fallen out again?"

"We never fell in."

Shifting her weight on the table, Blake let out a heavy

breath. She thought about all she had learned from her visit to the library. From the unsettling image of 'The Red Serpent' to the tragic family deaths and revelations of slavery, she was unsure where this case was heading. What she did know was that she was desperately lacking a lead, and she doubted she was going to find one at Stonecrop Gallery, her next stop. She stared at Judy, whose attention had returned to her computer screen. "Don't you think it's odd there's been so much death in the Trezise family? Both mothers, two of the five siblings . . ."

"Maybe," Judy said. "Or maybe it's just bad luck."

Or karma, Blake thought, then felt terrible for thinking it. Across the room, the bright blue door that led to the archive caught her attention. "How far back do The Cornish Press archives go?"

"Since its inception, I suppose," Judy said. "We're still in the process of digitising the earliest editions. Let's just say it's not a priority—we try to fit it in between jobs."

"But you have original copies?"

"Carefully preserved, yes. Why do you want to know?"

Blake leaned forward and flashed Judy a smile. "I need a favour. Can you look for anything about the Trezise family or Saltwater House? The British Newspaper Archive didn't include the Cornish Press."

"And when am I supposed to do that exactly? In between my full-time job and picking up the girls from school?"

"Maybe on your lunch break?"

"Oh, so now I'm your unpaid research assistant? You've got some nerve."

Blake held up her hands. "Fine. Just show me where to go and I'll look myself."

Across the room, Rod cleared his throat. "This isn't a library," he said. "We don't just let anyone in. Especially since *someone* left a coffee stain on one of our original editions."

"I told you that wasn't me." Blake rolled her eyes then tapped Judy's knee with her foot. "Please? The information well is dry and I can't get past the gates of Saltwater House to talk to that family."

"For God's sake, fine," Judy said. "I'll try to spend some time on my lunch hour. But there's one condition. You babysit the girls next Friday night."

"Me? I thought Kenver was your resident babysitter."

"Your cousin has been unreliable of late, and I really want to take Charlie out for dinner. He's been moping around ever since he lost his bid to become town mayor. It's getting annoying now, so I'm hoping that a little wine and good food will cheer him the hell up. Besides, it's been weeks since I've had a night out."

Blake wrinkled her nose. She liked children from a distance but taking care of two of them for an entire evening left her feeling uneasy.

"Deal or no deal," Judy said, crossing her arms.

"Okay fine, I'll babysit. How soon can you get me results?"

"As soon as you get your arse off my desk and let me get back to work."

Laughing, Blake got to her feet. "Thanks Judy. I appreciate it."

"You better. I'll call you if I find anything."

"And if you don't?"

"You're still babysitting Friday night."

8

STONECROP GALLERY WAS SITUATED down a side street close to Truro's city centre. It was a small space with a glass storefront and a typically minimalist interior. Blake introduced herself to the bored-looking receptionist and asked to speak to the owner. She had already called ahead to make an appointment, but that didn't stop the young woman from eyeing her suspiciously as she picked up the phone.

As Blake waited, she took a moment to observe the art hanging on the walls. Much of it appeared to be sourced from local artists, but none of it was to her taste. She had never really understood modern art. To her it was all emotionless squiggles and lines and geometric shapes that were outrageously priced. Not that she considered herself an art critic.

Behind the reception desk, a door opened and a tall man in his late forties stepped out. He had a wave of thick dark hair and deep-set eyes that flicked towards Blake as he entered.

"Why don't you take a five-minute break?" he told the receptionist in a French accent that had softened from years of living in England.

The young woman shrugged before rising and disappearing through the door.

Now that they were alone, the man strode towards Blake with an open hand. "Ms Hollow, I presume? I am Emanuel Arquette, the owner of this fine establishment."

Blake shook his hand, noting his expensive suit and rich, earthy cologne.

"Thank you for making the time to see me," she said.

"It's not every day I get a call from a private investigator. Especially one enquiring about Ms Kerenza Trezise. How may I help?"

"As I told you on the phone, I'm investigating the reason behind Kerenza's suicide. It's early days, but I'm trying to build a picture of her life. I was hoping you'd be able to tell me about the exhibition she was a part of two years ago."

Arquette's welcoming smile faded into confusion. "My time with Kerenza was fleeting at best. Wouldn't you be better off talking to her family?"

"Believe me, I'm trying. Please, Mr Arquette. If you could indulge me."

The gallerist was quiet for a moment, one hand tucked beneath his chin. "I read about her death in the newspaper. Truly terrible. A tragedy, really, for the art world to lose such an exciting talent. Yet at the same time you could say her suicide was not a surprise."

Blake stared at him. "Why would you say that?"

"Well, I suppose, from my brief dealings with her and the tone of her work, she seemed full of such sorrow and darkness. There's the old adage that an artist must suffer for her work, which just isn't true for everyone. But in Kerenza Trezise's case, I very much believe it was. Do you like art, Ms Hollow?"

The question threw Blake off-balance. She glanced at the framed canvasses hanging on the walls, trying to form an opinion.

"Forgive me for asking, only I noticed when I came in that you were looking at these pieces with a disapproving eye. They don't impress you?"

"I prefer photography. Landscapes, mostly."

"You're a nature lover?"

"Tell me about the exhibition. How did Kerenza become involved?"

Arquette smiled and slipped his hands into his pockets. "Well, the gallery had not yet opened, and I thought a clever way to generate interest would be to curate an exhibition showcasing local talent. I was a gallerist in London for many years, but I was not so well known on the Cornish art scene. It can be quite the clique, you know. So I advertised in the local newspapers asking for submissions. It's not the typical approach and probably frowned upon in certain circles because invariably everyone and their dog suddenly aspires to become a famous painter. But I have a keen eye and the publicity generated interest."

"And Kerenza?"

"She contacted me via email with photographs of her work. The paintings took my breath away. Her use of bold colours against pitch black, the fusion of flesh and nature, dark and light. And such aggressive brush strokes! The images she conjured were so bewitching in their nature yet dripping with such torment and isolation that I found myself almost brought to tears."

Blake recalled 'The Red Serpent', which had certainly left an unsettling impression.

"Kerenza's work was very different to the other submissions I received," Arquette continued. "But I knew I had to include her. We agreed that I would show four pieces."

"What was she like when you met her?"

"I didn't meet her. It seemed that Ms Trezise was painfully shy. The little communication we had was strictly via email. I was so intrigued by her that I dared to invite her to dinner one evening. Not with romantic intentions, I must stress, but out of pure curiosity and interest in her art. She ignored my invitation as if I had never made it, as is her right I suppose."

"She didn't even attend the opening night?"

"Alas, no. She arranged for her paintings to be delivered to the gallery a week before the exhibition. With them was a hand-written note suggesting the order in which they should be hung and a brief apology for being unable to attend. I was disappointed. I like to meet my artists at least once, but I think the idea of being present at the opening night of her first ever exhibition filled Kerenza with terror. I don't mean the act of putting the work on public display, but rather the vulnerability of being judged in person. There is nothing worse for an artist than rejection. Invisibility, perhaps. But at least then no one knows of your existence to be able to judge it."

Casting her gaze over the gallery space, Blake chewed the inside of her mouth. From what she had learned so far, which admittedly was not much, Kerenza Trezise had been intensely private and perhaps intensely shy. Yet she had still reached out to Emanuel Arquette, offering her art to display in his exhibition. Didn't that prove she had once believed in herself? Or did it mean she had been desperately seeking validation?

"What did people think of her paintings?" Blake asked.

Arquette grinned. "People were unsure of them. Not

because of the nudity—if that were the case, the Renaissance would have ended the art world centuries ago—but I think because Kerenza's work sparked an emotional response that made the viewer uncomfortable. And they were so different from everything else on the walls. You know, the usual still lifes and pretty landscapes, all nice and safe and devoid of adventure." He winked knowingly at Blake, who tried not to roll her eyes. "As much as they were a talking point throughout the exhibition, not one of Kerenza's paintings sold."

"She must have been disappointed."

"It's hard to judge how anyone is truly feeling when they hide behind the words of an email. In any case, I offered to buy two of her pieces for my own personal collection. But she refused. The next day, she arranged for a courier to collect her paintings." Arquette paused. "I suppose that does perhaps indicate disappointment."

"Did you hear from her again?" Blake asked.

"Sadly, no."

"And she didn't exhibit her work anywhere else?"

"Not to my knowledge. Believe me, as a fan of her work I kept an ear to the ground."

Behind them, the door to the back room opened and the receptionist returned. She cast a casual glance in their direction, then sat at her desk. Blake's five minutes were up.

"One more question if you don't mind," she said. "Do you know anything about the rest of the Trezise family? Anything at all, no matter how insignificant."

Arquette smiled again, showing his teeth. "Funnily enough, I once met Kerenza's father at a charity dinner. It was many years ago now, back in London. Griffin Trezise was a guest speaker. I didn't put father and daughter together until I read Kerenza's obituary."

"What charity?" Blake asked, her curiosity piqued.

"I don't remember now. I've been to many functions over the years. But I remember Trezise because of my encounter with him. I had no idea who he was at the time, but a friend mentioned he was one of the evening's main benefactors. I must admit he certainly gave a heartfelt speech, which was greeted with much applause. I was passing his table on the way to the bar, so I thought I would offer him my congratulations. But I was clearly beneath his breeding because he behaved like a pompous ass. He scalded me like a child for interrupting his conversation, much to the laughter and delight of his fellow table guests."

Arquette grimaced at the bitter memory. "This is the truth about people who come from Old Money—all these charity donations and sincere words are not about helping those in need. They're about elevating reputations and stroking egos. In London, I made a career of selling art to these people. Most didn't care about the art itself, or the artist behind it. All they cared about was that the price tag was high enough to brag about over an expensive dinner." He expelled a deep breath as his gaze returned to the artwork on the walls. "Griffin Trezise left an impression that night because he struck me as an unkind man. So, if you're searching for a reason why Kerenza Trezise was so afraid of the world, I suggest you look to her father."

Thanking him for his time, Blake gave him her card, then nodded at the receptionist who ignored her. As she walked back to the city centre, frustration punctuated every step. The more she learned about the Trezise family, the more she was intrigued by them. But they were still unobtainable, locked away behind the gates of Saltwater House. How was she supposed to discover why Kerenza jumped to her death when she couldn't get to the people who had all the answers?

Blake wondered if she should renege on her agreement with Campbell Green, even if it meant leaving him in a state of flux. Because taking a grieving man's money was making her feel uncomfortable, especially when she was struggling to bring him the closure he desperately needed.

She stepped out of an alley and onto Boscawen Street, slipping into the stream of shoppers who bustled in and out of high street stores.

Blake was not a quitter. She was too stubborn. Besides, she needed this money.

Removing her phone from her pocket, she made a call.

9

CAMPBELL GREEN LIVED on Old Bridge Street, a small road populated by nineteenth-century buildings that led towards High Cross and the Gothic Revival architecture of Truro Cathedral. His home took up the top floor of a three-storey redbrick building that had been converted into flats. Inside, the high-ceilinged rooms were painted white and the original floorboards had been restored and waxed. He had furnished the living room in a contemporary style that included a pair of bright orange sofas, a huge television with surround sound speakers, and an expensive-looking computer.

Blake stood in front of one of the latticed windows, warming her hands on a mug of coffee as she peered down at the small bridge that gave the street its name. Truro River flowed beneath it, the water brown and shallow.

"I'm not getting very far," she said, turning to find Campbell still on his feet and his expression slowly wilting. "With a case like this, I would be speaking to friends, work colleagues, family members. I'd be scouring social media pages. Kerenza didn't have any of those things, except for a family who I can't even get close to."

Campbell continued to wilt until he was seated on the sofa. "The social media thing was her choice. She said she found it all highly toxic. I've known a few people to come off it lately for the same reason."

"But none of her siblings have social media either, including the seventeen-year-old twins. Teenagers without social media doesn't strike you as odd?"

"Maybe they use pseudonyms. Or they're not like other teenagers. I don't know."

"But why don't you know, Campbell?" Blake stared at him. "You were getting married to Kerenza. Didn't you get to know her siblings at all?"

He shrugged. "Tegen, a little, I suppose. She was the only one to show me kindness. As for the others, Jack is a ball of anger who's going to explode one day, and just like her father, Abbie thought of me as staff until she found out I was seeing her sister."

"And afterwards?"

He shrugged again and shook his head.

Blake moved away from the window and leaned against the wall. "See, this is my problem. Short of breaking into Saltwater House and beating the truth out of the Trezise family, I'm running out of options. Which means I'm starting to feel bad for taking your money."

Hanging his head, Campbell expelled a long breath and stared at the floor. "What about Stonecrop Gallery? Why were you there?"

"To talk to the owner, Emanuel Arquette. I asked him about

the exhibition Kerenza had been part of a couple of years ago. Her first and last, apparently."

Surprise bloomed over Campbell's face. "What exhibition?"

"It was a few months before you met. Arquette said Kerenza's paintings dripped with torment and isolation. His words, not mine. He thought they were the work of a genius, but they didn't go down so well at the exhibition. Not one of them sold."

Campbell was quiet for a moment. "I didn't even know that she painted until Tegen let it slip. When I asked Kerenza about it, she got upset. She told me she didn't paint anymore and that she didn't want to talk about it."

"Did you ever see any of her artwork at the house?"

"No. Tegen said Kerenza burned them all."

Blake took out her phone, opened a bookmarked web page, then sat down next to Campbell and held up the screen. "I found one of her paintings in a promo piece for the exhibition. It's called 'The Red Serpent'."

Campbell's eyes grew round and bewildered. "Christ. I had no idea that . . . Kerenza painted *that*?"

"She did. Arquette also told me that he'd once met Griffin Trezise at a charity benefit. It was entirely coincidental and happened a long time ago in London. He said Griffin was a cold and spiteful man who ridiculed him in front of others. Would you say that's in line with your own impressions?"

"All I can tell you is that he's old and cantankerous. Most of my dealings with him were on a professional level, and although he seemed satisfied with my work, I got the distinct impression he didn't fully trust me, or anyone else for that matter. Then, of course, he found out about Kerenza and me, and it all went to hell."

Aware of her close proximity to Campbell, Blake got up and

moved over to the other sofa. "What about his relationship with his children?"

"According to Kerenza, he's never really shown them any affection. During my time at the house, Griffin was always in his study with strict instructions not to be disturbed unless it was an emergency. Makes you wonder why some people bother having children."

"So you think he doesn't love them?"

"That's not for me to say. But Griffin treated his children like possessions. Things to own and control." He clenched his jaw. "I think that's part of the reason Kerenza lived such an isolated life, because it's what her father wanted. The same goes for the rest of them."

"Except now there aren't many of them left," Blake said. Her thoughts momentarily turned to her own father. At least he had never been controlling like Griffin Trezise, and had shown her love, even if she now questioned whether that love was genuine. "Tell me about the son who died. Aidan Trezise."

"I don't know what else there is to say other than what I already told you. He and Griffin had a huge fight, which ended with him leaving and never coming back. Griffin told the rest of his children that he didn't want to hear Aidan's name again. From what I hear, he dropped off the radar, until they learned he was killed in a boating accident a couple of months before I was hired to manage the accounts."

Blake drummed her fingers on her knees. Another dead end. Quite literally.

"Tell me what happened when Griffin discovered you were in a relationship with his daughter."

A flash of anger lit up Campbell's eyes. "When he found out Kerenza and I were dating, he terminated my employment on the spot and told me to end the relationship. I refused. I told him he may rule his family with an iron fist, but he had no control over me. That didn't go down so well. He began making all kinds of threats about what would happen if I ever tried to marry Kerenza, or worse, have children with her."

"What kind of threats?"

"Nothing violent. Just the 'I'll make sure you never work in accountancy again' type of thing."

"Did he say why he was so against your relationship?"

"He didn't need to. I don't come from the right background to marry his daughter. I'm from a working-class family. My father is a factory foreman. My mother works for the post office. Growing up, we weren't poor, but there was never much left over for things like holidays. I was the first person to go to university in my family, and I worked three jobs to pay my way. I'm a self-made man, but apparently hard work and dedication doesn't count in Griffin Trezise's eyes. You have to be born into wealth before he'll even consider you as a potential in-law."

Blake wondered if now was the right time to inform Campbell about the appalling origin of the Trezise family fortune. She decided to wait a while longer. "So Griffin Trezise forbids you from marrying his daughter, and yet somehow you still ended up with your wedding day held on the grounds of Saltwater House. How did that happen?"

Campbell shrugged. "Kerenza threatened to leave, just like Aidan had. Her father wasn't happy, but I suppose the threat of losing another child outweighed his opinion." He paused, bowing his head. "Sometimes I wonder if I should have just walked away. Maybe if I hadn't pursued a relationship, Kerenza would still be alive."

"You don't know that," Blake said. "Sometimes people take

their own lives without ever leaving a clue that something was wrong."

Campbell looked up, and his face was stained with tears. "She jumped to her death right in front of her family. In front of me, on our wedding day. I'd say that was a big fucking clue, wouldn't you?" He hung his head again. "I'm sorry."

Blake was quiet, mulling over everything she'd learned. Which still wasn't much at all.

"I'm going to level with you," she said. "I'm a private investigator, not a superhero. I can't walk through walls or read people's minds. I don't have the resources that police detectives do. What I do have is years of experience, a decent internet connection, and the desire to try my best. But sometimes that isn't enough. Sometimes complex cases like this don't go anywhere. If I can't get access to Kerenza's family, I don't think it's fair to continue taking your money. So, help me out. Give me something I can use."

She watched as Campbell pressed his hands to the sides of his face and shut his eyes. He was silent for a long time, the veins in his temples throbbing. Suddenly he snapped his eyes wide open.

"The groundskeeper, Saul Bodily. He's a good man. He had a soft spot for Kerenza. After Griffin fired me, she would get Saul to open the gates and sneak me inside. Or he would take her on errands without the rest of the family knowing, and I would go meet her for a few hours. It was very Romeo and Juliet." He paused for a moment. Blake wondered if he was thinking about the tragic ending to that particular love story. "If you can get him alone, you can explain that you're trying to help me. Even if he can't get you inside, maybe he can send a message to Tegen. I know she would help if she knew it was about Kerenza. She worshipped the ground she walked on."

Blake nodded. "Sounds promising. Can you call him?"

"I don't have his number. Kerenza always arranged everything when Saul was at work."

"He doesn't live on the grounds?"

"No. He and his wife Violet—the housekeeper you talked to —they live nearby but I don't know where." Campbell chewed his lower lip, then sat up straight. "But I do know that they travel into town together once a week to get supplies for the house."

"No deliveries?" Blake said, surprised.

"Of course not. That would mean having to let strangers inside. Anyway, the point is that Violet will never talk to you because she's far too loyal to the family. But Saul will if you tell him you're working for me." He paused and heaved his shoulders. "I know it's not much, but if you can get him alone, even if it's for a minute, he'll be able to help."

For a last attempt to access the Trezise family it wasn't the most foolproof of plans, but Blake knew she had to try.

"What day do they go for supplies?" she asked.

"That's the thing," said Campbell. "It's tomorrow, around two in the afternoon. I know because Saul used to leave the gates unlocked for us when they left."

Blake picked up her coffee mug and raised it to her lips. "All right, then. Tomorrow afternoon it is."

Campbell breathed deeply as he sat back on the sofa. "Thank you, Blake."

Saying goodbye, Blake made her way back down to the street, where an icy breeze numbed her skin. She stopped by the bridge and peered down into the water. She wasn't sure how she was going to get Saul Bodily away from his wife just yet, and she was still doubtful this case was going to develop any further. But if there was one thing she'd learned throughout her years as a private eye, it was that sometimes you just had to show up and see what happened.

Tomorrow, she would do just that.

10

THE TEMPERATURE CONTINUED to plummet the following day, while the rain continued to hold off. It was 1:55 PM. Blake sat behind the wheel of her car, parked in a small lay-by on a country road, her gaze fixed on the mouth of the adjoining lane up ahead on the right. Violet and Saul Bodily would be appearing any minute now in their green Land Rover. Campbell had given her the license plate number and told her that the Bodilys' routine rarely changed.

She drummed her fingers on the steering wheel, feeling a twinge of excitement in her chest, the same she always felt when close to a break in an investigation. She still had no idea how she would get Saul alone, but even just a few seconds would be enough to give him her business card and explain why she needed to talk. Her gaze flicked down to the clock on the dashboard. She hadn't seen another vehicle pass by in the last twenty minutes, which meant that she would need to follow the Bodilys at a discreet distance until they reached the busier A3083 towards Helston.

As she continued to wait, her thoughts flicked back to last

night, when she had returned home to her mother. It had been an awkward exchange of words. First, Blake had apologised for storming out. Then her mother had apologised for inviting her father to dinner without telling her. But then Mary had tried to tell Blake about the evening, and Blake had quickly shut her down. She knew her mother had conflicted feelings about Ed, and she knew she wasn't helping her to resolve those feelings. But for Blake, there was nothing to resolve. She had already made her decision about her relationship with her father. End of story.

She wondered how long she would feel like this, the resentment towards him showing no signs of abatement. It couldn't be good for her own mental health to carry such hurt and anger. 'Forgive and forget' was the old saying, yet Blake wasn't ready to do either and didn't know if she ever would be.

As she lost herself in miserable thoughts, she barely registered the Land Rover emerging from the narrow track. It pulled onto the road in front of her then began moving away at a moderate speed.

Blake looked up, swore under her breath, and started the engine. Then she was following behind the Bodilys, keeping her distance as the narrow country road curved and twisted. The excitement returned, fizzing through her veins. Ten minutes later, the Land Rover joined the A3083. Just as Blake had predicted, more traffic appeared. She continued to follow, letting a motorbike insert itself between her car and the Land Rover. Then the Bodilys were turning off the road and into the large Sainsbury's car park, situated on the outskirts of Helston.

Blake slowed down, watching them park, then pulled into a space in the row behind. She switched off the engine and waited for the Land Rover's passengers to alight. The driver door opened, and a woman in her late fifties climbed out. Violet Bodily. She was a short, sturdy woman, with a bob of black hair streaked with grey, and small, furtive eyes. She wore a wax jacket over a plain dark dress that came to mid-shin, and thick winter tights. Blake watched the housekeeper pat down loose strands of hair, then reach inside the car to remove several shopping bags.

Now the passenger door was opening. But it was not Saul Bodily stepping out. It was the young woman Blake had seen wandering through the trees that stormy afternoon at Saltwater House.

Tegen Trezise. She was small in stature, with long blonde hair that reached down her back. Her skin was porcelain white, her large eyes round and curious as she glanced around the car park, then up at the huge supermarket building. Like Violet Bodily, she wore a wax jacket, but this one was oversized and clearly not her own. Beneath it was a flowing purple dress that looked too sheer to keep such a slight young woman warm in winter.

Blake's heart raced as she watched the two disappear through the supermarket sliding doors, Tegen Trezise skipping with excitement. This was an unexpected opportunity, one that she needed to play carefully. Leaving her car, she quickly followed them inside and grabbed a shopping basket from the stack by the entrance.

They were just ahead of her. Violet Bodily pushed a shopping trolley with one hand while clutching a shopping list in the other. Tegen flitted from shelf to shelf like a worker bee, gathering up armfuls of fruits and vegetables, then placing them in the trolley, before flying off again.

Blake shifted to one side, casually picking up a jar of manuka honey and pretending to check the ingredients.

Watching the teenager was like watching an excited young child. Her eyes were everywhere, flitting from shelf to shelf, then from shopper to shopper, as if the supermarket were the most exciting place she'd ever been. As for Violet Bodily, she smiled warmly at Tegen and exchanged pleasant conversation. This was not the hostile woman Blake had encountered over the intercom, or the cold-hearted housekeeper Campbell Green had described. Instead, Violet Bodily watched over the teenager in an almost maternal fashion.

The two continued to shop, Blake trailing behind while casually filling her basket with items. She wondered how she was going to talk to Tegen when she wasn't leaving Violet's side. But minutes later, as they reached the cash registers and joined the queue, the housekeeper unwittingly created the perfect opportunity.

"Oh, will you look at that?" she said. "This bag of flour is leaking."

Tutting, she looked around for a shop assistant. Tegen tapped her urgently on the shoulder.

"I'll get another one," she said.

Violet didn't look convinced. She glanced down the line of customers and saw the cashier hand over a receipt then begin scanning the next shopper's items.

"Please, Violet," Tegen said. "I can do it."

The housekeeper looked around one more time, shook her head, then let out a sigh. "Very well. But you'll need to hurry. Do you remember where to find it?"

"By the eggs. And don't worry, I'll be as fast as I can."

Tegen scurried off, light on her feet and far too enthused for such a mundane task.

Blake shot a look at Violet Bodily, who watched Tegen hurry

away, the sleeves of her oversized jacket flapping as she moved. Then Blake spun on her heels and darted back along the aisle. Reaching the end, she turned the corner and scanned the overhead signs, until she saw the sign for the home baking section. Half running now, she headed towards it then slowed right down. Tegen Trezise was halfway up the aisle, a puzzled expression crumpling her brow as she scanned the various types of flour.

Blake approached. Tegen bent her knees and ran a finger along one of the shelves.

"Baking something?" Blake asked, smiling warmly.

The teenager flinched and tensed her shoulders, startled by the stranger standing next to her.

"Sorry," Blake said. "I didn't mean to scare you."

Tegen blushed. Her gaze flitted to the shelf then back towards Blake. She smiled nervously.

"The flour burst," she said, in a quiet voice. "I mean the bag did."

She giggled, then her smile wavered and she returned to studying the shelf. She really was innocent and childlike, Blake thought, not at all like a typical seventeen-year-old.

Tegen plucked a bag of flour from the shelf.

"Got it," she said, and turned to leave.

Blake shot out a hand. "Wait. Are you Tegen?"

The teenager froze. Clutching the bag of flour tightly to her chest, she stared wildly at Blake. "How do you know that?"

"Because I'm a friend of Campbell Green."

Tegen's expression changed from bewilderment to shock, then to panic.

"Look, I know this is weird," Blake said, trying to calm her.

"And I didn't mean to ambush you like this, but I need your help."

"What kind of help?" Tegen glanced over her shoulder towards the end of the aisle. When she looked back again her eyes were misty with tears. "Is it about my sister?"

"Yes, it is. And I'm so sorry for your loss. But I'm trying to help Campbell find out what happened to Kerenza. The not knowing is eating him up inside. He told me you were the only one who was ever kind to him when he and Kerenza were together. He's hoping you'll be kind again and help him now."

"How?"

"I'd like to ask you some questions."

Tegen slid a foot back, then twisted around to check the other end of the aisle.

"I can't help," she said. "Everyone would be angry."

"Please, Tegen. All Campbell wants is to understand what happened. And maybe visit Kerenza's grave."

The teenager suddenly jerked her head. Violet Bodily was calling her name from somewhere nearby. She clutched the bag of flour even tighter to her chest, threatening to burst it. "I have to go now."

"Please," Blake said again. "I know that everyone is upset right now, but is it really fair for Campbell to be left out in the cold like this? All he ever did was love your sister. He and Kerenza were planning to spend the rest of their lives together. Isn't that worth something?"

The housekeeper's voice was closer now and sounded more exasperated. "Tegen! Where on earth have you got to with that flour?"

Pulling her wallet from her pocket, Blake removed one of

her business cards and held it out. "Please take it. Call me. I'm not trying to get anyone into trouble."

Tegen stared at the card but didn't take it.

"It's not safe for Campbell to come," she whispered. "It's not safe for anyone."

She peered over Blake's shoulder and drew in a sharp breath. Blake didn't need to turn around to know Violet Bodily was marching straight towards them.

"There you are!" she said, sounding more like the housekeeper Blake had encountered that afternoon. "Have you got the flour? We're holding everyone up."

"Please," Blake whispered, as Violet's footsteps grew louder. "One phone call, that's all."

Tegen hesitated, then snatched the card and slipped it inside her jacket pocket.

"Please don't tell my father I was here," she said, her voice trembling.

Then she was scurrying past Blake and towards Violet Bodily, who immediately began scalding her and pulling her in the opposite direction. When Blake peered back a few seconds later, the two were already gone.

11

BLAKE RETURNED HOME that evening to find her mother preparing the evening meal in the kitchen. She kissed Mary on the cheek, then plucked a cherry tomato from a salad bowl on the counter and ate it.

"Wash your hands," Mary said, batting her fingers away as they reached to take another.

Blake did as she was told, then pulled cutlery from a drawer and began setting the small kitchen table.

"How was your day?" Mary asked over her shoulder.

"Long. But I think I've finally made some progress on the case." She stared at her mother's back. Mary nodded but said nothing more. "How was yours?"

"Oh, you know. Your Aunt Hester came for a visit. She's upset because Mabel died."

"Sorry to hear that."

"Mind you, that cat lived the life of Riley. Probably had a better life than most people. And it was old. Can you fill the jug with water?"

Blake hovered for a moment, aware that her mother had still

not made eye contact with her. She went to the cupboard, fetched the jug, and began filling it with water and ice.

"Hester said Kenver is doing better with his drinking these days. That's good, isn't it? She was worried there for a while. Mind you, I'm still surprised he's stuck around here and not gone back to London."

"Me too," said Blake. "I thought he would at least move somewhere a bit more happening than Wheal Marow."

"There's nothing wrong with Wheal Marow. Anyway, why do you think he's still here and not gone back?"

"Maybe he realised London isn't the best place for him. Too many temptations." Blake set the water jug down on the table. "Can I do anything else?"

"Sit down. It's almost ready." Mary brought the salad bowl over, then removed a chicken casserole from the oven.

"Does he ever get in trouble?" she asked, bringing it to the table.

Blake frowned. "What do you mean?"

"Well, because of the way he looks."

"Everybody has tattoos these days, Mum."

"You don't. Anyway, it's more than that, isn't it? Kenver's quite different from most folk around here."

Blake unconsciously glanced downward. There was a small peace symbol tattooed just above her left hip bone, a casualty from her misspent youth, and one that her mother still didn't know about.

"Different is good," she said. "Otherwise it would be a very boring world, don't you think?"

With dinner ready, Blake's mother joined her at the small kitchen table. It used to be that they ate evening meals in the dining room, but after Ed's departure Mary had complained the room felt too large. Now they ate here in the kitchen, plates kissing, condiments squeezed into tight spaces.

Conversation was light and stilted as they dined together. Blake flicked occasional glances at Mary, who was still struggling to make eye contact. Blake's thoughts returned to today's events. She thought about Kerenza Trezise, and she wondered again why the woman had jumped to her death without leaving any kind of message. Had it been intentional? To punish, as Campbell had suggested earlier today. Or had Kerenza jumped spontaneously, her emotional state so unstable there hadn't been time to leave a note?

From what Blake had learned so far, Kerenza had lived a lonely and isolated life, her paintings the only escape from it. Until they were rejected. What a blow that must have been. Perhaps someone more resilient would have picked up the paintbrush again and started work on a new creation. But Kerenza hadn't done that, which made Blake wonder just how fragile she had become.

And what of Campbell? Meeting him had provided Kerenza with another opportunity to escape the isolation, whether she had loved him or not. Yet she hadn't taken it. Had Campbell come along too late? Or had jumping from the balcony been Kerenza's own way to escape without having to rely on anyone else?

But why did she do it on her wedding day, in front of her entire family? Was Campbell right? Had it been to punish? Even if that were true, the question of why remained unanswered.

Blake reached for her glass of water. Something didn't feel right about this case, and it was more than just missing information. In the supermarket, Tegen Trezise had demonstrated childhood wonder at visiting somewhere so mundane. But her excitement had quickly paled when Blake talked to her, and her last words had trembled with fear: "Please don't tell my father I was here."

The image that Blake was conjuring of Griffin Trezise was of an overbearing tyrant who kept a tight rein on his family from the confines of his study. How did someone exude such power like that? How did he make a seventeen-year-old young woman tremble when he wasn't even present?

"Blake?" Her mother's voice brought her back to the kitchen table. "Are you listening to me?"

"Sorry. I was just thinking about the case." Blake looked up and saw Mary had finally made eye contact. She looked tired, slight shadows circling her eyes. There was a sadness to them that made Blake sigh. "Mum, are you lonely?"

Mary flinched and stared at the table. She was silent for a moment before looking up again. "After forty years of marriage I'd be lying if I said I wasn't. How about you?"

"I don't know. Sometimes, I suppose. But I'm used to being on my own. You're not."

"I'm not alone, bird. I've got you."

"It's not the same."

Blake leaned back on the chair. Kerenza Trezise must have felt so alone in the world to no longer want to be in it. Now her absence had ripped a hole open in Campbell Green's heart, forcing it to bleed out. Blake felt lonely sometimes, now more than she ever had, but she was glad that she had never experienced the depths of loneliness that had plagued Kerenza Trezise. That were still tormenting Campbell.

She stared at her mother. "Tomorrow, I'm going to start looking for my own place. This was always supposed to be a temporary measure and I've been here long enough."

"Bird, you can stay here as long as you want. You know that."

"It doesn't matter. The longer I stay, the lonelier I'm making you."

Mary gasped, lines creasing her brow. "You're not —"

"Yes, I am. Because you miss Ed, and you desperately want to take him back. You can't do that while I'm here. I'm not going to pretend I like it, because I don't. But you have a right to be happy, and if that means Ed moving back in and me moving out, then so be it."

"Blake, you don't have to . . ." Mary's voice trembled then faded into silence.

Reaching for her mother's hand, Blake smiled sadly. "Yes, I do. I can't be in the same house as him."

She squeezed Mary's hand, then released it. Picking up her fork, she started eating again. Suddenly she was hungry and desperate to not say another word.

———————————————

Two hours later, Blake was in bed and trying but failing to read the crime novel she'd borrowed from Mary. It was the right decision to move out. She was pushing forty and the embarrassment she felt every time someone asked if she was still staying with her mother was slowly crushing her to death. And whether she liked it or not, her parents were getting back together. She didn't want to think about that any more than she needed to, hence the borrowed book. But Blake had never been a fan of crime fiction; she found the stories overly dramatic, and not at all like real life.

She was about to switch off the light when her mobile phone buzzed on the side table. She tiredly reached for it and saw an anonymous caller ID on the screen. She pressed the phone to her ear and said hello.

Silence answered her, followed by a trembling female breath that made the line crackle. Blake sat up straight. "Tegen?"

"I can't talk for long," a young voice whispered. "I'm not allowed to use the phone."

Pulling back the sheets, Blake got to her feet, crossed the room, and fetched a notebook and pen from her bag.

"Hello, Tegen," she said. "I'm glad you called."

The teenager let out an anxious breath. "I don't know why I did. What do you want?"

"The same thing you do. To understand what happened to your sister." She perched on the edge of the bed and opened the notebook, pen poised over a blank page.

There was a long pause before Tegen spoke again. "You're working for Campbell?"

"Not knowing why Kerenza ended her life is slowly destroying him. It's why he hired me. He knows it won't change anything or bring her back, but knowing why she died might help him to say goodbye. Don't you think that would be a good thing for Campbell? For all of you?"

The quiet was punctuated by Tegen's soft breathing.

Blake stared at the empty page of her notebook. "Don't you want to know what happened to your sister?"

"I already know." The young woman's voice trembled. "It's this house. Everyone dies here."

The fine hairs on Blake's forearms prickled as she scribbled into her notebook. "Why would you say that?"

"Because Saltwater House is a bad place. Terrible things have always happened here. I wish I could leave, but I can't. All of us are trapped here whether we want to be or not."

"Why can't you leave?"

Tegen fell silent. She was quiet for so long that Blake wondered if she had hung up. But then another long breath rattled the phone speaker.

"I shouldn't have called," the teenager said. "I shouldn't have talked to you in the supermarket."

"Wait. Please don't hang up yet." Blake's mind raced. How did she play this? Tegen was not old enough to be regarded as an adult, yet not young enough to be treated like a child. But she was still technically a minor, and Blake would be breaking all sorts of moral codes if she were to manipulate Tegen into giving her what she wanted. Besides, that was not her way of getting to the truth.

Softening her voice, Blake tried again. "You know, when I was about your age, my best friend disappeared. Her name was Demelza. She was like a sister to me. I spent most of my life wondering what happened to her. Where did she go? Was she still alive? Eighteen years of not knowing can really mess you up. I don't want that to happen to you, Tegen. Or to Campbell, or the rest of your family. Because what happened to your sister was awful, but I guarantee you that the emptiness and not knowing she left behind is only going to grow worse. It will eat away at you all, until there's nothing left. I can help you. I can fill some of the emptiness by finding out why Kerenza died."

"I told you," Tegen said. "It's this place. It drives you mad."

"And yet Campbell told me that even just a few days before their wedding, Kerenza was perfectly happy. She told him that she couldn't wait for their new life to begin."

"She was stupid to say that. No one is happy here because we're not allowed to be."

"But your sister was leaving Saltwater House. So it doesn't make sense why she —"

"You don't understand. You can't. This place doesn't let you go, even if you try to leave like Kerenza did."

"Then help me to understand. Let me come to Saltwater House."

"No. My father would never allow it."

"All I want is to talk to your family, maybe have a look around to see if I can find anything that explains what happened to Kerenza. Then I'll leave again, I promise."

"They won't talk to you. They don't like strangers coming inside. Not even Campbell. That's why they wouldn't let him come to the funeral."

"But you would have let him if you were in charge, wouldn't you?" Blake smiled, knowing it was true. "You like Campbell. He told me you were always kind to him."

"Campbell was funny. He listened to me," said Tegen, her voice cracking. "It's so lonely here."

Blake's chest swelled. It seemed that the gates of Saltwater House not only kept strangers out, but also the excitement and reckless abandon of friendship and youth. Better to be rich with love than poor with money was what Blake's father liked to say.

"I'm sure Campbell would love to hear from you," she told Tegen. "He's your friend. Friends help each other."

"I can't help him."

"But he needs you."

Silence. Then Tegen said, "Did you ever find your friend? The one that went missing?"

Blake swallowed, her throat suddenly dry. "Yes, I did."

"What happened to her?"

"Someone killed her."

More silence. Blake tightened her grip on the pen.

"Come tomorrow at two o'clock," Tegen said. "You'll need to hide your car somewhere. I'll wait for you by the gate."

The line disconnected before Blake could thank her. Excitement running through her veins, she stared at the only words she'd written in her notebook: *Everyone dies here.*

Tomorrow, she would find out why.

12

THE FOLLOWING AFTERNOON, Blake returned to Saltwater House. A heavy fog had descended, blanketing the road and surrounding woodland. Blake parked the car at the edge of the tree line as she had done days before, then continued the rest of the journey on foot. The fog was disorienting, twice making her step off the track and almost collide with a tree. Soon, the wrought iron gates of Saltwater House appeared before her. Blake peered between the bars. The fog continued into the distance, tree branches reaching out like ghostly hands.

Removing her phone from her pocket she saw that she was on time. So where was Tegen? She waited five minutes, the lack of birdsong unnerving her and the fog dampening her skin. She glanced up at the security camera on top of the gate pillar, then gave the gates a frustrated shake. She was about to give up and return to the car when she heard the crunch of foliage underfoot. A figure appeared from the fog on the other side of the gates, small and slight, moving nervously. As it came closer, Blake recognised the same young woman she had talked to in the supermarket. Tegen Trezise. She stopped inches from the gates and stared up at Blake with large, curious eyes. Her long white-blonde hair was as pale as the fog. She remained silent, the fingernails of her right hand clicking together.

"Hello," Blake said.

The teenager glanced over her shoulder, then smiled nervously. Reaching into the pocket of her long winter coat, she produced a large bunch of keys, selected one, and slipped it into the gate lock.

Blake felt a surge of excitement as the gates swung open with a metallic groan.

"Come in," Tegen said, her voice unsure of itself.

Blake stepped through the gates and waited as she locked them again. They stood for a second, assessing each other. Then Tegen turned on her heels and began walking away.

Blake followed her. "Won't we have been spotted on the security camera?"

"Saul and Violet have finished early today. Violet's got to go to the dentist. She's the only one here who checks the monitor."

There was a nervous energy about the young woman. She was light on her feet and she kept glancing back at Blake, as if she had just welcomed a fox into a chicken coop.

"Thanks for agreeing to see me," Blake said, trying to sound reassuring. "I promise not to take up too much of your time."

A sudden breeze cut through the fog, making it swirl and spin. Behind them, the gates had already been swallowed up.

"There are some places I can't take you," Tegen said. "Like the orangery because that's where Abbie will be. And if you want to see the house we'll have to sneak around. Jack and Father definitely won't be pleased you're here."

"Maybe we could talk first, just you and me. About Kerenza."

The path turned and Tegen stepped off it, heading for the trees. "Then I'll take you to where Kerenza is buried. I'm the only one who visits her, so we'll be left alone."

Blake slid to a halt. The breeze changed direction and the fog momentarily parted, revealing Saltwater House. It was an impressive three-storey manor house with a facade of silvery-grey stone and colonnaded wings of mellow brick, all covered in veins of ivy. A pillared porch stood at its centre, with three stone steps leading to an arched front door made of oak. Rows of latticed windows populated each floor including the roof, which was covered with slates and topped by four towering chimney stacks.

It was an impressive sight, like something out of a Jane Austen novel, but Blake could not forget that Saltwater House had been built from the dying breaths of thousands of Black slaves.

Tegen was growing impatient. She stepped back onto the path and reached for Blake's arm. "Come on, we don't want to be seen."

As Blake was guided through the woodland that surrounded Saltwater House, she thought about the strange ritual Tegen had performed. She wanted to ask about it but decided to wait. Revealing that she had been spying on the teenager was not the best way to build trust.

"Do you go to school?" she asked.

Tegen pulled her gently to the left, around a thick oak tree. She appeared unworried by the fog, easily navigating the terrain as if on a clear day.

"I've never seen inside a school," she said. "Kerenza used to teach Jack and me at home, but now that she's gone there are no more lessons."

"Can't Abigail teach you?"

"Abbie doesn't care about me. I wasn't grown in a plant pot."

"What about going to college or university? You must be around that age."

"What's the point when I have to stay here?"

"Kerenza went to Oxford University. So could you."

Tegen sighed. "She only went for a year. But then she was made to come back here and take care of me and Jack."

"What about friends?" Blake asked.

"Don't have any. Even if I did, it's not like I'd be able to stay in touch with them. Father won't let me have a mobile phone or internet access." She smiled sadly, then shook her head. "Anyway, it doesn't matter. I'm busy educating myself with all I need to know."

Blake stared at her. "What does that mean?"

But Tegen only smiled, then tugged on her arm again, skirting around a stretch of bog water. The crunch of foliage underfoot was the only sound. It was unnerving, like when snow falls to silence the world. Blake stared at her guide as they walked. To grow up as a child in such isolation with no friends would surely have taken its toll. At least the Trezise children would have had each other, and nature as their playground.

"How do you become a private investigator?"

The question surprised Blake. "Well, anyone can become a private investigator in this country. You still don't need a license, which I think is outrageous."

"Do you have one?"

"Yes, and I took every private investigator course under the sun, then worked for a few companies until I was good enough to go it alone."

Tegen stared at her with wide eyes. "Anyone can become a private investigator?"

"Anyone with half a brain who likes solving puzzles. But you need genuine experience and training to become a great one."

"Kerenza liked puzzles. She was always doing the ones from the newspaper."

They stepped out of the woods and into a grassy clearing. The fog was lighter here, revealing a small cemetery surrounded by a fence of iron bars. Tegen slowed to a halt and released her grip on Blake's hand.

"She's in here," she said, pushing open the gate.

Blake followed her inside and stopped still. There were at least twenty headstones, monuments, and sculptures, some crumbling and leaning to one side, others more recent and only slightly weathered. Just in front of where Tegen was standing was a fresh grave, the soil top still exposed.

"There's no headstone yet," Tegen said, dewy-eyed. "We have to wait for the earth to settle, otherwise it will sink."

"Tell me about her," Blake said softly.

"Kerenza was good and kind. She was like a mother to me and Jack. He's my twin, although you would never think it."

"Why not?"

"Well, I'm blonde and he's dark-haired. I like nature and he's, well, angry all the time. We argue a lot." She bowed her head and clasped her hands together. A small breath escaped her lips. "Our real mother died giving birth to us. It's terrible, isn't it? That she gave her life so we could live ours. I feel so guilty sometimes."

"I'm sorry," Blake said. "But you must know it's not your fault."

"That's what Kerenza used to say. At least my mother's free now."

Tree branches creaked above Blake's head. The breeze picked up, making the fog swirl and dance around the graves.

She stooped down in front of an ornate sculpture of a weeping woman draped over a small tomb. Words were engraved on the tomb wall: 'Olivia Trezise. Mother. Wife. Now in the calm after the storm.' She glanced up at Tegen.

"Do you think your sister was depressed?"

Tegen paused to wipe tears from her cheeks. "Kerenza used to get sad a lot. In fact, the only time she seemed happy was when she was painting. She was very good at it. But then one day she stopped. She took all her paintings out to the old coach house and burned them. I don't know why. Then she was sad again." A smile lit up Tegen's face. "But then Campbell came along and they fell in love, and it was the happiest I ever saw my sister. When Campbell asked her to marry him, she said yes straightaway. She told me she couldn't wait to leave this place, and even though she would be leaving me behind, I wasn't sad. Because I knew then what I know now. That if you ever try to leave Saltwater House, it will always pull you back."

"You don't know that. You're still so young with your whole life ahead of you. Besides, didn't your brother leave?"

Tegen pointed at the grave next to Kerenza's. "He still ended up here. Just like we all will."

Blake read the words engraved on the headstone: 'Aidan Trezise. Our brother.' She frowned. Hadn't he also been a son? His fight with his father must have been bitter and final, beyond forgiveness.

"Do you believe in God?" Tegen asked, staring at her curiously.

Another surprise question. "That's difficult to answer."

"You don't go to church?"

"No. My mother does, every Sunday like clockwork. How about you?"

Tegen frowned and shook her head. "What about your friend, the one you told me about on the phone? Demelza. Don't you ever visit her grave?"

Blake felt a pang of guilt. "Sometimes. Mostly I visit her mother."

"What's she like?"

"Faith is kind and gentle. She puts on a brave face, even though she's lost so much. I'm meant to be seeing her tonight, actually."

"What do you do when you're together?"

"We talk. Sometimes Faith cooks. Sometimes I bring Chinese food." She smiled. "I don't think she likes it very much though, but she's too polite to say."

"Then maybe you should stop bringing it," Tegen said.

Blake's smile faded. Her gaze returned to the recently dug grave. "Anyway, we're not meant to be talking about Faith Penrose. We're meant to be talking about your sister, Kerenza. It doesn't make any sense to me. If she was so happy and couldn't wait to leave, why is she buried right here?"

Tegen sighed. "How many times do I have to tell you? It's because of this place."

"But that's *all* it is." Blake could hear the frustration in her own voice. "A place, not a prison. You're almost eighteen, Tegen. You should be on the other side of those gates, living your best life, seeing friends, and getting up to mischief. Why aren't you?"

The teenager shook her head. "Why don't you get it? I *can't* leave. None of us can."

"So you keep saying. But I'm not hearing why."

"It's because of the —"

Suddenly the fog parted and the figure of a woman approached. As she came closer, Blake saw that she was in her early thirties, with a bun of black hair and a face that was pale and taut. She glared first at Blake, then at Tegen.

"Who is this?" she demanded, stabbing a finger in Blake's direction. "And what on earth is she doing here?"

Blake stepped forward and held out a hand. "My name is —"

"I'm not talking to you," the woman snapped. "I knew you were up to no good, Tegen. You need to explain what is happening right now."

Flinching, the teenager shrugged her shoulders and dropped her gaze to the ground. "This is Blake, a friend of Campbell's. She's helping to find out why Kerenza died."

The woman's eyes grew round and furious as she clenched her jaw.

"Please, Abbie," Tegen said. "We've been so cruel to Campbell. Doesn't he deserve to know?"

"Either she leaves now or I call the police and have her arrested for trespassing."

"But she's not trespassing! I invited her in."

Abigail Trezise caught her breath, then leaned in closely until her face was inches from Tegen's. "She leaves now. Then you and I are going to have a long conversation about inviting strangers into our home."

"I'm sorry this is a surprise to you," Blake said, stepping in between them. "I'm not here to cause trouble. I'm a private investigator hired by Campbell Green to investigate the suicide of his fiancée. I just need to ask a few questions, then I'll leave."

Slowly, Abigail straightened up. She was taller than Blake by a few inches and did a good impression of a Victorian school mistress. "I don't care who you are. And I don't care for Campbell Green thinking that he still has some sort of say over what goes on in this house. We all know what happened to our sister. We watched her die with our own eyes. So you can tell him to give up this ridiculous charade and leave our family alone."

Now it was Tegen's turn to step between the two women. She stared up at Abigail, her large eyes hard and narrowed.

"No," she said. "Blake is my guest. And I'm going to show her around and answer her questions, whether you like it or not."

Before her sister could reply, she grabbed Blake by the arm and pulled her through the gate and away from the cemetery. Then they were hurrying across a grassy lawn, the fog swarming all around.

Abigail bellowed behind them. "Tegen Trezise! You come back here right now!"

Tegen's grip tightened on Blake's wrist as she quickened her step.

"I'll tell Father!" Abigail cried. "I'll tell Father and then you'll be in terrible trouble."

Tegen marched on, dragging Blake behind her.

"Maybe this is a bad idea," Blake said, hurrying along. But what choice did she have? This was her only chance to be here and gain answers.

"No, you came here to help, so that's what you're going to do. You just might not have long to do it."

They heard Abigail growl, then take off after them, her feet heavy on the ground. Then she veered away, heading in a different direction.

"If there was one place you needed to go right now, where would it be?" Tegen asked.

Blake's mind raced. "Kerenza's room."

"Then that's where we'll go."

Saltwater House emerged from the fog like a leviathan rising from the depths of the ocean. It was the rear of the building, with steep stone steps rising to a terrace. As they raced up them towards the back door, Blake saw a large and faded blood stain. Then they were entering the house, and she wondered how much trouble she was about to dive into.

13

As Blake followed Tegen into the house through what would have once been the servants' entrance, the feeling that she had made a mistake tightened like a knot in her chest. But it was too late to turn back now. She let the teenager guide her through a laundry room and into the kitchen, where she half expected to see pheasants hanging from hooks. But the room was a surprising mix of old and new, with slate floor tiles, green marble counters, and an enormous range cooker.

Then the kitchen was left behind, Blake struggling to keep up with Tegen as they ducked down a narrow corridor, through an arched case opening, then took a sharp right and entered a square hallway with waxed floorboards and original framed portraits hanging from wood panelled walls. Stuffed and mounted animals, all covered in dust, watched Blake from side tables as she hurried by. She spotted a fox, a mink, even an owl with its wings stretched in flight. She grimaced. Taxidermy was an art form she did not appreciate.

Tegen swerved right, heading down another dimly lit corridor, then gripped Blake's wrist and put her finger to her own lips.

"My father's study," she mouthed and pointed to a large oak door. They tip-toed past. Tegen pulled Blake through another opening and into an even larger hall with more wood panels and a grand staircase that snaked upwards to the next floor. Blake felt dizzy and disoriented. Saltwater House was like a maze with no end.

"Come on," Tegen whispered.

They raced upstairs and along yet another gloomy corridor with doors on both sides. Despite there being a third floor of attic rooms there were no more staircases. Blake presumed there would be a separate access to reach what would have once been the servants' quarters.

"This is it," Tegen said, coming to a halt in front of one of the middle doors. She hesitated, her fingers trembling in front of the handle, then opened the door and ushered Blake inside.

An eerie silence descended as the door was shut again. The room was painted olive green, with a king-sized bed set against one wall, the bed sheets neatly laid and free of creases. Clothes were draped over a button back armchair in one corner, while a chaise longue sat next to a small bookshelf in another. Pressed against the far wall, a dressing table with an ornate mirror still held various makeup, lotions, and creams.

The balcony from which Kerenza had jumped to her death lay beyond a pair of French doors. The curtains were currently open, but all Blake could see through them was thick fog.

"It's a lovely room," she said softly, noticing a faint trace of perfume clinging to the air.

Tegen moved to the centre of the floor and turned in a slow half-circle.

"I come in here most days," she said. "I sit on the edge of the bed and listen. Sometimes I think I can hear her. Once I thought I felt her sitting next to me."

Tears silently spilled down her cheeks. Blake hovered, wondering if she should go to her. But as she stepped forward, Tegen flinched.

"You can take a look around if you want," she said, wiping her face. "But you need to be quick. They'll be here soon."

Blake let her eyes wander about the room. She moved towards the chair in the corner and touched the clothes that were draped over the arm. Then she stepped towards the dressing table, her fingertips grazing Kerenza's possessions. A corsage of white and purplish flowers, designed to be worn on the bride's wrist, sat in the centre of the table, its petals now shrivelled and slowly turning to dust.

"Tell me about the morning of the wedding," Blake said.

Tegen sat down on the edge of the bed and carefully smoothed out the crumples she had made. "Kerenza wanted to be left alone. That's what I remember most. I'd come upstairs to help with her hair and makeup. Abigail could have helped too, but she didn't approve of the wedding, so she was downstairs. Anyway, once she was in her dress and looking beautiful, Kerenza asked me to leave her alone. Not in a cruel way. She said everything was about to change, and that knowing she was about to leave Saltwater House was making her nervous. So she needed a moment to take it all in."

"So you left then?"

Getting up again, Tegen wandered over to the balcony doors and peered out. Without looking at Blake she bowed her head. "I wished her luck and told her that I loved her, then I went downstairs. I wish I hadn't."

There was a framed photograph of a woman on the dresser, next to the corsage. Blake picked it up. The woman was beautiful, dark-haired and with high cheekbones, but her eyes were filled with ghosts.

"That's Kerenza's mother," Tegen said, watching her. "Father said she got sick and died, but we all know she went mad."

Carefully setting it down again, Blake pulled open the top drawer of the dressing table and found another small picture frame inside. This one was empty.

"What happened then?" she asked. "After you went downstairs?"

"I joined the others outside. Jack was getting drunk even though we're not old enough. Abigail was taking her anger out on the catering staff."

"And your father?"

"He arrived a few minutes later, all smiles and charm, pretending he was so happy about the wedding."

Blake closed the drawer and ran a finger through the dust that had settled on the table surface. "Who else was at the wedding?"

"Some people Father used to know. Some of Campbell's family. They seemed nice, but none of my family bothered to talk to them."

"And friends?"

"I told you, we don't have any."

"What about Violet and Saul?"

"They were there, but not as guests. Father put them to work as usual, which I thought was wrong. Violet and Saul have been like family to us, especially to Kerenza and me."

"You're close with them?"

"I suppose. They never had their own children, and they feel sorry for me, I think."

"Is that why Violet sneaks you out to the supermarket?"

Tegen's eyes shot towards the door. "She says it's not good for me to be stuck here all the time. If my father found out he would fire her on the spot."

"So, the wedding. You came downstairs. Jack and Abigail were already there, and your father came a few minutes later. Then what?"

"And then Kerenza jumped out of the window."

"When you were with her earlier, did she show any sign that she was planning to end her life?"

Tegen shuddered and shook her head.

Blake touched a petal of the corsage and watched it crumble. She frowned, then gently moved the corsage to one side with her finger. There was powder beneath it, just a few fine grains that were red and earthy looking.

"Back in the cemetery, before your sister interrupted us, you were about to tell me why none of you can leave Saltwater House."

Tegen shrugged. "It's because of the curse."

Blake looked at her and almost laughed. "What?"

"There's a curse on my family. Has been for generations."

"Tegen, you don't really believe that, do you?" Blake said. "There's no such thing. Bad luck, yes. But curses? They're just fairy tales."

Tegen's face reddened as she glared at the floor. "I knew you wouldn't understand."

Suddenly there was commotion outside as thunderous footsteps stomped along the hall. The door flew open and Abigail Trezise marched inside. Her face was pulled into a sneer and her hands were clenched into fists. Then she was pushed aside by a young man, who was short and muscular, with black hair and eyes that crackled with rage. He glared at Blake before turning on Tegen.

"What the hell do you think you're doing?" he hissed, as he advanced into the room.

Tegen flinched but stood her ground. "Mind your own business, Jack. You're always interfering."

"This is all of our business, you stupid cow! You have no idea what you've done."

"Well, you have no idea what you're talking about because that would require a brain."

"Stop it, the pair of you," Abigail said.

Jack moved closer, the veins in his thick forearms almost bursting through his skin. Blake was about to jump in front of Tegen when an imposing figure pushed Abigail aside and stepped into the room.

Despite his silver hair and lined skin, Griffin Trezise was a formidable presence, towering over the others like a giant. Silence fell over the room. The fight left the young man, and he retreated like an attack dog that had been called off by its owner.

Ignoring Blake, Griffin Trezise fixed a steely gaze on his youngest daughter. When he spoke, his voice was deep and commanding. "Tegen, go to your room and stay there. *Now*. You too, Jack. Abigail, go back to whatever you were doing with your precious plants."

Abigail began to protest, but a stern look from her father immediately silenced her.

"Do I have to repeat myself?" The man said when no one moved.

One by one, the Trezise children left the room, Jack first,

fists pumping as he stormed away, quickly followed by Abigail, who flashed Blake a snake-eyed glare, then lastly Tegen.

"I'm sorry, Father," she whispered, as she hurried across the room. "I was only trying to help."

Griffin Trezise didn't look at her as she scurried away. Then Blake was alone with him.

She smiled, shifting her weight from one foot to the other.

"Well, this is awkward," she said.

Quickly removing her wallet, she produced her private investigator licence and held it up. "My name is Blake Hollow. I've been hired by —"

"We'll continue this discussion in my study," Griffin said, holding up a large hand. "Not in the bedroom of my deceased daughter."

He fixed Blake with a sharp look, then turned on his heels.

Blake hovered, her eyes shifting back to the dresser.

"Shit," she whispered, and followed Griffin Trezise out of the room, gently shutting the door behind her.

14

GRIFFIN TREZISE's office was just as Blake had expected. A large mahogany desk with a red leather top stood at the centre, bookcases lined every wall from ceiling to floor, the shelves filled with academic tomes of theology, anthropology, and ancient history, while a single leather armchair sat in front of the window, the plantation blinds shut. A beautifully carved antique drinks cabinet stood in the corner, with a silver tray containing two crystal whiskey glasses and a half empty decanter resting on top. A stuffed and mounted pine marten was perched on the edge of Trezise's desk, its beady glass eyes fixed on Blake, who sat on the other side of the desk.

"Tell me, Miss Hollow," Trezise said, his voice dripping with condescension as he peered over the half-moon spectacles balanced on his sharp nose. Whiskey soured his breath. "How is it that you came to be trespassing inside my home?"

Blake held his gaze. She had met men like him before, the kind who believed themselves the most important figure in the room, one of great authority who thought women had little purpose other than to breed and to serve.

"Technically, I wasn't trespassing," she said. "Your daughter invited me in and was willingly showing me around, until we were interrupted."

"And how exactly did Tegen come to be in a position where she could allow you in?"

"I asked, and she said yes."

"Playing games with me, Miss Hollow, is not an intelligent move. I need only make one phone call to have you arrested and your reputation in ruins, if indeed you even have one."

"Arrested for what exactly? I've committed no crime."

"We'll see what the chief superintendent has to say about that."

So, Trezise was a man with connections. She would need to play this carefully. Taking a breath, Blake relaxed her shoulders and placed her hands on the armrests of the chair. "I'll admit I did come here today with the intention of gaining entry, legally of course. As for Tegen, I happened to peer over the wall and see her walking through the woods."

"The perimeter wall is at least a foot taller than you, Miss Hollow. You weren't perhaps climbing over it?"

"Of course not, that would be trespassing. Besides, it's amazing how far you can stretch after years of yoga practice." She smiled. "When I explained to Tegen that I'd been hired by Campbell Green to investigate Kerenza's suicide, she agreed to let me in. I suppose she was curious for answers too, that's all. There was no manipulation on my part, and certainly no breaking and entering."

"And you didn't think to announce yourself at the gates instead of sneaking around like a thief in the night?"

"I tried that the other day. Your housekeeper very firmly told me to leave."

"Violet Bodily is a very loyal member of staff," said Trezise. "But tell me, what exactly does Campbell Green hope to gain by hiring a private investigator to infiltrate my home?"

"An explanation as to why your daughter ended her life on what should have been the happiest day of theirs. He's grieving, Mr Trezise. Just like your family is. He doesn't understand what happened, and because he was prevented from attending her funeral and continually denied the right to visit his fiancée's grave, his emotions are understandably raw."

Griffin Trezise looked away for a moment, staring at the shuttered blinds.

Blake leaned forward. "I understand this is a challenging time for you and your family. To lose a daughter, a sister, in the way that you all have, the pain must be indescribable. But what Campbell is struggling with is that there were no signs. He told me Kerenza was perfectly happy and looking forward to getting married. Tegen confirmed that just a few minutes ago. If that's true, why wouldn't you want to know why she killed herself?"

Griffin Trezise leaned back in his chair and emitted a sigh, appearing to sink into himself like a deflated balloon. "You don't know my family, Miss Hollow. There is a long history of ill luck. Sickness, madness, and death. None of us will truly ever know why Kerenza took her own life that day, but she was not the first. Her mother, my first wife, Olivia, was also an unwell woman. She had bouts of mania, followed by weeks of feeling so incredibly low that she could hardly get herself out of bed. If you've done your research correctly, and I'll assume that you have, you'll know that she was found dead in a field just a few miles from here. She'd gone mad, you see. She'd completely lost her mind, convinced that she was the next in line to die."

"Tegen mentioned a curse," Blake said, unsure of where the

conversation was heading, certainly not to a place where she'd been before. "She told me that none of you can truly leave Saltwater House for good."

Trezise surprised her by smiling, revealing crooked yellow teeth that had not seen a dentist's chair in several years. "Ah yes, the ridiculous family curse. Would you like to hear it?"

Blake nodded.

"A couple of hundred years ago, the Trezise family had amassed quite the fortune from, shall we say, international trade. At the time, a terrible famine had struck Cornwall. Crops had perished with no explanation, leaving the locals without food to eat and the farmers penniless. An elderly local woman, known as Mother Crow, lived in a nearby cottage and was said to be a witch. She came to the gates of Saltwater House one morning, pleading with the Trezise family to share their wealth by helping to feed the hungry. The master of the house at the time, William Trezise, refused. As a result, many people perished. Such was the anger of Mother Crow, she put a curse on Saltwater House and anyone who lived within it, condemning each family member to death and despair if they ever tried to leave."

Griffin sneered and raised his hands. "Obviously, it's nothing but a ridiculous story from a time when everyone believed in such nonsense. But I cannot deny there have been a number of tragic deaths and occurrences over the years. I've lost both my wives, my eldest son, and now my daughter Kerenza. However, I do not believe in curses, Miss Hollow. Nor bad luck. I believe in life and death, and the unpredictable nature of both."

"Tegen is utterly convinced the curse is true," Blake said. "Did Kerenza believe in it?"

"Tegen's head is always full of fanciful ideas. As for Kerenza, I'm a busy man. I don't have the time to discover every facet of

my children's lives. All I do know is that Kerenza's mother was
mentally unwell. They say it can be passed along, don't they? In
the same way as hair colour or the shape of one's eyes. Perhaps
Kerenza suffered from the same sort of affliction."

Blake stared at him incredulously. "If that were true, there
would have been signs. Surely you would have known. Did
Kerenza ever see a doctor? And your wife, Olivia, what was her
diagnosis?"

Trezise straightened his spine and cleared his throat, then
fixed Blake with a steely glare. "I'm not prepared to discuss these
private matters with a stranger. In fact, I've wasted enough time
talking to you. So, please return to Mr Green, and inform him
that we're as much in the dark about it as he is, and that hiring a
private investigator to wade into a business that does not belong
to her isn't going to help anyone."

"What about the toxicology report from the coroner?" Blake
pressed. "Maybe there's something there that could explain what
happened."

Glowering, Trezise slammed his palms on the desk. "Perhaps
you didn't hear me, Miss Hollow. Should I repeat myself?"

Blake was running out of time and options. She had one
wild card left to play, but it was a dangerous one.

"What keeps you so busy these days, Mr Trezise?" she asked,
coolly.

"I don't see how that's any of your business, but if you must
know, I'm involved in a great deal of philanthropy."

"Really? That's interesting. Because I did do my research, and
it looks like you *used* to donate to the odd fundraiser, now and
again, you know, for the sake of your reputation. But the much
more interesting little nugget I discovered was the source of your
family's wealth. What's that old saying? 'Behind every great

fortune lies a great crime.' Because it seems the privileged life-style the Trezise family has enjoyed over the past two hundred years comes from what you call international trading, and the rest of the world calls the slave trade."

Across the table, Griffin Trezise caught his breath. His sunken cheeks turned a shade of red, and his fingernails clawed the red leather of the desk.

"It wouldn't look good if it was made public, would it?" Blake said. "The benevolent philanthropist sitting on a pile of Old Money and living in a house that was paid for with the lives of thousands of Black slaves."

She leaned back, her heart racing as she waited for a response. It was a long time before Trezise gave her one.

"I don't care for blackmail," he said, his words slow and controlled.

Blake shrugged. "Blackmail is such an ugly word. Let's call it an exchange. You let me interview your family, and I won't tell anyone your dirty little secret."

Trezise's face was purple now, rage bubbling beneath the surface. "I'm very aware of how this family acquired its wealth. But the philanthropy I've done more than makes up for it, wouldn't you agree?"

"Except I didn't see any donations to Black causes in my research, Mr Trezise." Blake leaned forward again, meeting his furious gaze. "Look, I don't want to cause trouble for your family. All I'm asking is that you give me a chance to find out what happened to Kerenza. Campbell deserves to know. So do your children, come to that. And what about you? You already said you don't believe in curses, so there must be a legitimate reason why she did it. Do you really want to spend what's left of your life tormented by not knowing what it is?"

The silence was thick and cloying, pressing down on Blake, who was sure Trezise was about to reach across the table and throttle her with his bare hands. But he remained motionless, cold eyes boring into her.

"Exactly what do you want, Miss Hollow?" he said, at last.

"Five days, that's all. Five days in which I can visit Saltwater House and ask questions to try to ascertain what happened to your daughter. Hopefully I'll find some answers to help you all. Then I'll leave. You'll never hear from me again and I won't tell a soul about what I found."

"Two days," Griffin said, his eyes burning into hers. "Two days, and you sign a nondisclosure agreement."

"Three days, and I'll sign your NDA. But first you make a generous donation to one of the causes on this list." Blake fished a piece of notepaper from her pocket and dumped it in on the desk. "And you let Campbell Green visit Kerenza's grave."

She leaned back and held her breath as Trezise's face contorted into a grotesque caricature. For a moment she thought he was having a heart attack. But then his expression relaxed and his eyes glanced downward at the notepaper on the desk.

"You drive a hard bargain, Miss Hollow," he said. "But you're right. Knowing why Kerenza ended her life may help to appease my family's grief. I'll have my solicitor draw up the agreement."

Blake exhaled and slowly nodded. Then Trezise was leaning over the desk, his expression suddenly cruel and threatening.

"But mark my words," he said. "Cross me like this again and you will regret the very day you set foot in Saltwater House."

15

As Saltwater House disappeared in Blake's rear view mirror, the fog immediately began to lift. Excitement thrummed in her veins. She had played a dangerous move today, one that she knew was crossing all sorts of professional lines. But now she had three full days of unrestricted access to the Trezise family and their staff. She was still surprised that Griffin Trezise had agreed. Exposing the origin of the family wealth would certainly cause controversy, but the Trezises had already cut themselves off from society and Griffin no longer appeared to be involved in charitable ventures—so would the ensuing furore even reach them?

Perhaps then, despite his outwardly loveless persona, Griffin Trezise wanted to know why his daughter had taken her own life. Either way, three days wasn't a lot of time and the atmosphere was already hostile. If Blake was going to uncover the truth about Kerenza's death, she would need to be organised and ready to think fast on her feet.

Pulling over on the country lane, she checked she had enough phone signal, then made a crackly call to Campbell

Green. Upon hearing he was permitted to visit Kerenza's grave tomorrow, his voice cracked with emotion. He was to arrive at Saltwater House in the afternoon, where Blake would accompany him to the graveside and ensure there was no further trouble from the family.

"Thank you," Campbell said, close to tears. "I don't expect they'll cooperate with you over the next few days, but even if nothing comes of the investigation, at least you've given me the chance to say goodbye."

"Don't worry," Blake told him. "If the Trezises think they're stubborn, wait until they get to know me."

She hung up. She needed to make another call; one that she wasn't looking forward to. Instead, she sat for a moment, thinking about the strangeness of the Trezise family. They were a true anomaly of the twenty-first century, as if time had frozen at Saltwater House and stranded them in a purgatory where curses were real and the outside world was undiscovered territory.

As for the curse itself, Blake had heard similar stories before. Cornwall's rich history was full of hundreds of traditional tales and superstitions, borne from an era where people genuinely believed in magic and bad omens. There were still plenty of superstitious folk living in Cornwall today, throwing pinches of spilled salt over their shoulder to ward off bad luck or shuddering at the thought of opening an umbrella indoors. But a family curse? Even if Griffin Trezise thought it was nonsense, Tegen believed it was real. Blake didn't yet know where Jack and Abigail stood, but now that two of their siblings were dead, it wouldn't take much to convert even the hardiest cynics into believers.

Blake shook her head. A strange family indeed.

Heaving her shoulders, she picked up her phone again and called Faith Penrose.

The woman's voice was warm and soothing in her ear. "Blake? This is a pleasant surprise. How are you? I was just preparing dinner for tonight. Are you a fan of asparagus?"

Blake winced and peered through the windscreen. The sun was beginning to set over the field, the early winter night already drawing in.

"Actually, that's why I'm calling," she said. "I'm so sorry, Faith, but I have to cancel. I have a new case. A tricky one with a tight deadline."

She held her breath as the line went silent. She knew Faith would be disappointed; Blake was her only visitor these days, the rest of the town having turned their backs on her. But Blake also knew that if she didn't stay home and prepare, the next three days would be a wasted opportunity.

"That's exciting," Faith said, at last. She was doing her best to sound pleased for Blake. "I hope it's nothing too dangerous? You know how I worry about you."

"It's nothing I can't handle. I really am sorry, Faith. How about I come over this Monday instead, if you don't have any plans? We can watch some of those old Gregory Peck films you were telling me about. I'll even cook."

Another pause. "That would be lovely. I don't believe I've ever tasted your cooking."

"Don't get too excited. I can just about boil an egg." A pair of crows leapt from the hedgerow and flitted across the front of the car, startling Blake. It suddenly struck her that she hadn't heard a single bird the whole time she'd been at Saltwater House. "Faith? Are you still there? Are you sure you don't mind about tonight?"

"Of course not. It's important you take every case you're offered right now. We'll see each other soon." The words were light and jovial, but there was a tone to the woman's voice that suggested she'd grown used to disappointment. "How is your mother?"

"Oh, you know Mary." Blake didn't want to think about her mother right now, because it would inevitably lead her to think about her father. And a conversation about her parents always felt excruciatingly uncomfortable with Faith, particularly now there was talk of them getting back together.

"That's nice," Faith said. "Have you managed to find somewhere else to live yet?"

"I'm still looking."

More quiet. "You know, there's always a room here if you need your space."

"I —" Blake's voice caught in her throat. It wasn't the first time that Faith had suggested she move in with her. But as kind an offer as it was, Blake wasn't sure if she could live under the roof of a woman who had lost everything. It was selfish, she knew, but she could never replace the gaping hole that Demelza's death had left in Faith's life. And if she was brutally honest, she didn't want to.

"That's very kind of you. I'll keep it in mind," Blake said. "Well, I should go. I'm parked on a roadside in the middle of nowhere and it's getting dark."

"Oh yes, best to drive home as soon as you can. I'll see you after the weekend?"

Blake smiled. "It's a date."

She said goodbye and Faith hung up. The excitement she felt about spending the next three days at Saltwater House momentarily faded. Poor Faith, she thought. She wondered if the woman could ever find happiness again, or if this was her life now, empty and full of sorrow, with Blake her only company once a fortnight, sometimes not even that.

Pulling away, Blake drove through the oncoming darkness, thinking it was a terrible way to live.

16

REVEREND THOMPSON SWITCHED off the desk lamp, plunging her office into darkness, then stretched out her arms until she felt a satisfying pop in her upper spine. She had been hunched over the desk for the past hour, making last-minute amendments to tomorrow's sermon. It was going to be a special one, for the marriage of a local couple. The Reverend had always thought of herself as an old romantic, delighting in the love of the wedding couple, and their friends and family, so she liked to ensure her sermons reflected all those positive feelings. Her changes tonight would make tomorrow's marriage ceremony even more memorable.

Picking up her coat and bag, she exited the office and closed the door. The church was still and quiet. Built in the seventeenth century, its architecture was surprisingly ornate for an Anglican place of worship, which usually favoured a plainer aesthetic than the Catholic church. The lights she had left on cast the intricate stained-glass windows and sculpted cornice of the sanctuary in a soft, warm glow.

She had been the vicar of this parish for over two years. Her predecessor had been much loved by the local parishioners until sickness had forced him into early retirement. After an initial uneasy welcome, and the scepticism that came with being a female priest, she had gradually been embraced and was now considered a pillar of the community. Still, the struggle to fill the pews each Sunday was becoming greater with each passing month, although she knew it wasn't just her church experiencing a diminishing congregation.

Reverend Thompson walked along the left aisle of the nave, the soft clump of her shoes rising to the rafters, until she reached the front pew and sat down. Placing her coat and bag beside her, she smiled up at the large crucifix hanging over the sanctuary, then bowed her head in a final prayer for the evening. As her lips moved noiselessly, a sudden creaking broke her trance. It was late for a visitor. Nevertheless, Reverend Thompson finished her prayer and twisted around on the bench. At the far end of the nave the church door slammed shut, shattering the peace and quiet.

She looked left, then right, scanning the pews. For some unknown reason, her heart began to race and a cold sweat prickled the back of her neck.

"Hello?" she called out, but no one was there.

Sweeping up her belongings, the Reverend got to her feet and stared down the length of the central aisle. Then she was moving carefully along it, checking each row of benches. The homeless had been known on occasion to sneak inside, hoping for a bed for the night. The Reverend would have gladly provided, but there was a shelter in town and these days it was safer to keep the church door locked during the dark hours. But each pew was empty.

Reaching the heavy wooden church door, she stood, silently

listening to her own breaths and the low moan of the wind outside. Whoever had entered the church had clearly changed their mind and left again.

The Reverend relaxed her shoulders, looked across at the crucifix, and whispered goodnight. Switching out the lights, she opened the door and stepped outside.

Moonlight spilled over the front churchyard, illuminating the centuries-old headstones and the gravel path that led to the gates and the empty road beyond. It was cold, so the Reverend paused to button her coat before reaching inside her bag for a bunch of keys. Selecting a heavy brass key, she turned back to the door. As she slipped it into the keyhole, her hand brushed against the wood.

Reverend Thompson froze. Something warm and wet was smeared on her skin. And there was a smell, deep and coppery, clinging to the air.

The Reverend released her grip on the key and instinctively stepped back. She reached inside her bag again, removed her mobile phone, and activated the light.

Her hand was covered in blood.

Horrified, she pointed the light at the church door.

"Dear Lord!" she cried.

Painted on the wood in thick red blood was a large inverted five-pointed star enclosed in a circle. The blood was still fresh and oozing down the wood. The phone trembled in Reverend Thompson's hand. Her bag slipped from her shoulder as she fought for breath. She slipped one foot back, then the other, unaware that the strap of her bag had caught on her heel. The pentacle glistened like molasses in the phone light.

From the corner of Reverend Thompson's eye, she saw movement. She twisted around, wielding the phone like a weapon. As the light fell upon the headstones, her heart stopped in her chest.

The figure was dressed in black rags. A goat skull covered its face, the white bone gleaming, the horns sharpened at the tips. Behind the skull, eyes that were cold and violent bore into her own.

She screamed. Twisted around and tried to run. Reverend Thompson tripped over her bag and plunged forwards, landing on the grass. She rolled onto her back, clipping her left temple against one of the headstones. She felt warm blood on her skin. Then a surge of adrenaline pumping through her veins.

Ignoring the pain, she scurried back on her elbows until her shoulder struck yet another headstone. She held up a hand and squeezed her eyes shut.

"No!" she shrieked. "Please don't hurt me!"

She waited for the attack, sensed her bladder releasing itself. But no attack came.

Reverend Thompson opened her eyes. Slowly, she sat up. The figure was gone, leaving behind moonlit gravestones and darkness creeping in. The Reverend was alone again. Alone and filled with terror.

17

BLAKE RETURNED to Saltwater House at nine o'clock the next morning. The thick fog from yesterday had finally lifted, leaving the air crisp and cold, the sky iceberg blue. Approaching the gates, she climbed out of the car with the engine still running and went to press the intercom buzzer. But someone was already waiting for her on the other side. It was a tall, thin man in his sixties, with a ruddy face from years of outdoor work and soft brown eyes that regarded her politely from beneath a shock of thick silver hair. He was wearing a holey winter coat that was left unbuttoned, dirty blue overalls, and knitted fingerless gloves.

"Good morning," Blake said, holding up her private investigator licence. "Are you Saul Bodily?"

The man nodded as he reached inside his coat pocket for a large bunch of keys. "Mr Trezise mentioned you'd be coming. Thought you should make a proper entrance this time after yesterday's runaround."

He smiled wryly, his eyes twinkling, then unlocked the gates and pulled them open. The groan of rusty hinges filled the quiet.

Saul Bodily frowned then nodded to himself, as if making a mental note to come back with some oil.

"So, you're a private investigator?" he said, still standing there.

"That's right."

"Must be an interesting line of work."

Blake shrugged. "It has its moments."

The groundskeeper scratched at a stain on the front of his overalls. "S'pose you've come to ask questions about Kerenza."

"Right again. In fact, I was hoping I could talk to you while I'm here. Campbell told me that Kerenza liked you very much, and that you used to help them see each other without her father knowing."

Saul suddenly stiffened and glanced over his shoulder.

"Don't worry," Blake said. "I think what you did was a good thing. I won't be telling anyone else about it."

The man looked terribly sad. "I miss that girl something rotten. But I can't talk to you right now. Got things to do. Maybe later."

"I'll come and find you," Blake said, then thanked him and returned to her car.

Driving past, she smiled once then watched him lock the gates in her rear-view mirror before the lane twisted and Salt-water House appeared up ahead. Parking on a circular driveway with a stone fountain of running water at its centre, she switched off the engine and climbed out. Now that the fog had gone, she could see the house in all its grandeur. Yet it was also clear that the building was showing its age. Cracked and peeling paint clung to the window frames like wrinkles on elderly skin. Drain-pipes were rusted and the creeping ivy that covered the house was eating into the brickwork. It surprised Blake; she had assumed the wealthy kept their property in pristine condition, especially when they had staff to maintain it for them.

A cold wind chilled her neck and slipped beneath her clothes, aggravating the scar on her shoulder. Pulling her coat tightly around her body, she walked up to the front door and grasped the steel knocker. She rapped it three times against the wood then waited. And waited. When no one came, she tried again. A minute passed. Then another. Blake frowned. She had assumed the outcome of yesterday's encounter with Griffin Trezise would have gained her easy entrance. She stepped to one side and peered through the nearest windows, but the curtains were still closed.

Emitting a frustrated sigh, Blake started walking. As she rounded the corner, she began to get an idea of just how large the grounds of Saltwater House were. Woodland surrounded the estate on all sides, while large lawns and gardens filled the space in between. She saw myriads of flowerbeds, some overgrown with choking weeds, others filled with neglected plants in the throes of decay. She saw topiary hedgerows, sculpted into elephants and lions, others into chess pieces, all unkempt and in need of trimming. The ground changed beneath her feet from loose gravel to cracked pink paving. On her left was a large pond covered in duckweed. Ripples pooled on its surface as fish came up to feed.

The house continued into the distance, seemingly with no end. Then Blake passed beneath an arched hedgerow of yew and finally saw a side door next to three latticed windows. She peered through the first and saw the kitchen that she had followed Tegen through yesterday. Violet Bodily was standing at the kitchen island, her fists pummelling a large ball of dough. She wore a plain blue apron that was speckled with flour over her dress. Lines of concentration creased her brow as she worked.

Blake knocked on the window and Violet stopped kneading. She spotted Blake, who raised a hand and waved. Violet did not return the greeting. Instead, she wiped her hands on her apron, crossed the floor, and opened the door. She stood still for a moment, eyeing Blake with blatant disapproval. Then she returned to the kitchen island, leaving the door open, and continued kneading the dough.

"Thank you," Blake said, stepping inside. She shut the door and was thankful for the warmth that enveloped her. "I tried the front door but no one answered. I suppose it *is* a big house."

If the housekeeper heard her, she kept it to herself. Blake removed her wallet and reached for her license. "My name is —"

"I know who you are," Violet said, without looking up. "And I know exactly how you wormed your way in."

Blake opened her mouth and shut it again. "Anyway, I was hoping you could tell me where to find the family. They're expecting me."

Violet shrugged, tearing the dough in half then slamming it down on the counter. "Mr Trezise is in his study and is not to be disturbed. He gave me strict instructions about that. Abigail will no doubt be in the orangery. As for the twins, they've been up and had their breakfast an hour ago, so your guess is as good as mine."

Blake glanced around the kitchen. There were fresh fruits and vegetables stacked in piles on the counter, but still no pheasants hanging from hooks and waiting to be plucked. She was almost disappointed.

"Do you know why I'm here, Violet?" she asked.

The housekeeper bobbed her head. "That I do. You won't find anything though."

"Really? And why's that?"

"Nothing to find."

"Well, I guess we'll find out soon enough, won't we?" Blake said. "In any case, I'll need to ask you some questions. Griffin has given me permission to interview both family and staff."

"So I heard. But now's no good for me. I've got bread to bake and lunch to prepare."

"Sometime later?"

Violet grunted, then picked up the dough and dumped it in a bowl, which she covered with a cloth.

Blake hadn't been expecting a red-carpet welcome, but the frostiness of the housekeeper was giving winter a run for its money. She eyed the kitchen door that led to the rest of the house. Who did she speak to first? She wasn't quite ready to deal with Jack Trezise, not until she got to know him a little better and learned to diffuse his triggers. As for Abigail, she had made it her mission yesterday to make Blake leave. She had failed, which meant she would no doubt be harbouring resentment. Griffin Trezise had expressly requested that Blake leave him until last, so that she might share all she'd learned. And the Bodilys were clearly busy. Which left Blake circling back to Tegen.

She knew she would get a warm welcome from the teenager, and perhaps further insights into Kerenza's life. She could also help Blake find a way to talk to her siblings.

She glanced at Violet Bodily and tried on another smile. It was a tight fit. "Thank you for your precious time, Violet."

The housekeeper glanced over her shoulder. "S'pose you'll be wanting a cup of tea at some point. Something to eat too, no doubt."

"That would be lovely, thank you. I'll stop by again later, see if you're free for that chat."

Violet snorted, selected a large knife from a wooden block, then began attacking a bunch of carrots.

As BLAKE WANDERED through the halls of Saltwater House, the silence unsettled her. She heard no voices, no laughter, no music, only the soft thud of her boots on the floorboards, and the creaks and moans of a centuries-old home. She wasn't sure where to look for Tegen, so upon leaving the kitchen she had simply begun opening doors. So far, she had viewed a grand-looking dining hall with a long galley table and ornately carved chairs, a games room complete with snooker table, and a small library with wall-to-wall shelves crammed with hundreds of books. There she found a bone china cup on a round table next to a red leather armchair. The cup was half full of warm herbal tea, but there was no sign of the person who had been drinking it. Blake had also stumbled upon empty rooms with drawn curtains and furniture draped in white sheets, the air inside heavy with dust and the stench of decay.

Now, she wandered along another corridor, feeling increasingly lost and wondering if she should have troubled Violet Bodily for a map, if there was even such a thing. But then a sound reached her ears, a series of grunts and groans coming through a half open door on her right.

Blake softened her footfalls and came to a halt just outside. Peering through the gap, she saw yet another high-ceilinged room with wood panelled walls. This one was filled with gym equipment. Standing in the centre of the room was Tegen's twin brother, Jack. He was shirtless, sweat glistening on his surprisingly muscular body, as he raised one heavy-looking dumbbell, then another, his face taut and red, the anger Blake had witnessed yesterday still burning in his eyes.

As Blake watched him, she was struck by how different he looked to Tegen. Where she was slight and blond, he was short and stocky, his dark hair the same shade as the rest of his siblings. Yet twins they were, if only by blood. Blake wondered if she should approach him now; catching him off guard might disarm him. But as he lifted the weights and expelled a sharp breath between his teeth, she quickly changed her mind and turned to leave.

"You're not very good at surveillance, are you?" he called.

Blake swore under her breath, then pushed the door open wider.

"Busted," she said, holding her palms up in surrender. "But while I'm here, do you have time to answer some questions?"

"Father said you were coming back. How did you manage to convince him? Suck his dick?" Jack smiled to himself as he curled the weights, veins popping in his forearms.

"Actually, I think it had more to do with wanting to know what happened to his daughter."

"I doubt that. Father only cares about two things: his money and his reputation. He also used to care about the family lineage, but he's finally given up on that, thank God."

"You're not interested in having kids one day?"

"No thanks."

Blake took a few steps into the room, eyeing the array of exercise machines and racks of weights. The youngest of the Trezise family was serious about keeping fit.

"Why not?"

"Because it's what Father wants, and I never give Father what he wants."

"What about your sisters?"

"Abigail is incapable of loving anything that doesn't have leaves. And Tegen is a freak. She'd probably give birth to a goat or something. Kerenza was his only real hope of having grandchildren, and now she's dead." The teenager dropped the dumbbells to the floor and snatched up a towel. He pressed it to his face. "Do you have kids?"

Blake shook her head. "Can I ask you about Kerenza's wedding?"

"If you want, but there's nothing much to tell." Jack shrugged as he continued to towel the sweat from his body. "I got drunk. Kerenza killed herself. End of story."

"You saw her jump?"

"We all did." He froze for a moment. When he looked up, his face had changed. Instead of an angry young man, Blake was staring at a frightened child. He pressed the towel to his face again. When he lowered it, the anger had returned.

"Why do you think she did it?"

"Because she was sick and tired of everyone's shit. Isn't that why people kill themselves?"

"Then why go to the trouble of getting married? Why make plans for the future with Campbell?"

"Who knows how women's minds work? You're all crazy if you ask me."

Blake had been forming the opinion that the young man's vitriol was a front to protect the insecure little boy hiding inside. But now she thought he was just an arrogant little shit. Still, she forced a smile to her lips.

"Let's go back to before the wedding," she said. "Did you notice anything unusual about Kerenza's behaviour in the days leading up to it? Or anyone else's for that matter."

"I try not to pay attention to the rest of the family."

"So, you didn't care about Kerenza?"

"I didn't say that. She was all right, I suppose. It's just that she was twice my age, and we didn't have much in common."

He let the towel drop to the floor and began stretching his arms, wrists, and hands.

Blake eyed him shrewdly. "You don't seem very upset about your sister being dead."

Immediately Jack's shoulders tensed. But he continued, reaching one hand behind his back, then the other.

"She was my half-sister," he corrected her. "And you just get on with things, don't you? That's what Father says."

"I thought you didn't listen to your father." Blake shifted from one foot to the other, uncomfortable to be around such pent-up rage. "What about Campbell Green?"

"What about him?"

"Did you think he was a good match for Kerenza?"

"No. It was obvious Kerenza was marrying beneath her station. To tell you the truth, I think the only reason she agreed to marry him was so she could get away from here."

"And why was she so desperate to get away from here? It's a big house, you've got lots of money."

Jack snorted. "You met my father, didn't you? There's no love here."

"What about between you and your sisters?"

"Like I said, there's no love here."

Finished with stretching, the teenager cast a look in Blake's direction and rubbed his muscled stomach.

"How old are you?" he asked.

Blake narrowed her eyes. "Old enough to be your mother. Tell me what you thought about Campbell."

"I didn't like him. He didn't know his place."

"What does that mean?"

"My father employed him to manage the family finances, not to fuck his daughter. I mean, who did he think he was? He was our accountant, but he swanned around like he owned the place, thinking he was going to get a slice of the fortune just because he was marrying into the family. I'm glad he didn't get to go to the funeral."

"That's a cruel thing to say," Blake said.

"Maybe. But if you ask me, he loved Kerenza about as much as she loved him, which wasn't very much at all. He was only ever interested in the money."

"I'm assuming you have proof of that?"

"I don't need to prove anything to anyone. Anyway, I hear Campbell's being allowed to visit the grave later today. You better tell him to stay out of my way or there'll be trouble."

Blake stuffed her hands into her jeans pockets, because all she wanted to do was throttle the boy. He was entitled, indignant, and full of spite. Like father like son, she supposed. Which made her understand why Kerenza wanted to leave Saltwater House behind, but it still didn't explain why she killed herself.

Jack was staring at her again. She didn't like the look in his eyes, that of a horny teenager who thought he was about to get lucky.

"Do you have any more questions?" he asked. "Because I need to shower. You're always welcome to join me . . ."

He ran his fingers down his stomach, then up again, his eyes never leaving hers.

Blake grimaced. "No thank you. I already showered today, and children really aren't my thing. But I do have one more question. The family curse, do you believe in it?"

"Of course not. And I may be young, but I'm no child."

"Did Kerenza believe in the curse?"

"No one believes it except for Tegen. But I told you, she's a freak. She thinks she's a witch or something. More like a hag."

"If you don't believe in the curse," Blake said, "how come you don't ever leave this place?"

"How would you know what I do or don't do?"

"I'm a private investigator. So, what is it? No friends?"

Jack's face reddened as he turned away from her. "I can't leave."

"Because of the curse?"

"No, you idiot. Because I can't drive. If you hadn't noticed we're in the middle of nowhere. The nearest town is miles away and there aren't any buses that come close. Not that I'd get on one of those filthy things."

"I thought you wealthy types had chauffeurs," Blake said. "Why don't you learn to drive?"

"Because Father won't pay for lessons for the same reason that he won't let us have our own phones or the internet. He's a control freak. He likes to have us all here exactly where he can see us, even if he never leaves his precious study." He scuffed the floor with his shoe. "Saul keeps saying he'll teach me to drive, but he never does. I bet he's been teaching Tegen. The Bodilys think the sun shines out of her arsehole."

"So you're trapped here?" Blake tried to feel sorry for him, but his attitude had drained her of empathy. "I suppose that explains why you're so angry."

Fists clenching, Jack glowered at her. "Fuck off, woman."

"Nice to meet you, too," Blake said and turned on her heels. "Enjoy your cold shower. Maybe wash out that mouth of yours while you're in there."

She marched out of the room, plunging into the shadows of the corridor.

"Little prick," she whispered, as she stomped away. Jack Trezise was the kind of boy that would grow up to be a violent bully with a frightening attitude towards women. It was best that he couldn't leave Saltwater House, although perhaps not best for his sisters.

Blake had the impression that the Trezise family was made up of splintered factions, torn apart by death and lovelessness, yet imprisoned together within the grounds of their home. Curse or no curse, Saltwater House was a toxic, unhappy place. She wondered how Tegen managed to maintain her light, or if that too was a façade. As Blake continued to search for her, she truly hoped it wasn't.

19

AFTER CLEARING the rest of the ground floor except for Griffin Trezise's study, Blake found herself in the grand ballroom. It was where Kerenza and Campbell had planned to hold their wedding reception, until Griffin had intervened. It really was an impressive room, huge in size, with elegant coving and cornices, latticed windows and doors that overlooked the rear grounds. A huge crystal chandelier hung from the high ceiling, and a raised stage stood at the far end, where a string quartet would have once played. But the more that Blake looked, the more the decay became apparent. Large cracks and splinters ran along the ceiling. Mould spores grew over the windows. The chandelier was missing several crystal prisms, some of which lay broken on the floor below. Dust was everywhere. It coated Blake's throat and made her cough.

Retracing her steps to the central hall staircase, she climbed to the second floor. It was deathly silent up here. Even the old house had stopped complaining. Blake treaded softly along the corridor, knocking on each door she came to, then turning the handles when no one answered. Each room she inspected reeked of mildew, its furniture covered with dust sheets. Other doors were locked, including the door to Kerenza's bedroom, which prevented her from taking a closer look at the deceased woman's belongings.

She heaved her shoulders. Coming here was starting to feel like a waste of time. She wondered if Griffin Trezise had orchestrated this charade, so that Blake would give up and leave his family alone. If that were true, he clearly didn't know how stubborn she could be.

She came to the last door on the right. A sign hung from a hook, hand painted in bright colours: Tegen's Room. Fragrant red berries threaded on a length of red cotton hung around the sign. Blake knocked on Tegen's door, waited a moment, then turned the handle. It was locked, just like the others.

Returning downstairs, it took another five minutes for Blake to find her way back to the kitchen, where Violet Bodily now stood over the kitchen stove, adding salt to a pan of sauce. She eyed Blake as she entered the room.

"Found what you're looking for?" she asked.

"Not yet," Blake said. "I was wondering why all the doors are locked upstairs."

"Because those are the family's private rooms. Not for the likes of you to go snooping around."

"I need access to Kerenza's room so I can take a look around."

"Thought you did that yesterday," Violet said.

"I was interrupted." Blake stared at the housekeeper, who had turned her back on her. "What about the attic floor? I couldn't find a way up."

"Nothing much up there anymore. Used to be servants' quarters back in the day."

"How do I get up there?"

The housekeeper sighed and nodded to a door in the corner of the room that Blake hadn't noticed before. "Those stairs are the only way up. Staff used to have separate access, so they didn't bother the family with their comings and goings. But like I said, there's no reason for you to go up there now."

Blake started towards them. "I guess I'll find that out for myself."

"Guess you will," Violet said. "But if you're looking for Tegen, you won't find her up there. She's outside. I saw her duck past the window not a minute ago."

Blake crossed the kitchen towards the exit door. "Which direction?"

Violet smiled. "For the life of me I can't remember."

Muttering under her breath, Blake stepped outside. The cold hit her, making her shiver. She buttoned up her coat and slipped on her gloves, then looked from left to right. Choosing right, she headed for the rear of the house.

Soon, she was standing on the back terrace, looking down at the huge expanse of lawn that rolled out into the distance. At its centre was a hexagonal hedge maze with many intricate paths inside. It looked barely knee-height, more decoration than puzzle. Blake marvelled at how she and Tegen had escaped stumbling over it while dashing through yesterday's fog.

Moving along the terrace, she peered through the windows of the ballroom, until she reached the central steps that descended to the lawn. Her eyes immediately found the blood-stain. The steps had clearly been scrubbed since Kerenza's death, and the Cornish winter weather would have helped, yet the outline remained. Blake turned away from it and looked up to Kerenza's balcony on the second floor. If she had jumped from any other window she would have survived with a few broken bones. But the depth and angle of the steps had snapped her neck clean in two, severing the spinal column and killing her instantly. The blood suggested her head had burst open like a melon.

As grotesque as Kerenza's death had been, it was the height of the fall that troubled Blake. Most suicide jumpers picked heights they knew were impossible to survive.

Taking out her phone, Blake switched to camera mode and photographed the balcony then the faded blood stain. Something didn't feel right.

She descended the steps, carefully avoiding the stain. The lawn was soft beneath her feet, the soil still sodden with rainwater. In the distance, she saw the black railings of the family cemetery. The ornamental hedge maze was directly in front. Blake walked towards it. The closer she got to it, the clearer she could see how overgrown it had become.

She was beginning to wonder about the family finances. The signs of dilapidation were everywhere. Where were the gardeners to keep the grounds in shape? An estate this size was far too large for an elderly man like Saul Bodily to maintain alone. What about the abandoned rooms left to decay? Where were the painters and decorators? And why had Griffin Trezise ceased the philanthropy of which he was so proud? Either there was a cash flow problem, or the patriarch had grown miserly in his old age.

Blake reached the maze. As a child she would have enjoyed negotiating its many paths. As an adult, its height made it nothing more than a trip hazard. Skirting around, she searched the trees on her left for signs of Tegen. She thought about calling out. But then in the distance she saw movement. It was just for a second, but she swore she had seen a figure darting into the

trees. Blake quickened her pace, heading across the lawn. Had it
been Tegen? The figure had been too far away to say for sure.
Reaching the spot, she stopped to catch her breath, then entered
the woodland.

The fresh aroma of pine needles was intoxicating. Foliage
crunched under Blake's feet as her eyes darted from side to side.
There was still no birdsong, which wasn't unusual at this time of
the year, but here at Saltwater House, the silence was unnerving.

No one was here. Blake was about to give up and turn
around when she heard running water. She stopped still, trying
to ascertain where it was coming from. There was something in
the near distance, half hidden by trees. She stepped closer.

It was an old cottage, standing in a small clearing. The
dwelling was in bad shape, like it had been abandoned for
decades. All the windows were boarded up and its white frontage
was cracked and filthy. The thatched roof was pulpy and moss-
covered, the stench of rot choking the air. The chimney stack
had crumbled on one side, the rubble scattered on the ground.

Blake wondered who had lived here. Perhaps the previous
groundskeepers, from a time before the Bodilys.

A wind blew up through the trees, making branches creak
and the thatched roof rustle. She walked up to the door and saw
it was covered in mildew. She reached for the handle and turned
it. The door shifted an inch but wouldn't open any further. Blake
didn't think it was locked, rather that the wood had expanded in
the damp weather, leaving it jammed in the door frame. She
tried pushing it with both hands. When that didn't work, she
took her shoulder to it. But the door wouldn't budge.

Giving up, she brushed dirt from her coat, took a picture of
the cottage, and walked around to the back, Tegen momentarily
forgotten.

There was a small rear garden that was now overrun with weeds. The remnants of a wooden fence lay on the ground in rotten pieces. At the centre of the garden, what looked like a broom handle had been staked into the ground. Perched on top of it was the white skull of a large animal. Blake froze, staring in horror. What was it doing here? She couldn't tell what animal it belonged to, maybe a cow or a horse, and she had no idea of its purpose. Some sort of scarecrow? She stepped back, feeling its eyeless sockets on her, then snapped a picture.

The sound of water was louder here, and beyond the garden the ground dipped sharply. Tearing her gaze from the skull, Blake walked to the edge where trees grew precariously, their exposed roots reaching towards the wide stretch of water below.

Frenchman's Creek. In summer it would be beautiful, the amber riverbed and lush overhanging branches adding to its majesty. Here in the middle of winter, the dampness made Blake's shoulder ache.

She turned away from the creek and headed back to the cottage, giving the animal skull another wary glance. The rear windows were boarded up, just like the front. But the board over the window on the right was slightly loose.

Curious, Blake tugged at the corner. She wasn't sure why the cottage had got her attention, but now that it had she wanted to know what lay inside. She gave the board another tug, then scanned the ground for something to prise it open. Propped up against the section of fence that was still standing was an old rusty bar. Picking it up, Blake flipped it over in her hand, then glanced over at the skull. She wondered how much trouble she would be in if Griffin Trezise could see her now. She slipped the bar between the board and the windowpane, then spread her feet apart. Gripping the bar with both hands, she applied pressure.

"What are you doing? Stop that!"

The voice startled Blake. She spun around, wrenching the bar free and dropping it to the ground. Tegen stood ten feet away, staring at her in horror. Her complexion was horribly white, and her eyes were wide and round.

"You shouldn't be here," she said in a frightened whisper. Her gaze shot from Blake to the cottage, then back again.

"I was just taking a look." Blake shrugged guiltily. "It's just an old, abandoned house, isn't it?"

Tegen was trembling now. "Get away from there. It's not a safe place."

Before Blake could say another word, the teenager rushed towards her and gripped her tightly by the wrist.

"You shouldn't be here," she said again, and began dragging her away.

"What on earth are you doing?" Blake's expression was somewhere between shock and amusement.

But Tegen wasn't listening. She continued to pull Blake away from the house and back through the trees. Until Blake wrenched herself free.

"Do you want to tell me what's going on?" she said, rubbing her wrist. Tegen was frozen, peering over Blake's shoulder.

"Please," she begged. "You don't know what you're messing with."

"So how about you fill me in?"

"It's *her* house. We're not welcome here."

"Whose house?" Blake said, her patience fraying.

Tegen stared at her. Her lips were trembling.

"Mother Crow's," she said.

20

THE WIND HAD PICKED UP, rattling the windows. Blake and Tegen sat in a cushioned window seat, feet up and facing each other, drinking mugs of herbal tea and coffee made by a begrudging Violet Bodily after being admonished by Tegen for locking all the bedroom doors without permission. Blake had stood uncomfortably by, noting how even someone as seemingly good-natured as Tegen could still wield her entitlement over the housekeeper like a cane.

Now she glanced around the teenager's bedroom, which was immaculately tidy, although Blake suspected that had more to do with Violet and less to do with Tegen. The furniture was modern yet in keeping with the aesthetics of the house. Crisp yellow sheets covered the bed, while an analogue alarm clock ticked on the bedside table. But there were no band tour posters on the walls, no photograph collages of friends, no fluffy toys kept from childhood. Instead, rich, earthy incense hung in the air, candlesticks covered side tables and dressers, and cotton threads entwined around sprigs of drying berries, leaves, and herbs hung in the windows and from lampshades.

"What are those for?" Blake asked, peering up at the dangling greenery.

Tegen followed her gaze. "They're ingredients."

"For what?"

She smiled awkwardly and shifted on the window seat. "For charms and potions."

Blake nodded, unsure of what to think. "I met your brother Jack earlier. He's an incredibly angry young man."

Tegen scowled at the mention of his name. "Violet says he's going through a phase."

"That's one way to look at it. He told me you practice witchcraft. Is that what this is all for?"

The teenager blushed. Then she shook her hair and held her head up high. "Yes, it is. I'm a witch. Or at least, I'm trying to be. I'm only at the beginning of the cunning path."

Blake frowned. "What's the cunning path?"

"The journey to becoming attuned with both the physical and spiritual realms, to finding the forces that will empower and inform my craft."

"What kind of forces?"

"Spirit forces. The most powerful being the Red Serpent."

Blake recalled Kerenza's painting of the same name, depicting a fat red snake writhing through the countryside at night while naked women rode on its back. She had questions, but for now she let Tegen speak.

"The red serpent is the spirit force that flows through all things. Through land, through water, through rock. Even through us, giving us life. Witches get their power through harnessing the flow of the red serpent. To harness it we walk along the serpent's path, searching for the best places to draw it into our bodies and the staff we carry."

She pointed to a wooden cane propped in the corner of the room. It was beautifully carved with two wooden horns at the top. The afternoon that Blake had first spied Tegen, she had been carrying the same staff as she'd walked trance-like through the woods.

"How do you know where the serpent's path goes?"

"The path is everywhere," Tegen said. "It winds along Frenchman's Creek, through the trees, around Mother Crow's cottage, on and on, past the walls, in a never-ending coil. Some places hold more of the serpent's power than others. Like hills and cairns. Like standing stone circles." She paused, peering at Blake over her mug, who suddenly shivered. It wasn't so long ago that she'd found herself at the Merry Maidens stone circle, then at another, grislier incarnation. "To see the serpent's path, a witch must enter a state of consciousness that lies between the physical and spirit realms. It's what we call 'between the horns'."

"Between the horns of what?"

"Bucca, the goat god. The Horned One. The Devil."

Blake leaned back, her jaw slack.

Tegen laughed and shook her head. "Not the Devil of Christian beliefs, silly. Bucca is a deity of the old ways. Bucca is made of two halves: Bucca Gwidder and Bucca Dhu. Bucca Gwidder is the god of summer and healing magic. Bucca Dhu is the storm god, master of winter and dark magic, who rides a black horse with burning red eyes. They are opposing forces of nature, but they are one and the same. They cannot exist without each other, just like good and evil, life and death, day and night. In witchcraft, we worship both halves of Bucca, and we draw on each of them for our magic."

"So, you're trying to harness the power of the red serpent and this Bucca to do what exactly?"

"What do you think I'm trying to do?" Tegen stared at her with a look of disbelief. "Obviously, I'm trying to end Mother Crow's curse and heal this family."

Blake's head was reeling. "What about the cottage? How can you possibly know it belonged to Mother Crow?"

"The Red Serpent told me," Tegen said. "It warned me that place is full of bad magic. There are forces there that you can't possibly understand, which is why you need to stay away. Don't go back."

Blake turned her head to peer out the window, which overlooked the circular drive. She was deeply troubled by everything she'd heard. Tegen genuinely believed in magic curses and the spirit world. If she had lived three hundred years ago it would have been nothing out of the ordinary, but this was the twenty-first century.

To Blake, it seemed unhealthy for a seventeen-year-old on the verge of adulthood to be completely obsessed with such things. Still, she understood why. Tegen was friendless, isolated from other young people. Except for the occasional stealthy field trip to the supermarket with Violet Bodily, who surely had a good heart beneath her steely exterior, Tegen spent all her time within the boundary walls of Saltwater House. Isolation often led to fantasy as a mode of escape. The danger was that fantasy could sometimes cross over into the realm of delusion.

She glanced at Tegen, who had started humming to herself while swirling the tea around her cup. "How did you learn about witchcraft?"

"From books in the library. I like to read a lot."

"No one taught you?"

The teenager shifted her position on the seat and shook her head. "Why would you ask that?"

"Because I saw one of Kerenza's paintings," Blake said. "It was called *The Red Serpent*. Was she a witch, too?"

"Kerenza was interested in the power of nature, and how it can create both life and death. That's what she liked to paint." Tegen leaned forward, her eyes bright. "She wasn't a witch. But she told me her mother was."

"Olivia?"

"Yes. Kerenza's mother had strange visions all the time. She knew things that she couldn't possibly know. But I don't think she knew how to harness her power. Father thought she was mad, and so he kept her locked away from the world, never letting her leave the house. Until she finally did go mad, and they put her in the hospital for a long time. When she eventually came back home, she ran away. That was when they found her dead in the field."

"And you?" Blake said. "When did you decide to become a witch?"

"I didn't decide. The Red Serpent chose me."

Blake wondered if she should speak to Griffin about his daughter's obsessive nature. Yet at the same time, she didn't want to be responsible for Tegen being further isolated.

The rumble of an engine filled the air. Blake looked out the window and saw a silver car appear around the bend then pull into the circular drive.

Tegen appeared beside her.

"It's Campbell," she said, her face suddenly dour. "He's finally here."

21

CAMPBELL WAS CLIMBING out of the car when Blake stepped from the house and onto the drive. Their eyes met and Campbell gave her a curt nod. He was agitated, his hands twitching by his sides as he walked to the back of the vehicle and removed a large bouquet of roses, orchids, and lilies from the boot.

"They're beautiful," Blake said.

Behind them, Tegen emerged from the doorway. At first it seemed that she was about to run to Campbell and throw her arms around him, but instead she remained on the step and raised a hand.

"Hello," she said, not looking him in the eye.

Campbell smiled. "Hello stranger. It's good to see you."

Locking the car, he glanced up at the house and his agitation quickly returned.

"Don't worry," Blake said. "We're your only welcome party. But we should get going, just in case."

Campbell sucked in a faltering breath, then slowly let it out. "Tegen, are you coming?"

The teenager opened her mouth and shook her head.

They left her standing awkwardly on the doorstep. As they rounded the corner of the house. Saul Bodily appeared in the near distance on their right, the handle of a rake clutched in one hand. He waved in their direction. Campbell waved back.

"At least there are still some good people in the world," he muttered.

Blake didn't know what to say, so she remained silent, noting the way Campbell's gait was growing stiffer with every step.

"Talk to me," he said, when the silence became uncomfortable. "Tell me what you've found so far."

Blake gladly obliged. "There's not much to tell yet. This family, they're not like anyone I've met before."

"That's an understatement."

They were heading along the side of the house now, heading for the rear. Blake peered up and saw a silhouette watching them from an upstairs window. It quickly retreated.

She continued. "The Trezises are hostile, intensely private, and deeply unhappy that I'm here. Except maybe Tegen."

"She's a sweet girl."

"She is, but she troubles me."

"Why?" Campbell asked.

"Do you know about the so-called family curse?"

"When Kerenza told me about it, I laughed. I mean, it's preposterous. But Kerenza, she took it seriously."

"She believed in it?"

"She wasn't superstitious, and she didn't believe in ghosts or magic, not really. But she said the family had experienced so much misfortune that it seemed more ludicrous *not* to believe."

"Tegen is completely obsessed with it," said Blake. "She says there's no point in her trying to leave Saltwater House while the curse is still active because she'll end up dead, just like her brother and sister. Just like Kerenza's mother."

"I suppose when you've lived most of your life in isolation things like curses are easier to believe," Campbell said. His gaze flicked down to the bouquet of flowers, then up again. The far corner of the house was fast approaching.

"Did you know Tegen's practising witchcraft?" Blake said. "Apparently she's on a mission to break the curse and heal her family with dried berries and herbs. She's talking about drawing power from the Devil and something called the Red Serpent."

Campbell froze. They had reached the back of the house, where the vast lawn stretched out before them. "Wasn't that the name of Kerenza's painting you showed me? Please don't tell me she was into witchcraft too."

"According to Tegen, Kerenza was fascinated by it all, but she never dabbled. The occult only served as inspiration for her paintings."

Conscious that they were standing just a few feet away from the steps where Kerenza had died, Blake grasped Campbell by the arm and steered him away to the right, descending a bank of grass until they reached the lawn.

"Jesus," he said, shaking his head. "The more I learn about Kerenza, the more I wonder if I really knew her at all."

Blake shrugged. "Everyone has sides to them they don't want to share, even with the ones they love. But I'm concerned about Tegen. I don't pretend to know about witchcraft, but her obsession with it doesn't seem healthy."

"Is it really that bad? I mean, what else is there for her to do around here?"

Blake glanced at him. His answer had taken her by surprise. "I just don't know what to do about it, that's all."

"You don't need to do anything," Campbell said. "Unless it has something to do with Kerenza."

They were halfway across the lawn now, the hedge maze on their left. The black iron railings of the family cemetery loomed up ahead.

"What else have you learned?"

"Well, it's more of an observation than anything else, but have you noticed how Saltwater House is slowly falling into ruin? There are entire rooms left abandoned and covered in mould. The grounds are a mess and the gardens are full of weeds. It makes me wonder about the Trezise family fortune." Blake glanced at Campbell, who had slowed right down. "You worked for them. Did you notice anything untoward about their finances?"

His shoulders stiffened. "I signed an NDA. Which means that, despite my feelings about this family, it would be unwise of me to break their confidence. Griffin wasn't joking when he said he could ruin my career with just one phone call."

"But what if it's connected to Kerenza?"

"Believe me, it's not. She wouldn't have jumped just because the family's —"

Campbell stared at the ground, then picked up speed. Blake hurried to catch up with him again.

"Because the family's what?" she said. "Come on, Campbell. You hired me to find out answers. If you're not prepared to share important information, how am I supposed to do my job?"

He looked annoyed now, more with himself than Blake. "Look, all I'll say is that the Trezise family aren't as wealthy as they seem. Not anymore."

Blake wanted to press him, but now was not the time. They had reached the cemetery gate.

Campbell froze, hands clutching the bouquet of flowers as he peered through the railings. Blake opened the gate.

"I'll wait outside," she said.

Their eyes met. Then Campbell ducked inside, and Blake shut the gate behind him. She watched as he stood at the foot of the fresh mound of earth, scarcely able to comprehend that the woman he loved was buried beneath. He sank to his knees and gently rested the flowers on top.

Blake turned around, focusing on the house as Campbell quietly sobbed behind her. She thought about the family wealth. She was frustrated that he wouldn't share what he knew, so resolved to ask him about it again before he left. It was possible their financial crisis, whatever it was, had nothing to do with Kerenza's death, but Blake needed to explore every avenue if she was going to find the answers Campbell so desperately sought.

Her gaze shifted downward, suddenly spotting movement. A figure had emerged from one of the rear doors of the house and was hurrying down the steps. It was moving quickly, reaching the lawn then powering forwards, limbs swinging back and forth like pistons. As the figure came closer, Blake drew in a breath.

"Oh, shit," she whispered.

It was Jack Trezise, heading in her direction at a frantic pace. Now someone else was emerging from the house and descending the steps, female in shape but still too far away to identify.

Blake glanced over her shoulder. Campbell was still on his knees, tears streaming down his face in front of Kerenza's grave. She turned back to see Jack had already reached the maze and was now skirting around it. Behind him, the second figure was struggling to catch up. Too tall to be Tegen and too lithe to be Violet Bodily, it had to be Abigail Trezise.

Great, Blake thought. *Two pains in my ass for the price of one.*

Stepping in front of the gate, she spread her feet apart and sucked in a calming breath. She shot another glance in Campbell's direction, who was now standing and alert.

And then Jack Trezise was ten feet away from Blake, his fists clenched by his sides. But he wasn't interested in her. His hate-filled eyes were fixed on Campbell.

"You're not welcome here," he called, an ugly sneer contorting his face.

Blake cleared her throat, getting his attention. "Didn't anyone tell you to respect your elders? Campbell has every right to be here. Whether you like it or not, your father has given him permission."

"I don't care what my father said." The teenager turned on her. "He's got a minute to leave or there'll be trouble."

Behind him, Abigail had reached the maze.

"The best thing you can do right now is turn around and go back inside like a good boy," Blake said.

Jack stepped towards her, a cold smile on his lips. He laughed. "Are you seriously trying to give me orders in my own home? Mind your own business, woman."

"This *is* my business, you little shit. And if you call me that again I'll drag you by your ears to your father's study and tell him exactly what you've been up to."

The teenager's face flushed red as he mashed his teeth and took another step closer.

"Blake, it's okay." Campbell walked through the cemetery gate and closed it behind him. He took one last look at Kerenza's grave. "I'm ready to go now."

"Good riddance," Jack said. "You should never have come back here in the first place."

Ignoring him, Campbell turned to Blake. "Thank you.

Getting a chance to say goodbye means more than I can say."

"I'll walk you back to your car."

"That's right, fuck off!" Jack shouted.

Blake clenched her fists, desperate to whirl around and wipe the smile from his face. Instead, she followed Campbell as he headed away from the cemetery. But Jack seemed determined to get a reaction.

"Kerenza never loved you," he said. "She used you to try and get out of this place."

"Keep walking." Blake took Campbell by the arm and attempted to hurry him along. But he had already stopped and was turning around. Abigail was seconds away now, her arms swinging by her sides as she advanced.

"What did you say?" Campbell's eyes burned into Jack's.

"You heard me. Kerenza wanted out so she picked the first loser she met. But maybe she realised the shitty life she'd have with you would be no better than being stuck here. No wonder she killed herself!"

Campbell wrenched his arm from Blake's grip, and then he was rushing towards the teenager, filled with rage.

Jack was ready for him. He nimbly side-stepped as Campbell threw a punch, then countered with a sharp jab.

"Jack, no!" Abigail shrieked as she ran towards them.

Blood spurted from Campbell's nose as he fell backwards on the ground. Jack set upon him like a wild animal, kicking him viciously in the stomach. As he swung his leg back to deliver another blow, Blake grabbed his right wrist and twisted it sharply behind his back, pushing upwards.

Jack squealed in pain.

Blake drove her foot hard into the back of his leg. His knee collapsed and he went down, but as he fell, he swung his free arm back and drove his elbow into Blake's left eye.

The world flashed brilliant white. Then Jack hit the ground face first, punching the air from his lungs. Blake scrambled on top of him, pushing his wrist further up his spine and digging her knees into the small of his back. The pain in her eye was blinding, but Jack's screams were a satisfying tonic.

"Stop this now!" Abigail flapped around them, her face red and sweaty from running. Jack squirmed beneath Blake, but she refused to release him.

"Get off me, you fucking bitch!" He thrashed his legs about like a toddler in mid-tantrum.

Campbell was sitting up now and pinching the bridge of his nose. Blood splattered his shirt and jacket.

"Please," Abigail said, her eyes imploring Blake. "There's no need for this."

"Oh really? Tell that to your misogynist little brother." She twisted his wrist again, the soft tissue around her eye already beginning to swell.

Jack yelled and began to cry.

"Please," Abigail repeated. "He's just a stupid little boy who doesn't know his place. Please, let him go."

"How do I know he won't come at me with his fists flying?"

"He won't. Will you, Jack?"

"Fuck you!" Jack wailed.

Abigail's eyes grew dark and angry. "*Will* you, Jack?"

"Fine," he moaned. "I won't touch her."

"You see? You have my word. Now please, let him go."

Blake released her grip and staggered to her feet.

Jack rolled over and clutched his wrist, tears of pain and anger streaking his face.

"You bitch!" he hissed.

"Oh, shut up, Jack!" Abigail bellowed. "For God's sake, that's enough!"

He fell silent, nursing his wrist as he glared at the ground.

"Are you okay?" Blake asked Campbell, who was now on his feet and still clutching his nose.

He nodded.

"Right then," Abigail said. "You two better come with me, so we can clean up your injuries. Jack, you can go to your room. I'll talk to you later."

Jack wrinkled his face. "But she —"

"Go! Before I tell Father."

He stood up, glowering at Blake, then at Campbell. Still holding onto his arm, he stormed away.

Blake gingerly touched her eye and winced. She could feel the bruising already beginning to set.

"With me, please," Abigail said, then took off at a brisk pace, heading in the direction of the house.

Campbell and Blake stared at each other.

"This family will be the death of me," Campbell said.

Then he and Blake were following Abigail, back towards Saltwater House.

22

THE ORANGERY WAS a single floor extension on the south side of Saltwater House, with a low-pitched glass roof and brick pilasters between the wall-to-wall latticed windows. Inside, the air was thick and balmy with the smell of damp earth and vegetation. The plants were everywhere, standing in large ceramic pots on the tile-covered floor and sprouting from propagation trays on two long tables. Some had large, waxy leaves and woody stems, while others were more exotic-looking with intricate flowers. A coal oven sat at one end of the room, blasting out heat, while a workbench stood in the other, covered with various gardening hand tools and accessories. Through the glass roof, thick clouds could be seen swamping the sky.

Blake and Campbell perched on stools next to the workbench. Abigail had given Campbell a wad of tissues for his nosebleed. Blake's eye was already swelling shut and she had a headache. She had asked for an ice pack, but Abigail insisted she had something even better. Now Blake watched the woman pluck leaves from a small potted plant and drop them inside a stone mortar, then begin crushing them with a pestle.

The heat from the stove was overwhelming. Beads of perspiration beaded Blake's brow, yet Abigail remained unaffected. As she continued to crush the leaves, her furtive eyes kept flicking towards Campbell.

"Jack was right," she said. "You should never have come here."

Campbell removed the tissue from his nose to protest, but then a thin stream of blood slipped from his nostril, and he quickly replaced it.

Abigail continued. "Jack may not show it, but Kerenza's death has deeply affected him. He was only recently beginning to accept it, but you coming here has stirred everything up again. And as is the way of teenage boys, his grief is manifesting as anger."

"I get that he's angry, but we're all grieving," Campbell said, his voice muffled and nasally. "Perhaps if you hadn't prevented me from attending Kerenza's funeral, none of this would have happened today."

Setting the mortar down, Abigail selected a glass bottle from a shelf and extracted a few drops of golden liquid with a pipette.

"That wasn't my decision," she told him, as she squeezed the liquid into the mortar.

"Then whose was it?" Blake asked.

"Father's, of course. He blames Campbell for Kerenza's death."

Reaching up to the shelf again, she plucked a few dried leaves from a jar, then crushed them in her fist and sprinkled them into the mortar.

Campbell was incredulous. "He blames me? I didn't push her, she jumped. And if he wants to blame someone, he should take a long, hard look in the mirror."

"Perhaps. But if you'd kept to your job description and stayed away from her, Kerenza would still be alive today."

She began pounding the mixture again with the pestle.

"That doesn't make any sense," Blake said.

"Doesn't it?" Scooping up the contents of the mortar, Abigail squashed it flat between her hands then dumped it back inside. "Sometimes when people fall in love, they lose sight of their true selves. They begin to hide the parts they're afraid their lover won't like, for fear of being left alone again. They dampen down others, and they lie to themselves, pretending it's okay to give up who they truly are because love means compromise, even if they're the *only* one making compromises. And then when their lover inevitably hurts them in some way, they begin to feel resentment for having sacrificed those parts of them that made them whole. Resentment becomes anger. Anger becomes grief. And grief becomes the loss of hope."

"Wait a minute," Campbell said, his nasally voice adding a comical edge to his anger. "Are you suggesting I hurt Kerenza in some way that made her want to kill herself? That's an outrageous accusation."

"I'm not saying that at all. It's just an example of what can happen." Abigail stood over Blake, the mortar in one hand as she examined her eye.

"It's a very specific example," said Blake. "Talking from experience?"

Abigail froze for a second, then scooped up some of the green mash.

"Sit still and keep that eye shut," she said.

Blake leaned back. "What is that stuff?"

"A poultice. It will help to reduce the swelling and pain."

Abigail reached towards Blake again, who leaned even further back.

"How do I know it's safe?" she asked.

"Because natural medicine has been around for thousands of years, long before the pharmaceutical companies came along and spread lies so everyone would buy their drugs instead. Now, may I?"

Blake leaned forward again, reluctantly nodding. The poultice was cold and sticky on her skin as Abigail gently applied it around and over her shut eye. When she was finished, she stepped back and analysed her work. "Leave it on for the next few minutes, and don't open your eye. You don't want that getting inside."

She moved over to Campbell, pulled down the tissue, and examined his nose. It was swollen, but not broken. She began applying the rest of the mixture to his skin.

"Where did you learn to do this?" Blake asked, watching with interest.

"My mother taught me. She liked to grow herbs and plants."

Whatever the poultice was made from, it was already beginning to work. The pain in Blake's eye had subsided a little, and the skin around it had numbed.

"Tegen told me your mother used to practice witchcraft," she said.

Abigail's fingers hovered above Campbell's face, then began working again, nimbly applying the poultice.

"Tegen's head is filled with fanciful ideas borne from an overactive imagination," she said. "My mother had a fascination with botany, in particular the healing properties of plants. When she was well, she would spend her days right here in the orangery, nurturing and growing, and studying natural medicine. It was a passion, one that I try to continue. She most certainly was not a witch."

"What do you mean 'when she was well'?" Blake asked.

The poultice applied, Abigail put down the mortar, then leaned against one of the brick pilasters. "Mother was mentally unstable."

Blake regarded her through her good eye. The other was now pleasantly numb. "What was her diagnosis?"

When Abigail spoke, her voice was filled with contempt. "Father wouldn't allow her to see a doctor or take medication. He was a firm believer in the hysterical woman, putting her illness down to nerves. Until she had a very public breakdown at a charity ball. But instead of seeking help from a professional, he started locking Mother away, forbidding her to leave the grounds. That was when she truly lost her mind and had to be incarcerated." She paused, staring at Blake. "Why are you asking about my mother? You think Kerenza was mentally ill, too?"

"It crossed my mind," Blake said.

"She wasn't," Campbell said, sounding annoyed.

Abigail's expression remained neutral. "All I know is that my mother displayed very visible signs of instability. Bouts of mania, followed by bouts of depression. At the end, she was suffering from hallucinations and paranoia, convinced that Old Mother Crow was trying to possess her body so she could hurt us children. I'm assuming you've learned about the alleged family curse?"

Blake nodded. For now, she kept the fact that Tegen was practising witchcraft to herself.

"Did she hurt you?" she asked.

"Mother Crow isn't real," Abigail said. "It's just a nonsense story my father made up to keep us all from leaving."

"I meant your mother."

"Jesus, Blake," Campbell said. "That's got nothing to do with Kerenza. You shouldn't be asking questions like that."

Ignoring him, she glanced across at Abigail. "I'm sorry to ask, but I'm trying to build a picture, that's all."

Abigail was quiet, her eyes haunted by painful memories. "There are more ways to hurt a child than physical violence. The absence of affection, for one. The inability to say 'I love you', for another. When my mother was well, she was kind and loving. She never once lifted a hand to us. As for Kerenza, she was sometimes melancholy. Who could blame her with all the death we've suffered in this family? Our mother, our brother. Our step-mother too, I suppose. But no, I don't believe she was depressed enough to take her own life, and I don't believe she was unwell like our mother."

Blake pulled at the neck of her T-shirt, desperate to escape the humidity of the orangery. "So, if Kerenza was happy and mentally stable, why do you think she did it?"

Folding her arms across her stomach, Abigail shrugged. "You're the private detective. You tell me."

She turned her back on them, picked up a small watering can, and began tending to her plants. The conversation was over.

23

THEY WALKED BACK to their cars in silence, Campbell pensive and brooding, Blake's mind filled with troubled thoughts. Reaching the driveway, they slowed to a halt.

"How's your nose?" Blake asked. It looked a little swollen and slightly green from where the poultice had been applied. She imagined she looked the same.

"I'll live," Campbell said. "How about your eye?"

"Whatever was in that poultice is helping."

Up ahead, Saul Bodily appeared from the trees and began walking along the drive in the direction of the gates. Blake watched him before returning her attention to Campbell.

"I'm sorry your visit didn't go quite as planned," she said.

Campbell smiled. "On the contrary, it turned out exactly as I expected. Surely you didn't think I would be allowed to come waltzing in without any kind of trouble, did you?"

"I suppose not. They're certainly an interesting bunch."

"You're too polite. Anyway, I'm sorry you got hurt. I'd understand if you wanted to drop the case now."

Blake thought about it. It had certainly been an eventful first day, one in which she had learned all sorts of strange and shocking revelations. The only trouble was that none of it explained Kerenza's suicide. Still, she had another two days to go, and she was certain the Trezise family had much more to reveal.

"Don't worry," she said. "I'll be back here first thing tomorrow morning, bright and breezy. And if Jack Trezise wants to go another round, I'll be ready for him."

She smiled, but Campbell remained stony-faced.

"Just be careful. He may be seventeen, but that boy is dangerous. You can see it in his eyes." He turned towards his car, then paused, staring at Blake. "Be honest with me. What are you thinking so far? About Kerenza and why she did it."

Blake wavered, unsure whether to tell him what she was really thinking. She shrugged. "We don't have all the facts yet, and I'm hesitant to speculate."

Campbell lowered his head. "I see."

"How about you?"

"Honestly? Part of me wonders if I'm chasing ghosts. Maybe we already know why Kerenza jumped. You've met this family and seen how they live. They've grown up miserable and cut off from the world. Maybe the fear of leaving this place was too great for Kerenza, like some sort of Stockholm Syndrome. Maybe I wasn't enough to save her."

Blake shook her head. "You've had a difficult day. Go home and get some rest. I'll be back tomorrow, and I promise you as soon as I learn anything I'll be in touch."

"Okay." Campbell opened the door of his car. "You know you still didn't tell me how you convinced Griffin to let you inside."

"Do you know the origin of the Trezise family fortune?"

"I can't say I do."

"Their ancestors made a killing from the slave trade."

"What? Jesus. I had no idea."

"I don't think many people do," Blake said. "Griffin Trezise wasn't keen on anyone finding out about it either."

Campbell's jaw slackened. "You blackmailed him? Blake, I don't think that —"

"As I said to Griffin, blackmail is an ugly word. Anyway, I signed a non-disclosure agreement in exchange for him making a sizable donation to an appropriate charity. Except now I'm wondering if he can even afford to." She watched Campbell frown then look away. "It would really help if you could tell me what's going on with their finances."

"I told you, I can't."

"But what if it's connected to Kerenza?"

"It isn't."

"You can't know that for certain," Blake said. "You've already learned things about her you didn't know before. Who's to say there isn't more?"

Campbell winced and heaved his shoulders.

"I'm sorry," Blake said. "But I can't conduct a full investigation if I don't have all the facts. Hell, I'll sign another bloody NDA if that's what it takes."

Opening the driver door of his car, he peered back up at the house. "I'll think about it, okay?"

"Fine. But I have two day's left at Saltwater House, so don't think for too long." Blake said goodbye, then climbed into her own car and started the engine.

Campbell left first, with Blake following closely behind. Saul Bodily was already waiting for them at the gates. He waved them through then nodded at Blake as she drove by. Tomorrow, she was going to interview Saul and Violet Bodily to find out exactly what they thought of the Trezise family. But first she would take a second, closer look around Kerenza's room.

She watched the groundskeeper shut the gates in her rear-view mirror, then gazed ahead to Campbell's car. She understood his reluctance to share sensitive information, but he had hired Blake to investigate an extremely sensitive case that he knew would cause a great deal of upset and tension. So why was he keeping information from her? She was beginning to suspect it was more than just Griffin Trezise's threat to ruin Campbell's career. As for Kerenza, Blake was also beginning to suspect she hadn't killed herself at all. She knew it was irrational—everybody had witnessed her jump—and so far, there was no evidence to support her theory. But a seed of doubt had been planted and now it was starting to grow.

The track ended and merged with the country road that led back to civilisation. Campbell headed right, Blake left. As she drove along, her mobile phone suddenly buzzed in the cup holder. Pulling over, she checked the screen to find a text message from Judy: *I know you've forgotten—but don't forget you're babysitting tonight at 6 PM.*

Blake groaned. She hated it when Judy was right.

She quickly checked her eye in the rear-view mirror. It was still a little puffy and sore, but the poultice had prevented it from closing completely. Perhaps it would even prevent her from getting a black eye.

Starting the car again, she journeyed on towards Wheal Marow. Babysitting was the last thing she wanted to do right now, but a deal was a deal. She hoped Judy had fulfilled her side of the bargain, too.

24

IT HAD ALREADY GROWN DARK, the early winter nights drawing in, when Blake reached Wheal Marow. As she passed the small churchyard on her left, where her mother attended Sunday service every week, Blake slowed the car. Plastic sheeting hung over the church door, and a small perimeter of yellow police tape prevented entry. There were no police officers present, or anyone else for that matter. She frowned, wondering what had happened.

Driving on, she pulled into the midtown car park, paid for a ticket, then cut through a narrow alley that led to the high street. Most of the shops had already closed for the day, leaving the street empty. Passing the town square, Blake entered the off-licence and greeted the shopkeeper, Rodney Pellow, a middle-aged stout man with a bald pate and a penchant for gossip.

"Evening, Blake," he said, then frowned as he noticed her swollen eye. "What happened to you, then?"

Selecting a bottle of Rioja from the shelf, Blake made her way to the counter, where she picked up the latest edition of The

Cornish Press. She folded the newspaper neatly in half and set it down next to the wine.

"Teenagers," she said. "Never underestimate their mood swings."

"Oh, I see. Well, I hope you gave as good as you got. Need a bag?"

"No thanks."

The bell above the entrance door tinkled as two teenage boys walked in and nodded silently in Rodney's direction, who eyed them suspiciously.

"Hey Rodney, what happened at the church?" Blake asked. "I just passed there a minute ago and saw police tape."

The shopkeeper's eyes lit up. "You mean you didn't hear? Someone attacked Reverend Thompson last night!"

"What? Is she hurt?"

"A few cuts and bruises from what I hear. Banged her head on a gravestone."

"That's terrible. Did they catch who did it?" Blake swiped her debit card against the card reader.

"Well, people are saying all kinds of things. Apparently, it was a Satanist, if you can believe it! Someone wearing a sheep skull or something of the like. Painted satanic symbols all over the church door, he did."

Blake stared open-mouthed across the counter. "A Satanist?"

"That's what people are sayin'. *And* Reverend Thompson wasn't the only one to get a visit from devil worshippers last night. You know Ginny Martin?"

Blake shook her head.

"Yeah, you do. You *must* do—she's Martha Martin's girl. Anyway, last night she saw someone strange hanging around outside her house. Said it looked like they was wearing some sort of mask with horns."

"Did she call the police?"

"No idea. It's worrying though, isn't it? Who knows what makes people like that tick, and Lord knows we've had enough trouble around here lately."

Blake picked up her items from the counter and slipped them inside her shoulder bag. "Maybe it was kids playing a bad joke that went wrong," she offered.

"Oh, I don't think so. What kind of child would paint satanic symbols in blood on a church door?"

"Blood?" The fine hairs on the back of Blake's neck prickled.

"That's right. Couldn't tell you whether it was animal or human, though." Rodney turned his head to the back of the shop, where the two teenagers were hovering in front of shelves of cider. "Don't think you're getting your hands on booze tonight, fellas. Not unless you want me sent down for selling to the underage."

Blake thanked Rodney, who told her to be careful, and then she headed back along the empty street, her mind racing. She had heard of so-called satanic attacks happening before in Cornwall, but the ones she'd read about had involved the mutilation of animals, usually horses or sheep that had been left alone in fields at night. She wondered if she should call Rory Angove to see if he would tell her anything. But would he even know? The assault on Reverend Thompson was a job for uniformed officers, not a detective constable. Besides, she doubted Rory would share any pertinent information with her even if he did know something. Ducking down the side alley, she quickly changed her mind.

Blake was alone in the car park, with just a few other vehicles sitting in bays. As she hurried across the tarmac, the sky growing even darker above her, she clutched her car key fob tightly in her hand. Reaching the Corsa, she unlocked it, then glanced over her shoulder before ducking inside and dumping her bag on the passenger seat. Starting the engine, she pulled away and drove towards Judy Moon's house, an unnerving sensation twisting inside her stomach.

25

WHEN BLAKE ARRIVED at Judy's Moon's house at 6:25 PM, chaos was unfolding. Judy's children were fighting in the living room, while Judy stalked up and down the hallway searching for something.

"You're late," she called to Blake, who had let herself in and was now shrugging off her jacket.

"Sorry, long day," she said.

Judy stopped at the foot of the staircase and peered up at the landing. "Charlie, come on! We've got to be there in fifteen minutes."

She turned back to Blake, who was still standing in front of the door. The annoyance on Judy's face quickly dissipated.

"What the hell happened to you?" she asked.

Blake hung up her jacket and subconsciously touched the soft tissue beneath her eye. "I got into a fight with an angry young man. You look nice."

Judy glanced down at her dress and shrugged. In the living room, the children's screams rose to a crescendo. Judy swore under her breath then pushed open the living room door. "Lola!

Stacey! Stop fighting and go put on your PJs. Lola, while you're up there tell your father if he doesn't get downstairs in the next two minutes it will be dinner for one."

Blake watched as the girls filed out of the room. At ten, Lola was the oldest, while Stacey had recently turned seven. They both shared their mother's pale complexion and blonde hair. Blake waved as they approached. Stacey flashed a gap-toothed smile. Lola just stared.

Judy reappeared behind them, looking flustered and tired. "Upstairs, now."

The girls scurried up the steps, picking up their argument from where they'd left off.

"You've got your hands full with those two," Blake said.

"Just wait until they're teenagers." Judy frowned, staring at Blake. "Are you sure you don't want ice for that?"

"It doesn't hurt that much," Blake said. "Besides, I already had a poultice."

"A what?"

Blake followed Judy into the kitchen, where she continued searching for whatever she had lost.

"You know you're missing an earring," Blake said, pointing to the empty earlobe.

"No shit, Sherlock. Anyway, why are you beating up young men? Is it to do with your new case?"

"Something like that. And I wasn't beating up anyone. More like trying to break up a fight." She paused, watching Judy frantically sift through a pile of linen then scan the counters and floor. "Did you hear about the church getting attacked last night?"

"Everyone's talking about it. Apparently kids painted over the door and scared the shit out of the vicar. Honestly, if there was more for the youth to do in this town, they'd cause a lot less trouble. Charlie was going to build them a skate park if he was voted mayor."

"Rodney Pellow said it was a man in a skull mask who attacked Reverend Thompson."

"Rodney Pellow would tell you it was the prime minister if it got you to buy a bottle of wine. Which I hope you didn't, by the way. There's no drinking on babysitting duty."

Blake stared guiltily at her bag, then scratched her head. "It's probably bad timing, but I don't suppose you found any news stories about the Trezises?"

Judy flashed her a look. "I managed to find a few. That family is full of tragedy." She paused, throwing her hands in the air. "Where is the bloody thing?"

Heavy footsteps were coming down the stairs.

"Did you make copies?" Blake asked.

"They're in my study on top of my desk. Don't go snooping around in there."

Blake smiled wryly. "Says the journalist."

Judy's husband Charlie appeared in the kitchen doorway. He was freshly shaved and wore a blue cotton shirt and dark trousers. He greeted Blake, who nodded in his direction.

"Sorry about the mayorship," she said.

Judy winced and whispered, "Don't get him started."

Charlie held out his upturned hand, revealing a small diamond earring. "Looking for this?"

"I knew there was a reason I married you." Judy kissed him on the cheek, then took the earring and quickly put it in.

The children thundered downstairs and into the kitchen, both now wearing brightly coloured pyjamas.

"Ready?" Charlie asked Judy.

Judy turned to Blake. "There are leftovers in the pan if you're hungry. Stacey goes to bed at seven. Lola at eight."

"But Mum, I'm ten now," Lola complained. "Everyone else goes to bed at nine."

"Eight o'clock, on the dot," Judy continued. "Auntie Blake will read you both a bedtime story, won't you Auntie Blake?"

Blake nodded warily.

"Oh, and one more thing."

"Never feed them after midnight?" Blake said.

"Close. No sugar before bedtime. Not even a grain."

Judy bent down and kissed her children's heads, then turned back to Blake, frowning.

"Are you sure you've got this?" she asked.

"You're going to be late," Blake said. "Have a lovely time."

Charlie stooped to kiss the girls goodbye, then he and Judy left Blake alone with them in the kitchen.

She heard the front door open and shut, then silence. Lola and Stacey peered up at her with wide eyes. Blake shifted uncomfortably from one foot to the other. She glanced around the kitchen then back at the girls.

"So," she said. "Who wants popcorn?"

It was 9:28 PM and dark outside. Blake had put the children to bed and read them both a story. Lola had complained she was too old at first but then had fallen asleep before Blake had even finished the first chapter. Now she sat on the sofa in the living room, a glass of wine in her hand and the photocopies of the news articles Judy had printed resting on her lap.

To her disappointment, there was nothing of note that she

hadn't read before. There was a story about the death of Aidan Trezise, this time with a photograph taken next to his siblings at a charity gala for seriously ill children. He had been a handsome man, similar in appearance to his brother but taller in stature, and, with the exception of Tegen, shared his siblings' dark hair and eyes, and their aloofness, judging by his expression.

Another story from thirty years ago detailed the opening of a new cancer hospice in Bodmin, its construction part-funded by Griffin and Olivia Trezise. In the photograph, Griffin had a commanding presence, while Olivia stood quietly by his side, hands clasped together, eyes blank, her smile reserved. Five years later, she would be found naked and frozen to death in a field.

The next article detailed the death of Genevieve Trezise during childbirth. A grainy photograph showed her and Griffin at yet another charity function. She was blonde, like Tegen, with the same slight build and delicate features. Her hands rested on a surprisingly small baby bump for someone carrying twins— unless she had been in the early stages of pregnancy. But what did Blake know? When her sister-in-law had been pregnant, her belly had been the size of a beach ball, yet her nephew had barely registered on the scales after his birth. The caption beneath the image read: *Griffin and Genevieve Trezise open the Centre for Women's Health in Truro.* The age difference between the two must have kept the staff talking for days.

The final article was more recent and was about the death of Kerenza Trezise. She had been a beautiful woman, Blake thought. Beautiful and cloaked in mystery. The details of her suicide were scant and omitted the more delicate circumstances, such as leaping to her death in front of her loved ones. A post-mortem examination had been conducted to confirm the cause of death, but the coroner's final report was yet to be published.

Blake knew that in cases of suicide, an autopsy was common to rule out foul play. Also, blood and urine samples would be sent away for drug and alcohol testing to rule out accidental death. The wait for the toxicology results always delayed the coroner's final report, which meant it could take up to six weeks before the victim's family had conclusive confirmation of cause of death. In a place like Cornwall, where resources were limited and teams were understaffed, six weeks could turn into eight, sometimes even ten.

Blake checked her notebook. Kerenza Trezise had killed herself nine weeks ago. Yes, she had ended her life in front of several witnesses, but so far Blake had found no reason for her to do so. Was it because Kerenza had never intended to kill herself in the first place?

Blake needed to see the coroner's report.

An idea came to her. Picking up her phone, she called Kenver and waited for him to answer, which he finally did after her third attempt.

"God, you're persistent," he growled in her ear. "What's so damn important?"

"Do you remember that creepy guy you went to school with?" Blake said. "Jason something, who works at the coroner's office. Are you still friends with him?"

"Hello to you, too," Kenver said. "I'm fine, thanks for not asking."

Blake rolled her eyes. "This is what you get for being an unreliable babysitter."

"What?" Kenver said. "Wait, are you babysitting Stacey and Lola?"

"Not another word."

Kenver laughed. "You? *You're* babysitting? Miss 'I like children but I couldn't eat a whole one'?"

"Just answer the question. Are you still friends with creepy guy or not?"

"Jason isn't creepy, he's just socially awkward. And I haven't seen him in ages."

"What does he do at the coroner's office?"

"I think he's an assistant or something. Why do you want to know?"

"It's for work. Do you have his number?"

Kenver was quiet for a moment. He breathed deeply in Blake's ear. "I can't give out friends' phone numbers to random strangers without their permission."

"I'm not a random stranger. I'm your cousin."

"Exactly. My cousin, not his. Would you like it if I gave your number to someone you've never met?"

Blake huffed. "I suppose not."

"I could always give him yours, ask him to call you?"

"And what if he doesn't? Or he does and won't give me what I need? No, I need to see him in person. So, how about this? You meet him for a drink, then I turn up quite by accident and ask him a few questions." She waited for a reply, but Kenver said nothing. "Hello? Are you still there?"

She listened closely and heard muted whispers, followed by stifled laughter.

"Kenver, have you got someone there?"

"That's none of your business," he said, then fell silent

Blake heard the distinct smack of kissing lips. "Oh, Jesus. I'm not into threesomes, Kenver. Especially ones involving my cousin. Why the hell did you answer your phone?"

"Because you wouldn't stop calling!" Kenver said. "Anyway,

why do I have to meet Jason? You know I'm trying to stay off the booze right now."

"So go to a coffee shop. Please, I wouldn't ask if it wasn't important."

There was another pause as Kenver thought about it. "Fine. I could do with a night out anyway."

"A sober night out," Blake reminded him. "And thanks. You'll text Jason in the morning?"

"Yes. Now is there anything else?"

"I believe that's it. Please resume whatever it is I interrupted."

Kenver hung up.

Blake drummed her fingers on the arm of the sofa as she glanced up at the ceiling. The house was quiet, the children fast asleep. She picked up her phone again and began searching online for local properties to rent. As she scrolled through the results, she thought about her family and the animosity that had grown between them over the past year like a wall of thorns.

A shrill, piercing scream shattered the silence.

Blake leapt to her feet, dropping her phone on the floor. The scream came again, panicked and stricken.

Hurrying from the living room, Blake raced upstairs. Stacey's bedroom was open a crack, just as she'd left it. The landing hall light was still on. She pushed the bedroom door open further and saw Stacey sitting up in bed and sobbing hysterically.

"What's wrong?" Blake asked, coming into the room. She hovered at the foot of the bed, watching the young girl cry.

"There was a monster in my room!" Stacey wailed.

Blake moved closer, then sat on the edge of the bed, gently stroking Stacey's nest of hair. "It was just a bad dream. That's all."

"No, it was real! He had big horns and no skin, and he was standing right there." Her little body quaked as she pointed to the side of the bed.

Blake stared awkwardly. "But there's no such thing as monsters. Everybody knows that. And I can prove it to you."

The girl was still sobbing but she watched Blake stand up and move to the centre of the room.

"I'm going to search every inch of this place and show you there's nothing here," Blake said.

Stacey's sobbing subsided a little as she watched Blake first check the wardrobe, revealing its empty interior, then open the toy chest. Inside were enough toys for ten children, but definitely no monsters.

"You see?" she said. "Nothing here. And you know why? Because there's no such thing as monsters."

"What about under the bed?" Stacey started wailing again.

Blake's knees cracked as she sank to the floor. Her shoulder ached as she bent her elbow and peered beneath the bed.

"Oh my God!" she said.

She pulled out a dirty sock and held it in front of her face. "Now I know there are definitely no monsters because not even the nastiest ones would go near this."

She grinned. Stacey wiped her eyes and smiled back.

"It was just a bad dream, that's all," Blake told her, sitting on the edge of the bed again. "We all get them. Even your tough old Auntie Blake."

She dried the child's face with the tips of her fingers, then tucked her hair behind her ears.

"You want me to read another story?"

Stacey shook her head. "No thank you. You're not very good, not like Mummy."

"Charming. In that case, let's get your sheets tucked in and you back to sleep."

Blake gripped the edge of the bed sheet. A sharp stabbing pain made her snatch her hand back. She winced and saw beads of blood forming on her fingers.

"Don't move," she told Stacey, whose eyes were now glued to the droplets of blood, then carefully pulled back the sheet.

A wax figure, no more than five inches tall, was lying on the bed next to the child. It was yellow in colour, a roughly carved approximation of a girl. And it was covered from head to toe in sharp sewing needles.

Stacey stared down at it and began to cry again.

"I told you! A monster came into my room and put it in my bed!"

Blake's heart pounded in her chest as her eyes swept the room. Scooping Stacey up in her arms, she carried her from the room and out to the landing, where she pushed open Lola's door and flipped on the light switch.

Lola's eyes blinked open as she slowly sat up in bed.

"What —" she said, then winced at the sound of her sister's crying.

Blake set Stacey on the floor, then pulled Lola's bed sheets back. Satisfied it was safe, she picked Stacey up again and set her down next to her sister.

"What's happening?" Lola said, awake and alert now, as Blake checked under the bed, then pulled open the wardrobe doors. No one was there.

"Look after your sister for me," Blake told her. "And do not leave this room until I come back. Do you hear me?"

Both girls nodded, afraid.

"I'll be back soon, I promise."

She returned to the landing, shut the door behind her, then ducked back into Stacey's bedroom. The wax doll stared up at her from the bed, vicious needles covering every inch of its body. Grabbing a t-shirt from a chair, Blake quickly wrapped the doll in it, then carried it out of the room. She checked the bathroom, then Judy and Charlie's bedroom, finding them both empty. She went downstairs, her feet light against the steps, and checked the front door to find it still locked.

Hurrying along the hall, she slipped inside the kitchen, put the wax figure down, and snatched a knife from the block.

The back door swung into view. Blake reached out and tried the handle. There were no signs of forced entry, but the door swung open easily.

"Shit," she whispered.

She slammed the bolts across, then checked the rest of the ground floor. Judy's office and the dining room were clear, the living room as she'd left it.

Blake was at the foot of the stairs now. Lola was still crying, her sobs muffled by the closed bedroom door.

Whoever had been here was already gone. But were they still outside?

Blake unlocked the front door and opened it a crack. The cul-de-sac was dark and quiet. A pool of streetlight illuminated the pavement on the other side of the road. Somewhere in the distance, a dog barked and another answered. She wondered if she should check the rear garden, but that would mean leaving the children alone inside.

A horned monster, Stacey had said. It was the same description Reverend Thompson had given of her attacker two nights ago.

Blake shut the door and locked it again, pulling the deadbolt across. How had she not heard them creeping in and out of the house? She cursed herself for being so absorbed by her work, then hurried back to the living room to retrieve her mobile phone. In the kitchen, she set the knife down and called Judy's number.

"What is it?" Judy said, when she answered. "What's wrong?"

Blake let out an unsteady breath as she carefully unwrapped the wax doll and ran a finger over its many needles.

"You need to come home," she told Judy. "Come home now."

26

THE CRACKLE of police radios came through the closed living room door. Blake sat alone in the far corner, watching Judy and Charlie on the sofa, the children nestled safely between them as their tired eyes fought to stay awake to watch cartoons on the television. Blake had already given a statement to the police and was now waiting for permission to go home. The forensics team was not available, so uniformed officers had gloved up and were busy searching for fingerprints in the kitchen, hallway, and in Stacey's bedroom. The grotesque wax doll had already been photographed, bagged and tagged, but not before Blake had taken her own picture of it before the police had arrived. She wondered who had made such an awful thing and left it under the bedsheets of an innocent young child.

Her gaze wandered to the television screen, where animated characters were busy bashing each other over the heads with mallets while colours flashed like a kaleidoscope. On the sofa, Charlie was gaunt and pale. Judy's eyes were red from crying. She glanced over at Blake, and for a second her frightened expression gave way to anger. Kissing the girls' heads, she got to her feet and padded over to where Blake was sitting in an armchair. Her dress was creased and tear-stained, and sprigs of hair had sprung loose from her hair clip. She stood over Blake for a moment, then sat down on the carpet, awkwardly folding her legs beneath her.

"How are you bearing up?" Blake asked softly.

A fresh tear sailed down Judy's cheek. She wiped it away.

"I swear I locked the back door," she whispered, then glanced over her shoulder to make sure the girls weren't listening. "In fact, I know I did. I remember doing it."

"Maybe he picked the lock," Blake said, lowering her voice to match Judy's.

"Did you go out to the back garden? Maybe you forgot to lock the door when you came back in."

"I promise you I never left the house." She glanced over at Stacey, who was curled into her father's side and sucking her thumb. "Is she okay?"

"She's shaken up. The police want to interview her, but they're waiting for a female officer." Judy leaned in closer, dropping her voice even further so that Blake had to lean forward to hear. "What did she tell you, when you went into her room?"

Blake repeated what she had already shared with Judy, that Stacey had seen what she thought was a monster with large horns and no skin, and that it had come into her room and tucked the wax figure into her bed.

Judy shuddered. "What the hell was that thing? It looked like a Voodoo doll."

"I don't know," Blake said. "I've never seen anything like it."

Another tear slipped from Judy's eyes. She quickly swept it

away. "Whoever put it there, they wanted to hurt Stacey. But why? She's seven years old for Christ's sake."

Blake shrugged. "Maybe the intention was to scare more than to hurt."

"Well, they did a bloody good job!"

Over on the sofa, Charlie and the girls turned their heads in unison. Judy gave them an apologetic look then shifted her position on the carpet. She turned back to Blake. "Do you think it was the same person who scared Reverend Thompson?"

"Horns and no skin? Sounds like the same animal skull the Reverend described."

Judy's face twisted in horror. "Who is it? Why are they doing this?"

Blake didn't know so she said nothing. From the corner of her eye, she saw Stacey staring at them again.

"It's okay, sweetie," Judy said. "Watch the TV."

She waited until her daughter had turned away, then stared at Blake, long and hard, the anger that had briefly surfaced a minute ago returning.

"Where were you?" she asked. "How the hell did he get upstairs without you seeing?"

It was a question Blake had been repeatedly asking herself, until it hurt deep inside her chest. "I'm so sorry, Judy. But I was in the living room the whole time."

"Door open or closed?"

"Closed," Blake said, guiltily. "I went over the stories you copied for me, I called Kenver, then I heard Stacey screaming. Whoever it was, they were quiet. They must have known I was alone in here with the kids. It would have been too great a risk with both of you in the house."

"You're saying they watched us leave?" Judy's gaze involuntarily flicked to the living room window. The curtains were drawn now, but earlier Blake would have been clearly visible to anyone looking in from the street. "Christ. I'm getting the locks changed first thing in the morning."

Outside the living room, the clump of boots could be heard as police officers milled up and down the hall.

Blake felt terrible. She couldn't stop thinking about the masked figure. First Reverend Thompson was terrorised, now Judy's family had been targeted. Had they been picked at random or was there a design to what was happening? While both incidents had been horrifying, no one had been physically attacked, although placing a doll covered in needles was certainly a step up from painting occult symbols on a church door. What was next? Blake hoped they wouldn't find out.

Judy was staring at her, as if she had all the answers. Blake had none.

"It could have been worse," she offered. "A lot worse."

A dark cloud shadowed her friend's face. "Or it might not have happened at all if you'd been paying more attention."

Blake flinched and felt her face heat up. She couldn't disagree.

"Hopefully the police will find something," she said. "Maybe fingerprints that will help identify who it is."

"I hope so," Judy said, the cloud departing as fast as it had come in. "Otherwise, I don't think I'll ever sleep in this house again."

A soft knocking on the living room door made them turn their heads. The door opened, and a uniformed female police officer in her early thirties entered the room. She smiled warmly at the children, then at Charlie. Judy got to her feet and smoothed the creases from her dress. Noticing her, the police officer smiled then nodded at Stacey.

"We're ready for her now," she mouthed.

Judy turned to Blake. "If the police are done with you, you should go home."

"Are you sure you're going to be all right?" Blake asked as she got up.

Judy said nothing, only stared at her. Then she crossed over to the sofa, stroked Stacey's hair and scooped her up. She followed the police officer out of the room, leaving Charlie and Lola alone on the sofa, both staring helplessly at Blake.

———

With the police officers' permission Blake left Judy's house and hurried to her car, which was parked on the street. She checked the back seat, then climbed inside and started the engine. She drove away, heading through the darkness, the needle marks on her fingertips smarting as she gripped the steering wheel, a reminder of what had happened because of her own negligence. Guilt pressed down on her shoulders. Judy had been right to feel angry. Blake should have been paying more attention.

As she drove out of town and along the pitch-black country road that led to her mother's home, she repeatedly checked the rear-view mirror, unable to shake the feeling that she was being watched. Tomorrow, she would make amends. She didn't know how yet, but the wax doll was a good place to start. Why go to the time-consuming effort of creating such a thing then adorning it with a hundred needles when there were far easier ways to scare someone?

The doll had to have significance. A purpose. And if Blake

could figure that out, it would lead her to the man in the skull mask. And if it did, she would show that snivelling coward how it felt to be a frightened, vulnerable child. But first, she still had a suicide to solve.

27

A FINE MIST crept over the waters of Frenchman's Creek and snaked through the trees, heading towards Saltwater House. Blake had called ahead, and so was unsurprised to find Saul Bodily waiting at the gates as she approached. She was exhausted from a sleepless night, guilt twisting in her gut like the blade of a knife. Even now, she was unable to rid herself of the feeling. Judy's daughter had almost been hurt because she hadn't been paying attention. And what *was* that grotesque thing Blake had found in her bed? Perhaps Judy was right, that it was some kind of Voodoo doll. But in Cornwall? And who in their right mind would use it against a child? No one sane, Blake thought.

Saul waved her through then shut the gates again. Once inside, Blake applied the brakes and lowered her window.

"Frosty this morning," Saul said with a nod, as he came up beside the car. "Didn't expect to see you just yet."

"Lots to do." Blake smiled politely at the elderly man, wondering how far away from retirement he was. A year or two at most.

Saul squinted as he examined her face. "Heard about yesterday's scuffle. Got a bit of an eye there, haven't you?"

"It could have been worse."

When Blake had checked in the mirror earlier that morning, she'd seen a faint purple bruise over her eyelid. Abigail's poultice had thankfully reduced the swelling and prevented it from closing over. For that, she was grateful.

"That young scamp Jack is getting too big for his boots," Saul said. "One day he's going to get himself into real trouble."

Sooner rather than later, Blake thought. "I'd like to talk to you today, Mr Bodily. Like we agreed. When would be best?"

Saul crumpled his brow. "Well, let me see. Got things to do right now, but I'll be around all day, that is if you don't mind me fixing a few things while we talk."

"Of course. Where would I find you?"

Saul smiled wryly. "Oh, I'm sure a detective like you will have no problem tracking me down."

He gave another nod then strolled away, heading into the trees.

Parking in front of the house, Blake climbed out and walked around the side until she reached the kitchen door. Violet Bodily was at the kitchen counter making the day's bread, while an open fire crackled in the hearth. She turned her head as Blake entered but made no eye contact.

"Morning," Blake said. "Something smells good."

Violet grunted. "Just porridge oats. I suppose you'll be wanting a cup of tea."

Blake moved over to the hearth and rubbed her hands together, warming them in the heat.

"I'm a coffee drinker, but I'm happy to make it myself."

Violet wiped her hands on her apron, then removed a metal moka pot from a cupboard. "I don't think so. Everything has a place in my kitchen, and I like to keep it that way."

She added water and freshly ground coffee beans to the pot, then placed it on the stove. Feeling warmer, Blake shrugged off her coat and stared into the flames.

"You're here early," the housekeeper said, returning to the bread dough.

"Your husband said the same thing. I don't have much time left here, and I still have interviews left to do."

Violet's shoulders tensed. She kneaded the dough a little harder.

"Before that, I need to look over Kerenza's room again," Blake said. "I assume it's unlocked now?"

"It is," Violet said without turning around. "But you can't go up there yet."

"And why is that?"

"The children are still sleeping."

Blake felt a stab of irritation, but noted how Violet still referred to Jack, Tegen, and Abigail as children. There was fondness there, love even, but reserved only for the siblings.

"I suppose I can check the room later," said Blake. "In that case, perhaps now is a good time to ask you a few questions instead."

"Got things to do," Violet replied.

"Well, why don't I help you out in the kitchen for a bit? We can talk while we work together."

Violet stopped kneading and looked over her shoulder, surprised by the offer. "I don't need help," she said.

"All the same, I need to talk to you."

On the stove, wisps of steam rose from the spout of the coffee pot. The fire in the hearth sparked and crackled.

"Then you best sit down over there," Violet said, nodding at the kitchen table in the corner. "I'll bring your coffee over."

Blake did as she was told, pulling her notebook from her bag and laying it on the table. The rich aroma of coffee mingled with the smell of scorched wood. She watched Violet cover the dough with a tea towel, then pour coffee into a mug and bring it over.

"You need milk and sugar?" she asked, peering warily at Blake's notebook.

"Black is fine. Thank you."

If Violet had noticed Blake's bruised eye, she was keeping it to herself. She returned to the counter. "Got veg to peel. Ask your questions."

Blake picked up her pen. "How long have you and your husband worked for the Trezise family?"

"Why do you need to know that?"

"I'm trying to build a picture. It will help me to see things more clearly."

Opening a sack of carrots, Violet plucked one out and attacked it with a peeler. "I've been housekeeper for thirty-five years. Saul, the groundskeeper. We've been through thick and thin with this family. Good times and bad. And I don't care what you, Mr Green, or anyone else thinks of the Trezises, those children are good people."

Blake scribbled in her notebook, noting that Violet had referred specifically to the children, not Griffin Trezise. "You both live off the grounds?"

"That's right. Over Helston way. Been there for as long as I can remember."

"You were never invited to live here?"

"Of course not. Where would we live?"

"Well, there's the old groundskeeper cottage by the creek."

Violet froze, the peeler in her hand trembling slightly. Then it was put to work again with quick, fluid movements.

"That place is derelict," she said. "Ain't no one lived there for an age."

Blake sipped her coffee. It was smooth and thick, just how she liked it. "Thirty-five years is a long time to stay in a job. You must like working here."

"It pays the bills. The family has always been good to me."

"You must have been around when Olivia Trezise was still alive."

"I was, poor woman. God rest her soul." Violet set down the peeled carrot and picked up another. "She was a beautiful thing. Just lovely. It was unfortunate what happened to her, but I suppose some people aren't cut out for the harshness of this world."

"Do you remember the circumstances around her death?"

"What's that got to do with anything?" Violet said sharply. "I thought you were here to ask questions about Kerenza."

"Like I said, I'm building a picture."

"I see. Well, I do remember, but I don't feel much like talking about it. Feels disrespectful."

Blake tightened her grip on the coffee mug. She knew Violet Bodily was going to be difficult, but this was like pulling out teeth with a pair of blunt pliers.

"What about the children? Who took care of them after their mother's death?"

"Mr Trezise was a grieving man, not in his right mind to be

caring for children so young. Kerenza was just thirteen years old when Olivia passed. Aidan eleven, and Abigail ten. Far too young to be without a mother. So, I offered to take care of them."

"So you did live here?"

"Just for a bit." Violet suddenly sneered. "Until he hired a nanny, and in came Genevieve Parsons."

Blake looked up. "Genevieve? As in Griffin's second wife?"

"That's right." The housekeeper threw the carrot on to the chopping board and snatched up another.

"I take it you weren't a fan?"

"I wouldn't have an opinion either way. Besides, I don't like to speak ill of the dead."

"You're in a safe space here, Violet. Anything you tell me won't be shared with the family."

The carrots peeled, Violet picked up a large knife and began furiously slicing them into rounds. "Genevieve Parsons was only ever after one thing. Money. A gold digger is what they call her type. Mr Trezise hired her to live in and take care of the children, even though she was barely old enough to take care of herself. I offered to continue in the role, but he preferred I went back to housekeeping."

"How was Genevieve with the children?"

"Useless. She wasn't interested in being a mother to those three. No, all she liked to do was swan about the place like she was Lady Muck, trying to give me orders and leaving the children to run riot while she made eyes at Mr Trezise. It worked, too. Six months in, she was sharing a bed with him."

"Presumably they fell in love and got married?"

Violet snorted. "Don't make me laugh. Mr Trezise was vulnerable, still grieving for Olivia. And Genevieve knew it, too.

She took advantage of him, sunk her claws right in and convinced him that he loved her. They were married within a year. She enjoyed the high life, all right. Never saw her in the same dress twice and was always showing off her latest piece of jewellery. Mr Trezise wanted more children with her, but she wasn't interested. Good job, I thought at the time, since she could barely look after the three that were already here." She paused. "But then a few years later, she got pregnant. She wasn't happy about it, let me tell you. And then —"

Violet looked up, as if suddenly realising who she was talking to. She clamped her jaw shut and shook her head.

"And then what?" Blake prompted her.

"Then she gave birth and died." She turned and stared at the dancing flames of the hearth, her eyes growing misty. "Anyway, Mr Trezise was beside himself again. It was a tragedy, him losing two wives like that."

"For Genevieve, too, I suppose," Blake said dryly. "Seeing as how she died. And for the children. Losing one mother is terrible enough, but two . . ."

Violet shrugged as she scooped up the carrots and put them into a bowl, then began peeling potatoes.

"I suppose one good thing to come out of it all was Tegen," she said.

Blake frowned. "And Jack?"

Violet glanced at her. "Yes. And Jack."

"It seems like there's been a lot of death in the Trezise family. Olivia. Genevieve. Then Aidan. What was he like?"

The housekeeper was silent for a long time, as if trying to find the right words. "He was a lovely boy, until he became a teenager."

"What happened then?"

Violet was avoiding her gaze now, the vegetable peeler slicing through the potato skins with renewed fervour. "Nothing, just that he had a temper on him sometimes. He didn't like it if he couldn't get his way and would throw his weight around until he did. He and Mr Trezise fought like cats and dogs. Anyway, then Aidan joined the army at sixteen. I was shocked his father had given his consent, but by then I think he'd had enough and thought it would be good for the boy. Teach him some discipline and respect."

"And did it?" Blake asked.

Violet didn't reply at first but shrugged her shoulders. "He got discharged a few years later. I don't know the ins and outs, but I expect it was probably to do with that temper of his. When he came back home, he and Mr Trezise picked up where they left off."

Blake thought about her own brother, Alfie, whom she'd hardly seen since he'd become a parent. He and Ed had sometimes clashed in Alfie's teenage years, but not to the scale that Violet had described. And now Ed thought Alfie could do no wrong.

"What did Aidan and his father fight about on the day he left for good? It must have been something serious for Griffin to banish him from Saltwater House."

"I'm sure that's none of my business, or yours," the house-keeper said. "And I'm growing tired of these questions. You still haven't asked me about Kerenza."

Blake put down her pen and fought back her frustrations. "You're right, I haven't. So tell me about her."

Exchanging the peeler for a knife, Violet began cutting the potatoes into cubes. "She was a sweet thing. Kind and clever. The quietest of the children. Thoughtful. Always watching the world and everything in it. She doted on the younger ones despite the age gap. Practically half raised them after Genevieve passed, gave up university and everything else."

"I heard she liked to paint," Blake said.

Violet screwed up her face. "If you can call it that. I'm not sure where that girl got her ideas from, but those pictures were something dark. Not the kind of thing you'd expect from a lady of good breeding."

"I also heard she burned them all."

"Someone around here talks too much. I wouldn't know anything about that. Not my business."

Blake picked up her pen again. "Did Kerenza ever seem depressed to you? Mentally unstable or unwell like her mother?"

"You shouldn't be asking personal questions like that."

"I've been hired to ask personal questions exactly like that," said Blake. "And Mr Trezise has given me permission."

Violet muttered under her breath, set the knife down, then added the potatoes to the bowl of carrots. Blake watched her carry the bowl over to the sink and fill it with cold water.

"I can't say I ever saw her in the same state as her mother," Violet said, setting the bowl down on the side. "Sometimes she would mope around, or complain she wanted to get out and see the world, even though she'd already been to Oxford for a year. But mostly she was kept busy with the younger two, teaching them their lessons."

"And when Campbell came along?"

For the first time since Blake had met her, Violet Bodily betrayed her hardened exterior with a smile. "That girl was like a ball of sunshine floating around the house."

"She was happy?" Blake said, pen scratching on paper. "She was in love?"

"She was. Despite my personal feelings about Mr Green, I have to admit it was lovely to see her happy. There'd been so much tragedy, you see, I was beginning to wonder if there would ever be any more joy." Her smile faded. "What a fool I was."

In the hearth, the flames flickered and danced as a breeze blew down the chimney.

"Was she close to her other siblings? Was there any friction?"

"None that I could tell you about."

"And her relationship with her father?"

"You'd have to ask him."

Blake's annoyance was creeping back in. "What are your personal feelings about Mr Green?"

The housekeeper wrinkled her nose. "Well, it all happened so quickly, didn't it? One minute he was doing the accounts for Mr Trezise, the next he was asking for his daughter's hand in marriage. They'd barely spent two minutes together, then it was all love and roses, and secret shenanigans."

"Which your husband had a hand in, I believe," Blake said.

"Well, Saul Bodily is a fool, isn't he? It's lucky Mr Trezise never found out." She stared at Blake, daring her to run off telling tales. "Anyway, you don't just meet someone one day then get married to them the next, do you? Not if you want it to last."

"My parents got married after knowing each other for six weeks," Blake said.

"Still together, are they?"

Blake shifted on the hard wooden seat.

"Just my opinion," Violet said, "but I sometimes wonder if he really loved her or if he was more interested in her inheritance. But right or wrong, Kerenza loved the man, and I suppose that's all that matters now." The housekeeper tucked loose strands of hair behind her ear. "Anyway, is that it? I've got plenty more things to get on with."

"Just a few more questions," said Blake. "You were working on the day of the wedding. Did you see what happened?"

"No, I didn't, thank the Lord. I was in here all morning, overseeing the catering staff Mr Trezise had hired. A bunch of buffoons, they were. Made a right mess of my kitchen."

"You weren't invited to the wedding as a guest?"

"No. Why would I be? I'm just the housekeeper."

"But you've worked for them for thirty-five years, Violet. You weren't even invited to watch the ceremony?"

Violet was silent, staring at the floor.

"Did you see Kerenza that morning?"

"I did. She came down to the kitchen, all in a panic because she'd torn the sleeve of her wedding dress. Just here." Violet pointed to the centre of her forearm.

"How did she tear it?"

"She was trying to put on her corsage. Must have used some force because the pin pricked the skin on her wrist and made it bleed. Anyway, first I scolded her for wearing her wedding dress around the house for everyone to see, *and* in the kitchen where it would only get dirty. But I was glad she did because it was the last time I saw her. She looked like an angel, and —" Violet paused, her voice catching in her throat. "I patched up the hole as best I could, then she kissed me on the cheek and went on her way."

"How did she seem?" Blake asked softly.

Violet looked away and wiped her face. "Full of jitters, but she was happy. It was the happiest day of her life."

It was quiet as Blake scribbled in her notebook. "Did you see anyone else that morning? Anything that struck you as out of the ordinary?"

"No. Just Tegen coming into the kitchen and getting in the way of the catering staff. Then Abigail a few minutes later, looking annoyed. No doubt Tegen had wound her up again. Abigail reckons she's always doing something to rile her up. If you ask me, she's too hard on that girl."

"You're close with Tegen, aren't you?"

"I look out for her. She's young and impressionable, and she's suffered something terrible since Kerenza passed. The girl's lonely. She's never been close with Abigail, and she and Jack don't get on."

"What about her father? Does she spend time with him?"

"I told you, Mr Trezise is a busy man."

Blake nodded. "That's why you sneak her out for trips to the supermarket?"

Violet stiffened as her eyes shot to the kitchen door. "It's not right for a girl her age to be left on her own all the time. Anyway, it does no harm. She keeps me company and it frees Saul up to do his job. You've seen this place; it's falling apart at the seams."

"Aren't you worried about losing your job if Mr Trezise finds out? Tegen told me he doesn't allow her to leave Saltwater House. He won't even let her have a phone."

"Wouldn't you keep a tight rein on your family if half of them had died?"

The woman was squirming now and glaring at Blake.

"Relax," Blake said. "If I were in your position I'd do the same thing, which is why I'll keep your secret. But I'm concerned about Tegen."

"Why would you be concerned?" Violet said. "You don't even know her."

Blake hesitated, wondering if she should say what was on her mind. "What do you know about the family curse and the tale of Mother Crow?"

The question took Violet by surprise. Her jaw swung open, then snapped shut again. "Well, I suppose there's got to be some truth in it, don't you think? How else could one family have so much tragedy if it wasn't by design?"

"So, you believe in witchcraft?"

"I didn't say that, and don't you write down that I did."

"Tegen believes," Blake said. "Did you know she's practising witchcraft? She thinks if she can break Mother Crow's curse, she'll set her family free and stop anyone else from dying."

Violet paused, the corner of her mouth twitching. She waved a dismissive hand. "Tegen doesn't know what she's talking about. She's just a child playing games with herbs and berries, thinking she can heal this family of its pain."

"But she seems obsessed with it. You think that's healthy for a seventeen-year-old?"

"I think that's none of your business. Now I really need to get on. I'm running behind."

Blake stopped herself from rolling her eyes and instead scanned her notes. "To sum up then. You don't believe Kerenza was depressed or suffering from mental illness, and you can't think of anything that would drive her to take her own life. In your own words, she was a ball of sunshine floating around the house. And on her wedding day, she was happy. So why *do* you think she killed herself?"

Violet stared at her with unblinking eyes. "I don't believe she did."

Blake caught her breath. "What do you mean? There are multiple witnesses who saw her jump, including her own family."

"I know," Violet said. "But I'm telling you that girl couldn't wait to get married. She was in love, and she was excited about the future. There is no way on God's green earth that she willingly jumped to her death."

28

DOWNSTAIRS WAS QUIET AND STILL. Blake walked through dimly lit hallways and corridors, heading towards the main staircase. The gnawing feeling in her stomach grew in intensity, along with her conviction that Kerenza had not killed herself. Violet Bodily thought it, too. Of course, that didn't mean it was true. So, if not suicide, then what? An accident? She didn't think so—Campbell had told her they'd all witnessed Kerenza climb onto the balcony balustrade before jumping. A murder? But Kerenza had been alone. Even if someone had pushed her from behind, why had she climbed onto the balustrade?

No, Blake's intuition was wrong. Kerenza *had* jumped to her death, and the reason for her doing so was still hidden somewhere, waiting to be found. Blake hoped she would find it tucked away in Kerenza's bedroom.

Reaching the foot of the stairs, she gripped the railing and climbed the first step. From somewhere to her right, she heard hurried footsteps followed by the opening and closing of a door. She turned around, staring down the length of the hallway that led to Griffin Trezise's study. No one was there.

Climbing the rest of the stairs, Blake reached the landing and peered into the gloom. She walked quietly, slowing down in front of each bedroom door and listening for signs of life. She reached Kerenza's room. Over on the right was Tegen's bedroom door. The brightly painted name sign was still hanging, but the wreath of dried berries was gone.

Blake entered Kerenza's room and quietly shut the door. She stopped still, her eyes growing wide.

The curtains were open. Pale winter light leaked through the French windows and fell on an empty room. It had been picked clean. The bed was stripped of sheets and pillows. Bedside cabinets had been cleared, and so had the dressing table, Kerenza's makeup, photographs, and wedding corsage all vanished into the ether.

Blake stalked to the centre of the room and turned full circle, anger and suspicion catching in her throat. Someone was attempting to sabotage her investigation. Whether it was because they had something to hide or because they didn't appreciate Blake's intrusion upon their insular world, she didn't know. But she was going to find out.

Moving over to the dressing table, she removed each empty drawer, then turned it over in her hands, searching for secrets taped on the underside. Finding nothing, she pushed the dressing table away from the wall and scoured every inch of it, feeling for hidden compartments. She swore under her breath, then crossed the room and threw open the doors of the built-in wardrobes. A thorough search revealed nothing but dusty shelves. Whoever had cleared the room had been meticulous.

"This family," Blake muttered and shook her head. Her eyes found the French doors. She carefully opened them and stepped outside.

The balcony was small and narrow, standing room only. Blake gripped the top of the stone balustrade and leaned over. A fine blanket of mist was spreading across the lawn, smoky tendrils reaching towards the house. Directly below, steep granite steps led down from the terrace, forever stained by Kerenza's blood.

Blake shivered, her head dizzy with vertigo and a sudden urge to climb onto the balustrade. She shut her eyes and pictured Kerenza in her wedding dress, the hem bunched in her hands as she peered down at her family, at the man she was supposed to marry. Then jumping, her gown billowing like a parachute and fluttering like an angel's wings, the screams and gasps of her loved ones ringing in her ears. Then a sickening crack. Her body slamming into the steps. Her neck snapping like dry tinder. Her head bursting open like an overripe melon. Then blackness. Nothing. A void.

"Why did you do it?" Blake whispered.

She removed her hands from the balustrade and took a step back.

Who had cleared the room? Had it been Violet Bodily? She had locked all the bedroom doors yesterday in a bid to prevent Blake from doing her job, and she was fiercely loyal to the Trezise family. Perhaps the morsel of trust Blake thought she had earned back in the kitchen was nothing more than a ruse.

A more likely suspect was a member of the Trezise family. But which one? Despite tending to Blake's injured eye, Abigail had made it clear she was not welcome here. She had also been the first to object to her presence, running off to fetch her father.

Or was it Jack Trezise? Blake had humiliated him yesterday by pinning him to the ground and making him cry. He was the type of young man whose world would end if it were made public that he'd been immobilised by a woman. Emptying Kerenza's room could have been a petty act of revenge.

Griffin Trezise wouldn't bother himself with such trifles, although he might delegate the task to one of his children. But Griffin Trezise also had the threat of exposure hanging over his head.

Which left Tegen. But Blake ruled her out; the teenager had been the only one actively helping her so far, the only one who had shown any interest in finding out what had happened to her sister.

Blake breathed in damp air and the minty aroma of pine needles. She would need to talk to all of them, one by one. Again.

Leaving Kerenza's room, she moved along the landing, trying every door handle and once again finding them all locked, including the door to Tegen's bedroom. Her irritation building, she made her way downstairs and began searching for the Trezises. She stayed away from Griffin's study, deciding to save him as a final intervention if reasoning with his children failed to make them cooperate. Two minutes later, she heard Abigail's stern voice coming through a closed door near the old ballroom. Blake entered without knocking.

It was an old classroom that looked positively Dickensian. Five wooden desks stood in the centre of the room in two rows, facing a large blackboard covered with white chalk handwriting. Abigail sat at a teacher's desk next to it, dressed in black with her hair pinned back. Jack Trezise was slouching at a front row desk and tapping a pen against the empty page of a notebook. Tegen was hunched over a desk in the back row. She was terribly pale, the shadows of a sleepless night circling her eyes, and there were finger-shaped bruises on her exposed right wrist.

All three of them looked up as the door swung open. Tegen quickly pulled down her sleeve.

"Sorry to interrupt Victorian Week," Blake said, staring at Abigail. "But I was wondering if one of you could tell me what the hell happened to Kerenza's room?"

Jack smirked. "Must have been witchcraft."

He glanced over his shoulder at Tegen, who immediately lowered her head.

"Shut up, Jack," she muttered.

"Why don't you make me?"

"Why don't you just kill yourself?"

"Tegen, that's enough!" Abigail's eyes filled with thunder as she glared from one sibling to the other. "Get on with your work, both of you. And Jack, stay in your seat. If you get up, I'll know about it."

Jack rolled his eyes, then shot a look at Blake. His face reddened, as if yesterday's events had suddenly returned to mock him.

Brushing past Blake, Abigail stepped out of the classroom.

"Tegen, are you okay?" Blake asked. "What happened to your arm?"

At the desk, Tegen pulled her sleeve right over her hand, then turned away until her face was no longer visible.

Concerned, Blake closed the door and focused her attention on Abigail.

"What's going on here?" she asked.

Abigail gave a curt nod. "The children needed to take up their studies again. At the very least it will keep them both out of trouble."

"I'm not talking about that. I meant the bruises on Tegen's arm."

"Bruises?" Abigail said. "I hadn't noticed. But she can be a clumsy oaf at times. Perhaps she fell."

Blake didn't believe it, but she decided not to pursue the matter just yet. Instead, she crossed her arms over her stomach. "So, let's hear it. Because your father gave me permission to both examine and question, which includes taking a look at Kerenza's belongings."

"That may be," Abigail said, with a slight shrug of her shoulders. "But I believe we've had enough disruption in our lives without some random stranger entering our home and rifling through our dead sister's personal possessions."

She stared at Blake, a challenge in her eyes. Blake stared back.

"Are you saying you're the one who emptied her room? Where did you put her things?"

Abigail smiled. "I'm sure I don't know what you're talking about."

"Oh, come on, Abigail. We're both adults here. You emptied that room because you didn't want me to find something. What was it? Incriminating evidence? Or perhaps something that would cause a public outcry if it were to get out."

"I hardly think the public would care about anything we do."

"Really? You're telling me that you'd be happy for everyone to know your family made its fortune from the slave trade?"

Abigail flinched as if she had been slapped. It took her a moment to regain her steely composure.

"You may think you're some sort of private investigator extraordinaire," she said, "but you know nothing about my family, and what we've had to endure over the years. If it wasn't for you manipulating Tegen, you wouldn't even be here right now. But I think you'll find she won't be of any further help to you. So, I suggest you leave now and save us the pain and anguish that your so-called investigation is forcing us to suffer. We've lost our sister for God's sake!"

Abigail blinked twice and her eyes shimmered with tears. But Blake knew the woman would never let them fall, at least not in front of another person.

"All I'm trying to do," Blake said softly, "is find out what happened to Kerenza. Don't you want to know? Wouldn't it make it easier to grieve?"

Glancing back at the classroom door, Abigail let out a breath.

"We already know what happened to Kerenza," she said. "Everyone does. It's only your employer who refuses to accept it."

"But it's not really a question of what happened is it? It's a question of 'why'? And if you know why, please enlighten me. Because the sooner I know the truth, the sooner you'll be left alone."

Abigail glanced at the floor. When she looked up again, a dry smile was on her lips.

"I don't know what to tell you," she said. "Except perhaps that I did see something yesterday evening."

Blake stared at her. "What?"

"Smoke. From a bonfire. It looked like it was coming from near the old coach house. I hope it wasn't anything to do with Kerenza's belongings."

Blake swore under her breath. Anger bubbled in the pit of her stomach.

"You better hope I don't find anything in the ashes," she said, leaning in. "And if I find that it's you who left those bruises on Tegen's arm, you'll be sorry you ever laid a finger on her."

Abigail's smile remained frozen as Blake walked away.

"Your eye is looking better," she called after her. "I have a salve that will prevent the bruising from getting worse. Come by the orangery later and I'll give you a jar."

"No thanks," Blake said.

She heard the classroom door open and close, then she turned a corner and stalked towards the kitchen. She had no idea where the old coach house was, or if Abigail was even telling her the truth. What Blake did know was that she was tired of scurrying around the maze that was Saltwater House and only finding dead ends. And she was sick and tired of the Trezise family.

She was starting to wonder if something had transpired since yesterday's visit. A family meeting. A gathering to conspire against her investigation. More worrying though was Tegen. Someone had hurt her, punishment for inviting trouble into the family home.

Blake clenched her jaw, barely able to contain the anger that was threatening to erupt. First, she would find what was left of Kerenza's belongings. Then she would find the person who had hurt Tegen. She hoped they were one and the same, because then she would have two good reasons to knock them out cold.

Violet Bodily was no longer in the kitchen. Blake stood for a moment, the aroma of cooking stew and the warmth of the open fire helping to sooth her frustrations. Then she was grabbing her coat from the back of a chair and heading out into the cold, in search of the old coach house.

29

IT WAS another fifteen minutes before Blake found the old coach house. There was a dirt track close to the west wing of the house that she had not seen before. It trailed through the gardens and into the trees, eventually opening onto a cobbled courtyard flanked on two sides by outhouses with corrugated roofing that was rusty and full of holes. The old coach house stood on the north end, a single-storey granite building with large wooden doors that were now badly weathered and hanging off their hinges. A long time ago, it would have housed the Trezise family's horse-drawn carriage and associated tack, while the horses would have sheltered in the moss-covered stable next to it. Now both structures looked abandoned and ready to return to the earth.

The smell of burnt wood and ash hung heavy in the air. Blake crossed the courtyard, the cobblestones slick beneath her boots, then went through the gap between the coach house and stables. The acrid stench grew stronger. She slowed to a halt. Behind the buildings was a stretch of wasteland where nothing seemed to grow. A large in-ground stone fire pit had been built in the centre. Blackened remains of a fire covered the bottom.

Blake found a stick lying on the ground, then leaned over the pit and began poking through the charred remains, disturbing fine flakes of ash that were snatched away by the wintry breeze. Chunks of scorched wood had survived the fire, along with what looked like blackened bed springs and a charred tin can.

Crouching on her haunches, she continued sifting through the debris for another minute. Her anger returned. Nothing had survived intact.

"That part of your job, is it? Poking around fires?" The voice startled her, and she almost fell headfirst into the pit. Steadying herself with a hand on the ground, Blake got to her feet.

Saul Bodily was standing behind her with a wheelbarrow piled high with broken tree branches. He smiled. "Didn't mean to startle you. And I don't think you'll find much in there apart from old rubbish."

"It wouldn't be the first time I had to wade through people's crap," Blake said. She looked down at the remains of the fire. "Kerenza's room has been emptied. Abigail told me she saw a fire burning out here yesterday evening."

"She told you that, did she?" Saul pushed the wheelbarrow to the edge of the fire pit and set it down. "That Abigail will run rings around you if you're not careful. She's sly and clever, and she doesn't suffer fools gladly."

"Then it's a good job I'm no fool," Blake said.

"You done rooting around? Only there's more of this to come." Saul nodded at the contents of the wheelbarrow.

Blake tossed the stick into the pit and stepped to one side. "It's all yours."

The groundskeeper began throwing tree branches into the fire pit, creating small explosions of ash.

"Anyway," he said. "Abigail wasn't lying to you about there being a fire yesterday evening. I lit it myself, like I do most days. If you hadn't noticed, the grounds of Saltwater House are overgrown and turning to rot. Ever since Mr Trezise got rid of the gardeners, it's just me here fighting a losing battle."

"You lit the bonfire yesterday?" Blake said. "And no one else came by to add more fuel?"

"No. It was just me on my ownsome."

"You didn't leave at any point?"

"I ain't daft enough to leave a fire this size burning on its own. And I put it out before I went home, too." He nodded to the tap and hose attached to the coach house wall behind them, then upended the wheelbarrow and shook it violently, emptying the last few stubborn twigs into the pit.

Blake shoved her hands inside her coat pockets. Perhaps she was a fool, after all. Unless the man was lying about being alone with the fire. But she didn't think so. Which meant Abigail had been playing more of her games. If she wanted to lower Blake's opinion of her, she was doing a stellar job.

Saul was busy clapping his gloved hands together, ridding them of sawdust. Blake cleared her throat.

"Seeing as you're here, can I ask my questions now?" she said.

The groundskeeper nodded. "Suppose. Don't you need your notebook?"

"I can record instead." She pulled out her phone and opened the audio recording app. "If that's okay with you."

Saul looked uneasy but didn't say no.

"Let's begin with a few general questions," Blake said. "Your

wife Violet told me you've both worked for the Trezise family for
over thirty years."

"That's right. Almost half of my life."

"You must like it here."

"Pays the bills, I suppose."

"That's exactly what your wife said."

Saul shrugged a shoulder. "Just our little joke."

"How do you feel about the family?" Blake asked. "Have
they been good to you over the years?"

There was a pause, as if the man was carefully considering his
options.

"They've had a lot of pain, that family," he said, staring into
the empty wheelbarrow. "Pain can go one of two ways with a
family. It can either pull them together, or it can tear them right
apart."

Avoidance tactics, Blake noted. But it was an interesting
observation, one that made her think of her own family situation. "Which do you think happened to the Trezises?"

Saul eyed Blake's phone screen, where the timer counted the
passing seconds and the red 'record' icon was like a drop of
blood against the bleak morning mist. He shifted uncomfortably. "Not for me to say. But you've spent time with them, so
I'm sure you can answer that question yourself." He lifted the
handles of the wheelbarrow. "Got more deadfall to collect."

Blake walked with him, passing through the courtyard of
ruined buildings and back onto the dirt track, the wheelbarrow
bouncing along its uneven surface. Mist coiled around the tree
trunks on both sides.

"Talk to me about Kerenza," Blake said. "You helped her and
Campbell to see each other in secret before their relationship got
out. Why did you do that?"

Saul remained silent, his eyes flicking to Blake's phone clutched in her hand. He turned the wheelbarrow off the track and into a clearing on their left, where fallen branches lay in stacked piles. Blake followed him, foliage crunching beneath her feet.

"You can give me a hand if you like," Saul said. "Might want to put that phone away for a minute though, in case it gets smashed."

Blake nodded, understanding. Pretending to switch off the recording app, she tucked the phone inside the breast pocket of her coat. Saul moved over to one of the stacks and began hauling branches into the wheelbarrow. Despite his age, he still possessed strength and vigour borne from years of outdoor work. Blake watched him for a second, then stooped to pick up a branch. Her shoulder twinged as she added it to the already growing pile.

"I helped Kerenza because she deserved to be loved," Saul said. "She was a good girl. Kind and warm-hearted. She gave everything up to help raise the youngsters, and she did it all without making a fuss." He paused to snap a branch in half over his knee then tossed both pieces into the wheelbarrow. "Griffin's never really loved his kids. After Olivia died there was no affection for any of them, not even from the second Mrs Trezise. So, you can see why they behave the way they do. But when those two younger ones came along, Kerenza took on the motherly role. It didn't matter that it trapped her here until they were old enough to take care of themselves. She loved them anyway."

"Did she ever tell you that she felt trapped here?" Blake picked up another branch and threw it into the wheelbarrow.

"Didn't need to. Working here for years, you get very good at noticing all kinds of things from a distance. Anyway, I was glad when Campbell came along and those two fell in love. He's an honest man, and I'd never seen Kerenza so happy. She deserved love. And with the young ones soon turning eighteen, she'd earned the right to have her own life." He froze for a moment, a broken branch pressed against his chest. Slowly he shook his head. "Which is why I still don't understand what happened when I went to see her that morning."

Blake looked up. "What morning?"

Saul tossed the branch into the wheelbarrow, then glanced over his shoulder into the trees. He turned back to Blake and dropped his voice to a mutter. "It was her wedding day. I went upstairs. I know I'm not supposed to, but me and Violet, we can't have children, and we watched them kids grow all the way up into adults, as if they were our own. We weren't invited to the wedding. Thirty-five years of employment ain't good enough to be considered a guest in Griffin Trezise's eyes, the miserly sod. But I wanted to give Kerenza a gift. Nothing fancy, just a few flowers picked from the garden to wish her well. I knocked on her bedroom door, and she answered. She was in her wedding dress, and she should have looked radiant. But she didn't. She looked something awful."

Blake stared at him, open-mouthed. "What do you mean?"

"Something was wrong with her. She was trembling and sweating, and her skin was the colour of bone."

"Was she sick?" Blake asked.

Saul shook his head. "To me, she looked terrified. I asked her if she was all right, if she needed help. But she stared at me like I was a stranger, then screamed at me to leave her alone." Saul stood rigid, his face haunted by the memory. "I didn't know what to do, so I apologised for disturbing her and put the flowers on the side table outside her room. When I looked back Kerenza was staring into the corner just behind the door."

Blake was deeply troubled by what she was hearing. "Was someone there?"

"I tried to peer through the crack, but I couldn't see anyone. Then Kerenza caught me staring and slammed the door in my face." The groundskeeper hung his head. "I should have fetched someone, but I didn't. Instead, I went downstairs, back to work. Ten minutes later, I heard the screams. I came running and there she was, a bloody mess on the steps." He peered up at Blake, suddenly showing his age. A single tear sailed down his cheek. "I didn't tell anyone. The police didn't bother questioning the staff. Everyone had seen her jump, so I suppose they thought there was no need."

Blake stared at him incredulously. "You didn't tell the family? Or your wife?"

"Everyone was talking about suicide. And all I kept thinking about was how much in those final moments Kerenza reminded me of her mother. You see, Olivia lost her mind in the days before running off to her death. We used to hear her wailing and shrieking, her cries so full of anguish, while her husband went about his business like he was deaf as a post." He paused, trembling with anger and shame. "The sickness in this family goes way beyond nonsense about witches and curses. It's something rotten. Hidden all the way down in the blood. I was wrong about Kerenza. She hadn't been fine all those years, not making a fuss while locked away from the world in this lonesome place. She'd been slowly crumbling, just like Saltwater House. And now I'll have to live with my own curse for the rest of my days, because if I'd fetched someone that morning Kerenza would still be here with us."

He bowed his head again. Silent tears splashed on the foliage. The only sound was the moan of the wind and the creak of the trees.

Blake let out a breath and struggled to suck it back in. Was Saul right? Had Kerenza's mind irreparably snapped, just like her mother's? The fear of escape severing the final cord of her sanity?

Or had someone been in the room with her, tucked away in the corner so that Saul couldn't see them?

From somewhere in the woodland came a loud crack, like a branch snapping underfoot. She turned her head. Saul did the same, his body stiffening. Then he stared into the distance over Blake's shoulder, before his eyes wandered back into the trees.

What did Blake do with this new information? It was a small yet significant piece of the puzzle, but it made no sense on its own and would only cause distress if passed on to Campbell without context. The same went for the Trezise family. None of them could know. Because if someone *had* been in the room with Kerenza, one of them was the likely suspect.

"Do me a favour, Saul," she said. "Keep this information to yourself for a bit longer."

He slowly nodded then leaned in, his face lined with concern. "I know you haven't got long left here, but you be careful. It's not just misery that haunts Saltwater House. It's full of ghosts. Some more real than others."

"Exactly what does that mean?" Blake said, unsettled by his expression and the way he kept looking over her shoulder.

"Just keep an eye out, is all I'm saying. You never know who's watching."

The wheelbarrow now full, Saul gripped its handles, gave Blake a mournful nod, then headed back onto the track in the direction of the old coach house.

Blake stood in the clearing, watching him leave. And then she was alone again, the mist thickening all around her. She turned full circle, unease prickling the back of her neck, her mind racing with all that she'd learned.

Removing her phone, she switched off the recording app and stared at the screen. Suddenly the phone vibrated in her hand. Kenver had texted.

"Finally," she whispered.

I'm meeting Jason tonight. Be at Crystal's Bar for 6.30. You owe me big time.

She texted back: *You're my hero. But a bar? Is that wise?*

She waited a minute, watching the trees and listening to the unnatural silence. But Kenver did not reply. Blake put her phone away. As she began walking back towards Saltwater House, she scanned the woodland on both sides, unable to shake the feeling that someone was hiding among them, watching her every move.

THE CLASSROOM where Blake had encountered the Trezise children earlier that morning was empty, the lesson finished for the day. She was still concerned about the bruises on Tegen's arm and wanted to check that she was okay before heading to her office in Falmouth. Blake knew that leaving now meant giving up an afternoon of her limited time at Saltwater House, but she needed space to think. Besides, she still had tomorrow.

Wandering the corridors, she passed Jack's gym room, where she heard the metallic clang of weights and pulleys. Violet was back in the kitchen, busy scrubbing the counters. She eyed Blake and gave a nonchalant shrug when asked for Tegen's whereabouts.

Blake headed upstairs, but the teenager wasn't in her room either. Which meant she was probably outside somewhere, walking the serpent's path or whatever she had called it. Blake peered through the open door of Kerenza's bedroom and found it still empty. Heaving her shoulders, she returned to the ground floor and headed to the orangery. She stopped still outside.

Hushed voices were seeping through the door. Blake pressed

her ear to the wood. She couldn't hear what they were saying, but both voices were taut with worry.

Blake opened the door and stepped inside.

Tegen and Abigail were sitting side by side on a chaise longue in the far corner of the room, their brows creased with lines. They both looked up as Blake entered and immediately fell silent. Abigail sat up straight and placed her hands on her knees. She smiled coldly.

"Did you find what you were looking for?" she said.

Blake moved between the tables of germinating plants, tugging at the neck of her pullover. She had forgotten how hot it was inside the orangery.

"Strangely enough, I didn't," she said. "But I did discover something else of great interest. And tonight I have a meeting that I'm sure will finally help us get to the truth, once and for all."

Of course, she had no idea if her statement was true or not, but the frozen smile on Abigail's face more than satisfied her pettiness.

"And what truth is that?" the woman asked.

Blake returned her smile. "I suppose I'll find out tonight. Anyway, I thought I'd come by to accept your kind offer of a salve."

Tegen watched the women intensely, eyes flicking between the two like the pendulum of a clock.

Abigail rose to her feet, her smile so tight that Blake thought her face might crack. "Of course. I have some right over here."

She crossed the room, avoiding Blake's gaze as she headed in the direction of the workbench. Rummaging through the shelves next to it, she selected a small glass jar, checked the label, then returned to Blake. She held it out and Blake took it, noticing the tightness of Abigail's grip.

"Apply it up to three times a day," Abigail said, her smile gone. "No more than that, unless you want a terrible rash."

Blake unscrewed the lid and sniffed the gloopy contents. It wasn't the most pleasant smell she had encountered. Replacing the lid, she slipped the tub inside her coat pocket. "Thank you. It's much appreciated."

Abigail gave a stiff nod, her eyes never leaving Blake's.

"Tegen, I wondered if you might walk me to my car," Blake said, staring right back.

"Leaving so soon?" Abigail said. "What a pity. But I'm sure you know your way out without needing a guide."

Tegen stood up. "It's fine, Abbie. I need some air."

"But we haven't finished our conversation. You can go for a walk afterwards."

"Oh, I'm sure you have plenty of time to talk about me after I've gone," Blake said. She turned towards Tegen. "Shall we?"

Abigail's face turned red. She shot a warning glare at Tegen.

"You're looking a bit hot and bothered there, Abigail," said Blake. "Might want to open a window."

She smiled and walked to the door. Tegen scurried after her, with her head down and her eyes fixed on the floor.

"Don't be too long, Tegen." Abigail's voice was sharp with anger. "We still have lots to discuss."

When they were alone in the corridor, Blake shut the door and moved away, gesturing for the teenager to follow. They walked in silence, heading through another door and into a gloomy passage.

"Are you all right?" Blake asked.

Tegen nodded, even though her desperately sad eyes said otherwise.

They continued walking, heading in the direction of the front door.

"How did you get those bruises on your arm?"

The teenager remained silent, but Blake sensed her body stiffen.

"It's not okay for someone to hurt you," she continued. "Ever. No matter what mistakes they think you made."

"No one hurt me." Tegen's voice was no more than a whisper.

"I saw the bruises, Tegen. They were shaped like fingerprints. Believe me, I've seen enough bruises like that in my time as a private investigator to know what they are."

They entered the main lobby. Wood panels covered the walls. Mounted heads of hunted exotic animals stared at Blake with lifeless eyes. She grimaced.

"All I'm saying is that if Abigail hurt you, I want to know about it. I can help."

Tegen stared hard at the floor. "It wasn't Abigail."

"Then who? Jack?"

Of course. It had to be Jack. He had already shown a penchant for violence and a disdain for women.

But Tegen shook her head. "It wasn't anyone. I told you, I fell."

"Tegen —"

"Will you stop going on about it? You're not even my family, so why do you care?"

Blake reached the front door. She pulled it open and the cold rushed in. "I don't have to be family to worry about someone who's been hurt. If you won't tell me who did it, can you at least tell me why?"

Tegen remained tight-lipped, a scowl pulled over her face.

"What were you and Abigail talking about in there? It looked tense."

The teenager shrugged and let out a small, frustrated breath that froze as it was expelled.

Gravel crunched under Blake's feet as she stepped onto the drive. The mist had reached her car, wrapping it in a white blanket. Removing the tub of salve from her pocket, she handed it to Tegen.

"Take it. Use it on those bruises."

She wanted to press further, but Tegen was already slipping away from her, the trust she had built beginning to fracture. Instead, Blake stood in silence at the driver door as Tegen clutched the tub of salve in a limp hand.

An idea came to Blake. One that might smooth over the cracks and help solve a mystery at the same time. Removing her phone from her pocket, Blake swiped the screen and found the picture she had taken last night. She hesitated, staring at the ghastly wax doll and its savage needles.

"You won't let me help you," she said. "But maybe you can help me."

Tegen was staring at her now, her curiosity piqued. "How?"

Blake held up the phone. "You know a lot about the occult. So maybe you can tell me what this is."

The change in Tegen's expression was unnerving. Her skin paled, her eyes grew wide, and her mouth fell open. "You took this picture?"

"Just last night."

"In your home?"

"Someone else's."

Tegen took the phone from Blake's hands and stared intently at the photograph.

"It's a poppet," she said.

"A poppet? That's a cute name for something so vile. What is it used for?"

"It's an effigy. A representation of a person, used in magic."

"Good magic or bad?"

"Poppets can be used to both heal and harm. This one is definitely to harm."

Shivering, Blake glanced down at the scabby pinpricks on her fingertips. "How does it work?"

"The person creating the curse makes an effigy of the person they intend to hurt. Poppets are at their most powerful if you make them using a lock of the victim's hair or a piece of their clothing. Once it's made, the curse is spoken and the poppet is either pricked, stabbed, burned, or mutilated. The pain is then transferred onto the living victim as an act of revenge."

"Revenge?" Blake gasped. "Jesus, I found it in the bed of a seven-year-old girl!"

Tegen glanced up from the phone screen. "Perhaps the revenge was for one of her parents."

She gave the image one last look then handed the phone back.

Blake's mind was reeling. "There have been other incidents," she said. "Satanic symbols painted on a church door. Sightings of a figure wearing the skull of an animal on his face."

"Bucca," Tegen whispered. "The Horned One."

"I know you believe in that stuff," Blake said. "But I don't. Whoever is behind this is a real person, clearly with a lot of issues. A child was almost hurt last night. I'm worried about what might happen next."

"Whether you believe or not doesn't matter," Tegen said, her eyes round and large. "Most witches stay away from this kind of dark magic and will only ever use it to defend themselves and others. Whoever is doing these things in your town, they mean to cause harm. You need to be careful."

Blake's breath caught in her throat. "I didn't say it was in my town."

"Didn't you?" Tegen held her gaze. "I suppose I just assumed. Anyway, you better take this."

She removed a ribbon from her pocket that was attached to a small pouch of red velvet. A pungent aroma of herbs seeped from the pouch as she looped the ribbon over Blake's head.

"What is it?" Blake said, wrinkling her nose at the smell.

"A protection charm. It will keep you safe."

Blake reached for the ribbon and tried to remove it. "Thanks, but I don't need –"

"Please," Tegen said, clasping a hand over hers. "For me."

Frowning, Blake slowly nodded then opened the car door. "You have my number. Call me if you need help. It doesn't matter what time it is."

The teenager instinctively glanced over her shoulder at the house. "I won't need to. I'll be fine."

Blake climbed into the driver seat. A chill had slipped beneath her clothes and into her bones. She nodded goodbye and went to shut the door.

"Wait," Tegen said. "Who are you meeting tonight?"

"Someone who works at the coroner's office."

"What does a coroner do?"

"When someone dies in unusual circumstances, it's a coroner's job to determine the cause."

"You mean work out how they died?"

"Yes. Based on the evidence, they'll confirm whether it was natural causes, a suicide, an accident, or a murder."

"A murder?" Tegen said. "We definitely know it wasn't that."

Blake stared up at her through the gap. "I'll be back tomorrow."

She closed the door and started the engine, then drove away with the heating cranked up to maximum. In the rear-view mirror, she saw Tegen still standing out in the cold, pale and unmoving. Saul Bodily's words echoed in Blake's mind: "It's not just misery that haunts Saltwater House. It's full of ghosts. Some more real than others."

The smell of herbs filled the car. Blake pulled at the ribbon around her neck, until it snapped. Flipping open the glove box, she tossed the protection charm inside. Then she pressed her foot down a little harder on the accelerator pedal, until she cleared the bend in the drive and the wrought iron gates swung into view. She hoped that Jason Harris would give her what she needed tonight, because after tomorrow, she never wanted to see Saltwater House again.

31

RETURNING TO HER OFFICE, Blake spent the afternoon hunched over her laptop, researching the unsettling world of poppets. Magical dolls and effigies dated back to ancient times and from all over the world, including India, Africa, and Europe. They could even be found in Cornwall, with the *Museum of Witchcraft and Magic* in Boscastle housing a collection of frightening specimens, most of them crafted in the twentieth century and employed by everyday people seeking revenge on cheating spouses and back-stabbing friends.

Blake thought about what Tegen had told her, that dark magic was rarely used by witches for malicious purposes. Whoever was hiding behind the skull mask and roaming the streets of Wheal Marow at night seemed very much intent on doing harm. But why had Judy's daughter been targeted?

Or maybe she hadn't.

Tegen had suggested that one of Stacey's parents had been the target, which made more sense. And hurting their daughter would certainly cause them distress. But what had Judy or Charlie done to attract the attention of someone obsessed with the occult? And what about the attack on the church and Reverend Thompson? Blake stared at the pinpricks on her fingers. She had been in the house that night and been the one to find the poppet. Was it simply a coincidence?

Getting up from her desk, she moved over to the window and peered out across the harbour. The sun had already set. Seawater swelled and churned, tugging at moorings, trying to free the boats. On the other side of the bay, the village of Flushing had already been swallowed by the incoming darkness.

Blake had tried calling Judy earlier, but she hadn't answered. Which was understandable. Judy would be with her children and was probably still angry at Blake. The guilt pressed down on her chest a little harder as she peered at the wall clock. 6:02 PM.

Her mind returned to Saltwater House and the information she had learned from Saul Bodily. She pictured Kerenza's pallid face greeting the groundskeeper, her terrified eyes flicking to the shadows that lurked behind the bedroom door.

Blake crossed the room and grabbed her jacket from the coat stand in the corner. The situation with Judy would have to wait. Right now, Blake had an accidental meeting to get to.

————————

Crystal's Bar in Truro had a contemporary look with chrome edgings, charcoal walls, and neon blue lights in the windows. Mostly populated by people in their twenties and early thirties enjoying after work drinks, it was busy but not overcrowded, and the music was at a respectful volume. There hadn't been time to change or freshen up, but Blake didn't care. She spotted Kenver sitting at a corner booth, having an animated conversation with a scrawny-looking man of similar age, who had short, spiky hair and an oversized Adam's apple poking out from his shirt collar. He was wearing a tie, which had been loosened, and his shirt sleeves were rolled up.

Jason Harris, the coroner's assistant.

Blake was in no mood for putting on a performance, and Kenver already looked drunk, but this was her only chance to get the information she needed. Forcing a smile to her lips, she walked over and stopped still, her eyes widening in mock surprise.

"Kenver? I thought that was you!"

Kenver was in his usual black attire, tattooed arms on display, and his pitch-black hair flattened in a side-parting. "Blake? No way! I'm just having a drink with an old friend. This is Jason. Jason, this is my cousin Blake."

Blake leaned over the table and stuck out a hand. "Nice to meet you," she said, flashing a warm smile.

From the glassiness of his eyes, Harris was drunker than Kenver. He shook her hand and flashed her a leery smile. "Likewise."

Blake slipped her hand inside her jacket pocket and subtly wiped away the clamminess.

"What are you doing here?" Kenver was clearly enjoying his role.

"I was *supposed* to be meeting a friend, but they cancelled just as I arrived."

"Some friend."

"I know. Anyway, I thought, well I'm here now, so I may as well have a quick drink." She flashed another smile at Harris, who was busy downing the rest of his beer.

"You should join us," Kenver said, moving over. "You don't mind if my cousin stays for a bit, do you, Jase?"

"Not at all. The more the merrier." Harris stared pointedly at his empty glass.

"In that case it's my round," Blake said. "Same again, Jason? And Kenver, perhaps a soft drink?"

Kenver laughed. "My cousin thinks she's hilarious, but she needs to work on her routine. I'll have a beer, thanks."

She went off to the bar, some of her bad mood giving way to anticipation. Returning with a tray of beers, she carefully set them down on the table then squeezed in next to Kenver.

"Cheers!" They clinked glasses, and Blake took a swig of ice-cold lager. "So, what do you do for work, Jason?"

Harris cleared his throat and put down his glass, spilling a little on the table. "I work at the coroner's office."

"Really? Cutting up bodies and things like that? You must have a strong stomach."

"Oh, no. I don't work in the mortuary."

Blake flashed a side-eyed glare at Kenver, who shrugged.

"I'm the coroner's administrative assistant," Harris continued. "But I'm thinking about applying for medical school, if I'm not too old already."

Blake let out a quiet breath. "Still, you must get to read all the gory details of the coroner's reports, things like that?"

"I do indeed. Some of them would make your hair stand on end." He grinned and swallowed more beer.

"Blake recently moved back to Cornwall from Manchester," Kenver said.

Snorting, Harris raised an eyebrow. "Why would you want to do that?"

"I guess I fancied a quieter life. Not that it turned out that way."

"What do you mean?"

Blake shook her head and sipped her drink. She was driving tonight, and this beer had to last until she got what she needed. "I keep meeting interesting people with exciting lives, such as you."

Across the table Harris laughed. It was a loud, drunken din that made Blake wince. "Me? I'd hardly call what I do exciting. Some people think it's weird to work in a place full of dead people. They think I must be creepy or something."

"Well, I think it's fascinating." She held his gaze, slowly reeling him in. Not that he needed much prompting.

He picked up his glass and drained the contents. "Who wants another one?"

Kenver held up a hand as he chugged the rest of his drink.

Blake stared at them both open-mouthed, her glass still three-quarters full. "No, thank you."

She watched Harris zigzag his way through the growing crowd on unsteady feet, then she turned back to Kenver.

"Jesus, how much did you both put away before I got here?"

Kenver rolled his eyes. "I know right. And you thought I had a drinking problem. No wonder I stopped hanging out with him. He's a prize dickhead."

"Yeah. So much for being socially awkward." Blake wrinkled her brow. "I'm sorry. I shouldn't have put you in this position. Just one more and I'll drive you home."

"You think you'll get what you need with one more drink?"

"Please. Do you even know me?"

She winked at him. Jason returned with a tray of beers. He was even more unsteady on his feet, and Blake wondered how many shots he'd done at the bar. Reaching the table, he clumsily put the tray down. One of the glasses tipped over. Blake shot out a hand to steady it, but not before a third of it sloshed over the edge and onto Kenver legs.

"Shit," Harris said, slurring. "Sorry, mate."

Kenver jumped up, alcohol soaking into his skinny jeans. "Forget it. I'll grab a towel from the bar." Scowling, he made Blake move so he could climb out of the booth. He leaned into her as he brushed past. "Work fast. I'm over this muppet."

He flashed a smile at Harris then disappeared into the crowd. Blake sat down again.

"Tell me more about your job," she said. "I bet you've had to catalogue some really strange deaths."

Smiling, Harris reached for the full glass that he hadn't spilled. "Oh, I have. But I'm not supposed to talk about them outside of work."

"Oh, come on! You can't tease me like that. Anyway, I don't even know you. Who would I tell?" Blake reached out and touched his hand. "Just don't name any names. Go on, tell me something gross."

Harris gulped more beer, then tugged at his tie, until it was loose enough to remove. Stuffing it in his pocket, he leaned across the table. His alcohol-fermented breath assaulted Blake's senses. "All right. There was this lady brought in a couple of years ago. Car accident. Lost control while driving and went off the A30. Visible signs of injury, but no major blood loss and no obvious cause of death." He flashed a sleazy smile. "Until they did an X-ray."

"What did they find?" Blake wasn't sure she wanted to know.

"A tube of lipstick. Inside her fucking brain!" Harris wheezed with laughter. "She'd been putting on makeup while driving. Her head hit the dashboard and, well, you can guess the rest."

Blake recoiled, horrified by the image. "That's disgusting."

Encouraged, Harris snorted and swigged more beer. "Believe me, it's nothing. I haven't told you the one about the human soup inside a body bag. Or the one about the crab."

"Crab?"

"Fishing trawler got hit by a storm. One of the men went overboard, got his foot stuck in the net and drowned upside down. He was taken to the mortuary, bagged and tagged, and put in the fridge. Anyway, after a while, the attendant suddenly heard this knocking, coming from the cold chamber. He opened the drawer, pulled out the body. That was when he saw the dead man's stomach moving."

To Blake's relief, she saw Kenver returning with a towel. She desperately waved him over.

"What did I miss?" he asked, as he mopped up the spilled beer from the table.

Blake moved over so he could sit down. "Your friend Jason's just been telling me some really messed up stories."

"What? And you didn't wait for me?"

Harris giggled, spittle flying across the table. "Don't worry, there's plenty more."

"Actually, I've got one," Blake said. "Do you remember that local news story from a couple of months ago? About the rich family's daughter who killed herself on her wedding day?"

Kenver nodded. "Sounds vaguely familiar."

"The bride jumped to her death in full wedding regalia, right in front of her family and her husband-to-be. No one could explain it. One minute, she'd been excited about getting married, the next she was a pulpy mush on the floor. Apparently, her death remains unexplained to this day."

Harris grinned, his face lighting up. He scanned the bar then leaned in, dropping his voice to a whisper. "That's not strictly true."

Blake frowned. "What isn't?"

"I probably shouldn't say anything, but the coroner's report for that one was signed off a few days ago."

"What? You're joking!" Blake glanced at Kenver, then back at Harris, unable to contain her excitement. "What did it say?"

"Toxicology took a while to come back, but . . ." He paused, his bloodshot eyes shining with glee. "That woman was tripping her tits off when she died. High as a kite on her wedding day!"

Blake shook her head, wondering if she'd heard correctly. "Tripping? You're saying she was on drugs?"

"Dangerous levels of tropane alkaloids were found in her blood. Atropine, hyoscyamine and scopolamine." He pronounced the words with surprising eloquence despite his slurred speech. "They're from a plant. *Datura stramonium.* Otherwise known as Jimsonweed, thorn apple, or the Devil's snare. It's a member of the nightshade family."

"*Datura*," Kenver said. "I've heard of that. Isn't it a hallucinogenic?"

Blake shot a glance at him. "Of course *you'd* know that."

"I looked it up out of curiosity," Harris said. He told them that the plant had originated from North America, but now grew all over the world, the seeds carried by birds and spread in their droppings. Despite its toxicity, indigenous tribes used to ingest *Datura* in sacred ceremonies, believing it opened the mind to intense spiritual visions. "Maybe your bride thought she'd make her wedding day that little bit more special. Probably didn't think to read the warning label, though."

"What do you mean?"

"If you don't know what you're doing with *Datura*, it can be fatal. If it doesn't poison you first, the terrifying hallucinations and extreme paranoia might be enough to make you do something stupid. Like jump off a balcony in front of your wedding guests."

Blake's head was spinning. "So, it wasn't a suicide?"

"The coroner was going to rule Death by Misadventure, which includes suicide. But now she's questioning whether further investigation is needed." Harris suddenly looked worried. "Don't tell anyone I told you, okay? The family hasn't been informed yet."

Datura stramonium. In all honesty, Blake hadn't known what to expect from tonight. But this? It didn't make any sense. She glanced at Kenver, who only shrugged.

Harris picked up his glass and pulled a face when he found it empty. "Whose round is it?"

32

IT WAS JUST BEFORE ten when Blake returned to her mother's house. She had given Kenver a lift home and watched with a guilty weight in her chest as he'd staggered inside and shut the door. He had been doing well with not drinking, and now she had potentially ruined it all by using him to get to Jason Harris. She would check in with him tomorrow evening, and the day after that if necessary, to make sure she had only caused a blip. If it turned out to be worse, then it was on Blake to put things right.

Mary was waiting for her in the living room, nervously twisting the wedding band she still wore despite her husband's infidelities.

"There you are," she said, getting to her feet. "I've been worried sick."

Blake arched an eyebrow. "Why? I'm a grown woman and it's not even ten."

Her mother reached up and kissed her cheek, then beckoned her towards the kitchen. "Have you eaten?"

"Not yet."

"Well, it's a good job I saved you a plate. I'll heat it up."

Blake thought about the turgid tales Jason Harris had glee-fully relayed, and her stomach churned. "Thanks, but I'm not hungry."

"It's no good going to bed on an empty stomach. You won't be able to sleep."

Mary removed the foil from the plate of food as she put it in the microwave and set it to warm. She smiled nervously then glanced towards the kitchen window.

"What's with you?" Blake said, sitting down at the table and dumping her bag on the floor.

"It's nothing. Cup of tea?"

"No thanks."

As Mary topped up the kettle with water and switched it on, Blake rested her elbows on the table and shut her eyes.

"Long day, was it?" her mother asked.

"The longest." Blake's head was still spinning from all that she'd learned. Blake had found no evidence of Kerenza ever being a drug user, recreational or otherwise. And even if she had, why take something as potentially dangerous as *Datura stramo-nium* on her wedding day of all days? She would have been hallucinating through the entire ceremony.

Blake was unconvinced that Kerenza had deliberately ingested a mind-altering plant before marrying the love of her life. And if she hadn't taken it, the only other explanation for its presence in her bloodstream was much more sinister. The coroner was right to think further investigation was required.

"How is Judy doing?" Mary hovered by the kitchen counter, twisting her wedding ring around and around.

Blake shook her head. "No idea. I don't think she's talking to me."

"I'm sure she will come the morning. It's frightening, what happened. Everyone in town is talking about devil worshippers. I was scared to be here on my own tonight."

"I don't think whoever it is will come out here just to give you a fright, Mum. It's probably just kids playing stupid games."

"Dangerous games, more like. It was lucky the child wasn't hurt. And your fingers, it could have been worse." The kettle clicked off. Mary poured boiling water into a mug. "Anyway, where are the police? Why aren't they doing anything about it?"

"They are. They were over at Judy's last night, dusting for fingerprints."

Mary's eyes wandered back over to the kitchen windows. Blake got up and gave her a hug.

"Try not to worry, okay? I'll call Rory tomorrow and see if he knows anything."

"I didn't know you two were talking again."

"We're not," Blake said. "Why don't you go up to bed? I'll check all the windows and lock the doors."

Mary didn't look convinced.

"No one's coming, Mum. They wouldn't dare, not while I'm here."

"Didn't stop them last night, did it?" The microwave dinged. Mary took out the plate and set it on the table. "Sit down and eat your dinner."

Blake slumped back in the chair and stared at the food. Pork chops, boiled potatoes, and greens. Her stomach heaved again.

Her mother kissed the top of her head. "I'll go up then. Make sure you lock up properly. Bolts and all."

Mary fetched her mug of tea from the counter then hovered a minute, looking lost and afraid. Blake knew what she was thinking: if only Ed was here right now.

"Get some sleep, Mum. I'll see you in the morning."

Mary said goodnight and left Blake alone in the kitchen, who immediately pushed the plate of food away. There was no way she was going to eat tonight. Instead, she got up and went from room to room, locking the windows and doors, and sliding all available bolts across. Stopping at the front door, she peered out of the side window into the darkness of the drive beyond. Skeletal tree branches swayed in the wind. The sky above was black and full of stars. Blake shivered then returned to the kitchen. She picked up the food plate and scraped her dinner into the food recycling bin.

"Sorry, Mum," she whispered.

Datura stramonium. She needed to call Campbell and tell him what she'd found, but she was reluctant because she only had half an answer.

Pulling her laptop from her bag, she powered it up and opened a web browser, then typed in: '*Datura stramonium*'. Before she could hit the search button, her phone began to buzz. It was Judy calling.

"I'm so glad to hear your voice," Blake said without saying hello. "Are you okay?"

Judy breathed in her ear. "What do you think?"

So, not forgiven yet. "You're right. I'm sorry. How's Stacey doing?"

"Surprisingly fine. Better than her parents, anyway. We're staying at my Mum's for a couple of nights. I couldn't face being in the house."

Blake stared at the table. "Did you get the locks changed?"

"The locksmith came around this morning, after the police were done. But it doesn't change the fact that a stranger entered our home. That he was in my daughter's room, hovering over her bed."

"I'm sorry, Judy." Blake was surprised by the tears stinging her eyes. "I don't know what else to say, but I'm so sorry."

Judy was quiet for a long time. Then she said, "It's fine. I mean, it's not fine, obviously. But it happened and no one got hurt. And I keep thinking about the back door. Maybe I didn't lock it after all. Maybe they would have still got in if it had been me and Charlie at home instead."

It wasn't forgiveness, but Blake felt a tiny surge of relief. "Did the police find anything?"

"Nothing. Not even a print."

No fingerprints. No signs of forced entry. It sounded a lot like it wasn't the first time the intruder had broken into someone's home.

"What about the wax doll?"

"Nothing yet." Judy let out a faltering breath. "Why was my family targeted, Blake? What did we do?"

Blake thought about what Tegen had said about the nature of poppets, that they were used as an act of revenge. But it was late and dark outside, and Blake didn't want to add more fuel to Judy's nightmares tonight.

"I doubt you did anything," she said.

"But it feels so personal."

"Try to get some sleep," Blake told her. "Hopefully, the police will lift something from the doll and catch the bastard."

"I hope so. I'd hate to think of him doing this to someone else."

"I'll call you in the morning, okay?"

"Okay. Good night."

"Good night."

Blake hung up and stared at the laptop screen. Her vision was bleary. She was tired and her head hurt, spinning with a myriad of thoughts. At least Judy was talking to her again.

She yawned, suddenly exhausted. She needed to sleep, to allow her brain time to process the events of the day. Then tomorrow morning, she would return to Saltwater House one last time, and she wouldn't leave until she had answers.

Switching off the kitchen light, she padded along the hallway, checked the locks on the front door once more, and headed upstairs. And when she was in bed, the softness of the sheets lulling her to sleep, she tried not to think of the figure in the goat skull mask. She hoped no one would hear from him again. But she had a terrible feeling that he was only getting started.

33

FAITH PENROSE SAT in her living room with the curtains drawn and the table lamps switched on, watching a late-night repeat of an antiques show on the television. She was watching, but not really watching. She found it hard to concentrate on anything these days. Her mind constantly wandered into the past, getting lost for hours. It wasn't Alzheimer's disease or anything terrible like that. The past was where she could find her daughter still alive. The present was so empty now, her home like a charnel house, where she watched over the bones of the dead. Sometimes it felt like she was dead herself, and she would blow softly into her hand to check she was still breathing. The warm breath on her skin was always a bitter disappointment.

She sipped her third sherry of the evening. There had been a lot of third sherries lately, but who could blame her? She was alone. No one visited anymore. Except for Blake Hollow, who had already cancelled this week's visit, and who had only been coming to see her for the past year. Before that, she had actively avoided Faith for eighteen years. But Faith did not resent her for it. Blake had been Demelza's best friend, and her disappearance had torn Blake's world apart almost as much as it had destroyed Faith's. But Demelza wasn't missing anymore. What was left of her had been laid to rest in the cemetery.

And now the people of Wheal Marow, people who had once been Faith's friends, no longer saw her as the tragic mother reeling from years of loss. Now they only saw her as the wife of a serial killer. How had she not known her husband was a deranged monster? A killer of seventeen young women, including her own daughter? It would have been impossible for him to hide his depravity, to keep up the pretence of a sane human being twenty-four hours a day. There would have been cracks. Tell-tale signs. Faith Penrose must have noticed them. She had to have known but then kept it to herself. Which surely made her just as guilty as her psychopath of a husband.

It didn't matter that Faith had been divorced from him for seventeen years. Seventeen years in which he'd done most of his killing. And it didn't matter that she hadn't even spoken to him for the longest time.

Guilty by association. That was Faith's name now, even though the police had found no evidence connecting her to the crimes. Even though her husband had fooled everyone else, not just her.

Guilty by association. She was forced to wear it like a sign around her neck.

Lately, she had been thinking it would be better to leave Wheal Marow, just like Christine Truscott had last month. Faith admired the woman. It must have taken guts to pack up her home and go elsewhere to start again. When most parents lost a child, they felt compelled to remain in the same house, leaving the child's room exactly as it had been left, frozen in time, like a shrine or mausoleum. It helped to keep their child alive in their minds, Faith supposed. It certainly had for her. Demelza's room was still exactly as she had left it eighteen years ago. Sometimes Faith would go in there and stand quietly, not daring to touch anything for fear of disturbing the layout. But since her daughter's remains had been recovered, she had been in there less and less.

For the longest time, visiting the room had given Faith hope that Demelza would one day return home. Here are your things, she would tell her living, breathing daughter. Here is your life, just like you left it. But Demelza was dead now, and there was no longer need for hope. Only a grave covered in wilting flowers. And yet Faith could not bring herself to empty her daughter's room. To turn it into something else.

The TV show ended and advertisements began to play, fake people with fake smiles speaking to her in patronising tones that made her feel like a child. She reached for the remote and switched the television off. She drained her sherry glass and got to her feet.

Her eyes felt heavy, but she already knew sleep would prove difficult tonight. Lately, her insomnia had grown worse. Her doctor had prescribed sleeping pills, with a warning only to use them when she was in desperate need. She hadn't had the heart to tell him she'd been desperate for eighteen years. But the pills did help her sleep, immersing her in a dark and dreamless slumber. And even though the hopelessness returned the next morning, at least the pills erased most of her terrible nightmares.

Padding over to the mantelpiece, she picked up a framed photograph of her daughter. Demelza was seventeen in the picture, beautiful, with intelligent eyes that were old beyond her years, and a smile that was as warm as a meadow in summer. It was how Faith liked to remember her, filled with hopes and dreams, completely unaware of the horrors lying in wait for her just one year later. Pressing the photograph to her lips, Faith kissed her daughter goodnight.

In the kitchen, she rinsed out her sherry glass and placed it on the drainer. She locked the back door, sliding the bolt across, then returned to the hallway and locked the front door.

Yesterday, she had gone to the corner shop for milk and the day's newspapers. She had heard Iris Babcock and Norman Wells gossiping in one of the aisles. They were talking about an attack on the church and Reverend Thompson, something about satanic symbols and a man wearing an animal skull on his face. The image frightened Faith, who had been a regular churchgoer until the day Demelza disappeared. But then Iris Babcock, who oversaw the church's foodbank where Faith had occasionally volunteered until last year, said, "Ever since poor Lucy Truscott was murdered by that monster, Wheal Marow has felt tainted." Then she went quiet as she saw Faith standing in the aisle, desperately reading the ingredients on a tin of tomatoes and pretending she hadn't heard. Faith supposed she was a reminder to the town of all the terrible things her ex-husband had done.

Upstairs, she brushed her teeth and washed her face, then climbed into bed. A blister pack of sleeping pills sat on the bedside table. Popping one out, she swallowed it with a drink of water, then picked up the historical fiction novel she'd been trying to read. Two pages in, her mind began to wander. She sighed, realising she hadn't absorbed a single word, then returned to the beginning and tried again, focusing on the text, trying to lose herself in each letter.

A loud creak from the landing outside made Faith look up. She rested the book on her lap and stared at the bedroom door. For some unknown reason, her heartbeat began to flutter. She listened carefully, wondering if she should get up and investigate. But the noise didn't come again. The house was old, and sometimes creaked and groaned. The doctor had also warned her the sleeping pills had possible side effects, including auditory hallucinations. The creak she'd heard was probably nothing more than that.

She read for another ten minutes, until she felt the pills beginning to work. Her limbs grew heavy and tired. Her eyes began to droop. Setting her book down on the bedside table, Faith tiredly fluffed up her pillows, then switched off the lamp. She lay on her back, staring at the ceiling, moonlight spilling in through a crack in the curtains. Her eyelids grew too heavy, until she could no longer keep them open. She shut them, still awake but not for much longer.

As she began to drift off, consciousness slipping away, she was unaware of what was lying just beneath her.

A hand emerged from under the bed and gently pressed against the frame. Two curved horns appeared, growing larger, followed by a terrifying mask made of bone, a goat skull that glinted in the moonlight. Then came a neck and shoulders, followed by another hand. This one was holding something, curved and sharp with a serrated edge.

Faith shifted on the bed. The figure froze, the eyeless sockets of the skull staring upwards. Faith was still again, her breathing settling into a steady rhythm.

Little by little, the figure continued to ease itself out from under the bed, limbs moving like liquid in the dark. Then it was on its feet, growing like a shadow, the tips of its horns almost touching the ceiling. It leaned forward, watching her sleep.

And then, as if sensing a disturbance in the air, Faith Penrose opened her eyes. At first, all she saw was darkness. But as her vision began to adjust to the gloom, she saw the white glint of bone and the sharp curve of horns.

And then she was fully awake, adrenaline fighting the lull of her medication. She scrambled for the light switch.

The room lit up and she saw the figure in all its awful glory.

Death had come for her, a cruel-looking sickle in its hand. And even though she had yearned for it repeatedly, now that it was finally here, she wasn't ready.

"Please," she gasped. "Not yet."

The goat skull tipped to one side, the bony sockets observing her. A whisper came from its skinless mouth.

"This is what she gets," it said. "For not leaving things alone."

Faith drew in a breath. The sickle cut through the air and plunged into her flesh. The scream died in her throat.

34

A FRANTIC KNOCKING on Blake's bedroom door woke her from troubled sleep. Confused and disoriented, she lifted her head from the pillow as her bedroom door opened and her mother hurried in.

"Blake? Are you awake?" Mary said in a half whisper.

"I am now." Blake groaned and pushed herself up on her elbows. The room was still cast in shadows, the remnants of night still fading outside. Mary switched on the overhead light. Blake winced. "What's going on? What's wrong?"

Her mother was still in her nightdress, her hair sticking out at awkward angles. But her eyes were alert and her complexion was pale.

"Winifred called," she said.

"Who?" Blake tapped her phone screen on the bedside table and checked the time. 7:01 AM. The gossip grapevine started early in Wheal Marow.

"You know Winifred. Her boy, Ben, was a year below you at school. Anyway, she called to say the police are all over her street. They've shut half of it off."

Blake was sitting up now, rubbing her eyes. "Why?"

Mary opened her mouth, then shut it again, her fingers knitting together. "Well, it's just that . . ."

"Spit it out, Mum."

"Winifred lives four doors down from Faith Penrose. She says people in white suits are coming in and out of Faith's home. It's all taped off."

Blake's eyes snapped open, fully awake now. A chill crawled up the back of her neck and she shivered. "What did you say?"

"You were over there just the other day, weren't you?" Mary said. "I do hope she's okay."

Her heart was pounding, her breath catching in her throat. *People in white suits.* Blake pulled back the duvet and jumped to her feet. The room spun a little.

"What are you doing?" Mary asked.

Blake grabbed her jeans from the back of her chair and began pulling them on. "I'm going over there."

"But you haven't had your breakfast yet."

She threw on a t-shirt. Nausea climbed her throat. Panic made her dizzy. "I'll grab something later."

"But —"

"Mum," Blake said. "Faith is my friend. She's been to hell and back. I'm going over there."

Blake drove with her foot down, weaving in and out of the morning traffic, her heart and mind racing together. Faith Penrose lived in a small cul-de-sac near the outskirts of town. Blake pulled over at the end of the street and switched off the engine. A cordon of blue and white police tape prevented her from going any further. Uniformed officers stood guard, keeping sharp eyes on the gathering crowd, made up of nearby residents who were all staring and whispering to each other. It wouldn't be long before the press arrived and chaos ensued.

Jumping out of her car, Blake hurried towards the cordon. From here, she could see Faith's house standing at the far end of the cul-de-sac, a red and white inner cordon surrounding the perimeter of her front garden. More uniformed officers stood guard, while an ambulance and the CSI van were parked nearby. Two crime scene investigators dressed head to toe in white were busy examining the lawn. In adjacent houses, neighbours peered worriedly through their windows, unable to leave their homes until the police gave them permission.

Blake's throat was dry. She was finding it hard to breathe. Eyeing the nearest police officer, she marched up to him.

"Is Faith Penrose all right?" she asked. "Where is she?"

The officer, who was at least ten years younger than Blake, stared at her with probing eyes. "And you are?"

"Blake Hollow. I'm a friend. I've known Faith all my life."

His face softened a little. "I see. But I'm unable to give out any information at this time."

"Can you at least tell me if she's alive?"

"I'm sorry. Now I need to ask you to step back."

Walking away, Blake shoved her hands in her pockets to stop them from trembling. She slid to a halt and stared back at the house, feeling helpless and afraid. Someone tapped her on the shoulder, and she turned to see Judy. Her winter coat was half-buttoned and her hair was unbrushed.

"What's happening?" she asked, following Blake's gaze. "I got a tipoff. I didn't realise it was Faith's house they were talking about."

Blake tasted bile in the back of her throat. "The police aren't saying anything. But I know what it looks like."

"Me too." Judy nodded grimly.

They both watched in silence as another white-suited figure emerged from the house and walked towards the CSI van, a bag of evidence in hand.

"How are the kids?" Blake asked, unable to take her eyes off Faith's house.

"They're fine. Still at Mum's. Christ, Blake. What's going on in this town? First the church, then our house, now Faith?"

"We don't know if they're connected yet."

"Don't we?" Judy let out a trembling breath. "Seems a bit too coincidental if you ask me."

Blake was silent, her thundering heart deafening in its panic.

"I'll see if I can find out more," Judy said. "Back in a second."

She paced over to a female police officer who was guarding the cordon. Judy smiled and the police officer said hello. They seemed to know each other. Blake watched them talking for a moment before her gaze was drawn back to Faith Penrose's house. The crime scene, she thought, and felt a sudden urge to vomit.

The front door opened again. Two more figures dressed in white overalls were emerging. They stood to one side and began stripping off, revealing suits and ties beneath. Blake caught her breath. It was Detective Constable Rory Angove, along with Detective Sergeant Will Turner. The street seemed to tip to one side before righting itself. Their presence could only mean one thing.

Blake returned to the police cordon and waved her hand above her head. "Rory! Hey, Rory!"

Heads turned in her direction. DS Turner handed his protective suit over to an officer, then stared at Blake across the distance. He leaned towards Rory and said something. To Blake's surprise, Rory started walking over, a dour expression on his face.

Judy was still talking to the uniformed officer, but she eyed the detective constable as he drew closer to Blake.

He reached the cordon and stood on the other side, staring uncomfortably. Despite the situation, Blake felt the awkwardness, too.

"Hi," she said, her words stuck in her throat.

Rory stared at her. "What are you doing here?"

"Mum got a call from one of the neighbours. I came as quickly as I could. Faith is a friend, you know that. Please, Rory. Tell me what's going on."

He heaved his shoulders, then glanced over at Judy, a crease wrinkling his brow. He turned back to Blake.

"Listen, DS Turner needs you to come along to the station. You can follow me in your car. He'll be along shortly."

"Me?" Blake said. "Why? What for?"

"We need to ask you some questions."

"What about?"

Judy was saying goodbye to the police officer and heading back over.

Rory's almond-shaped eyes filled with worry. "Please. Just follow me in the car over to Truro."

Judy joined them, saying hello to Rory then staring at Blake. "Any news?"

Blake clenched her jaw and shook her head. Her stomach churned and fluttered with dread. She peered over at Rory.

"Okay, fine, I'll come with you. But first you tell me if Faith is alive."

"Go where?" Judy said. She looked tired, Blake thought. As if she hadn't slept all night. "What's going on?"

"Police business," Rory said.

Blake leaned into Judy. "I'll tell you later."

Rory frowned. "No, you won't."

And then a sudden murmur rose from the crowd of onlookers. Over at the Penrose house, a pair of paramedics stepped from the doorway, wheeling a stretcher between them. And on the stretcher was a body bag covered in a white sheet.

The blood drained from Blake's face.

Next to her, Judy drew in a shocked breath. "Faith! Oh no!"

The paramedics wheeled the body to the back of the ambulance, the wheels collapsing as they pushed the stretcher inside.

"We should go," Rory said. "Wait for me by your car."

He moved along the cordon towards a uniformed officer, who was logging people in and out of the crime scene.

"Go where?" Judy asked for a second time, her voice barely a whisper.

Blake reached out and squeezed her hand. The ambulance engine started up, the red and blue emergency lights dazzling against the grey of the houses.

"I'll call you," she whispered.

Then Rory was stepping outside of the cordon and staring in her direction. Blake turned and walked away from the crime scene, heading towards her car with Rory close behind. She felt numb. Confused. Terrified.

Faith Penrose was dead. Just like her daughter.

Now Blake was on her way to the police station and didn't even know why.

35

THE INTERVIEW ROOM was small and square, with a desk and chairs at the centre and a second smaller table in the corner. There was nothing on the walls and there were no windows. Blake sat at the desk, her lower spine aching from sitting on the rigid plastic chair for forty minutes now. The cup of bitter coffee she'd been given was still full and had gone cold. Her mind was reeling, thoughts scrambling over each other. Faith Penrose was dead. Murdered. But why? And by whom?

For Faith's life to end in violence felt like the punchline to a sick and twisted joke. She had lost her daughter, twice, and had spent the past eighteen years in deep mourning, only to discover her ex-husband had murdered their child and another sixteen women. A memory flashed before Blake's eyes. She was a teenager. She and Demelza were in Faith's kitchen, laughing at something silly, while Faith smiled and shook her head as she made them cheese sandwiches. It was such a small, random moment to recall but it crushed her.

Blake had avoided seeing Faith for eighteen years. It was the grief in her eyes that she couldn't stand; grief that Blake had repressed for nearly two decades. Since Demelza's remains had been found and laid to rest, Blake had been making an effort to visit Faith while others had turned their backs. Now those visits felt small and pathetic, nowhere close to recompense.

She leaned back on the chair, drumming her fingers on the table. The tears were inside her somewhere, too afraid to come out of hiding. Only numbness had dared to show its face.

Footsteps were approaching. The door opened and Detective Sergeant Will Turner entered the room. He was a handsome man, in his late forties, who had permanent shadows beneath his sad eyes. Blake knew he had witnessed the aftermath of terrible cruelty during his time on the police force. She had shared her own horrors with him just last year. Back then, they had clashed and fought against each other, until Blake had single-handedly stopped a serial killer in his tracks. Gradually, Turner had grown to respect her. And she supposed she had grown to respect him.

The detective sergeant nodded as he sat down on the opposite side of the desk. The door opened again and a female detective in a charcoal trouser suit entered the room and took a seat at the corner table. She was young, Blake noted, late twenties or early thirties.

"I'm sorry for the delay in getting to you," Turner said. "This is Detective Constable Collins. She'll be joining us for this interview."

DC Collins took out a notebook and placed it in front of her, pen poised over a clean page.

"Where's Rory?" Blake asked Turner.

"DC Angove has a personal connection to you, so it would be inappropriate for him to participate in this interview."

"I see. And what exactly is this interview about?"

"We'll get to that in just a moment."

Blake slid her cold cup of coffee to one side. "Please, just tell me what's going on. Was Faith murdered?"

Turner cleared his throat. "Perhaps we could begin with you confirming your whereabouts last night."

"What?" Blake almost laughed, then realised the gravity of the situation. "I was with my cousin, Kenver Quick. We met at a bar in Truro around six-thirty, then left at around nine. I drove Kenver home, then I went back to my mother's."

"You still live there?"

"For the time being."

"Which bar were you at?"

"Crystals. It's on Duke Street. If you'd like to know what happened when I got back to my mother's, she warmed up a plate of leftovers for me—pork chops, potatoes, and greens—which I didn't eat. Mum went to bed, I followed soon after. Anything else?"

Turner ignored the hostility. "Anyone join you and Kenver last night?"

"Kenver had a friend with him called Jason."

"Last name?"

"Sorry, I don't know. You'll have to ask my cousin." Blake stared at Turner. "Am I a suspect?"

The detective sergeant shrugged. "I'm just building a picture. Are you working on a case right now?"

"Yes, I am. But what's that got to do with Faith Penrose?"

"Indulge me. What kind of case is it?"

"The personal kind. I'm investigating a woman who took her own life on her wedding day."

"Which woman?"

"Kerenza Trezise. Her family is wealthy. They live on an estate out by Frenchman's Creek."

Turner stroked his chin. "Was that in the papers? It sounds familiar. If I remember correctly, she jumped to her death in front of the whole wedding party."

"Good memory." Blake narrowed her eyes. "Seriously, Turner. Why are you asking?"

"Any leads yet?"

She heaved her shoulders. She'd forgotten how annoying Turner could be. "If you must know, the investigation's just taken an interesting turn."

"In what way?"

"In a confidential way."

"Who hired you?"

"Again, confidential. And it has nothing to do with your investigation."

"All right. Let's talk enemies. Have you made any lately?"

"Of course. It comes with the territory. Currently, the entire Trezise family wants my head on a plate. They haven't taken kindly to me probing into their private lives." Blake leaned forward, staring at Turner with unblinking eyes. "Are we done with the getting-to-know-you questions? My friend is dead. Undoubtedly murdered if you're involved. So why don't you stop pissing around and tell me why I'm here?"

At the corner table, DC Collins paused from her notetaking to arch an eyebrow. Turner's expression remained grave.

"All right. What I'm about to tell you is extremely confidential," he said. "It does not leave this room. If the press gets hold of it, I'll know exactly who to come for."

Blake's throat was dry. "Go on."

"I'm sorry to tell you that, at six o'clock this morning, Faith Penrose was found murdered in her home."

She had already known what Turner was about to say, but the shock still took her breath away. "Who found her?"

"The milkman. Her front door was wide open. He was concerned, so he looked inside."

"How was she killed?"

"I'm afraid I can't divulge that information at this time."

The grief that Blake had been concealing began to stir. "Did she suffer? Was it violent?"

Turner stared at the tabletop. "Yes."

Christ, Blake thought. Poor Faith.

"You were friends with her?" Turner asked. His body language had softened a little, along with his tone.

"Yes I am. *Was*. You know that from last year."

"When was the last time you saw her?"

"Four or five days ago. I try to visit Faith at least twice a month. She doesn't—she *didn't*—get out much after her daughter's remains were found."

"How did she seem to you?"

"Quiet, like she always is. She asked after Mum and the family, about my job. We didn't ever really talk about what happened, but you could tell it destroyed her. How do you recover from knowing your ex-husband is a serial killer, and that he murdered your daughter?"

"I suppose you don't." Turner shifted on the seat. "Did Ms Penrose seem worried about anything or anyone in particular? Did she express any concerns to you?"

Blake shook her head.

"Can you think of anyone who wanted to harm her?"

"Most of Wheal Marow turned their backs on her after Dennis Stott. Which was unfair, but I'm sure you've been here long enough to know how small towns work. Still, I don't think anyone here would want to murder Faith because of her ex-husband's crimes."

Turner tilted his head to one side. "And how about you? Have you or your family received any threats lately?"

"What? No, not that I'm aware of." Blake glanced at DC Collins, then back at Turner. "I mean, this isn't about my family, but there was an incident the night before last at Judy Moon's house."

Turner wrinkled his brow and glanced at Collins, who shook her head.

Blake's eyes widened with disbelief. "Don't you detectives talk to your uniformed friends? Someone broke into Judy's house while I was babysitting her kids. Whoever it was, they left a nasty little doll covered in needles in one of the girl's beds. I suppose you didn't hear about the church either?"

Turner stared at her.

"A few nights ago, someone painted satanic symbols in blood on the church door and frightened Reverend Thompson half to death. Apparently, whoever it was wore an animal skull mask on their face."

Turner was sitting up now, eyes fully alert. "The break-in at Judy Moon's house happened while you were there?"

"That's right." Blake clasped her hands together and stared uncertainly at the detectives. "What's going on? Why are you looking at me like that?"

The temperature in the room seemed to drop by a few degrees. She rubbed her arms in response.

Turner nodded at DC Collins, who produced a digital tablet from her bag and brought it over, placing it on the desk in front of him.

Blake watched as he switched it on and swiped the screen. His face was deadly serious.

"I'm going to show you a photograph from the crime scene. It doesn't show the body," he said. "But please remember my warning about confidential information leaving this room."

Blake swallowed, desperate for air. Turner slid the tablet over, turning it a hundred and eighty degrees.

Sucking in a deep breath, Blake blew it out through her nose then stared down at the screen. Her heart smashed against her ribcage. She gasped, glanced up at Turner, then back down again, scarcely able to believe what she was seeing.

The image was of the wall above Faith Penrose's bed, the bedposts just visible in the lower quadrants. Arterial sprays splattered the walls. And drawn among them in what Blake assumed was Faith's blood was the inverted Cross of Saint Peter. Beneath it were three words, the letters dripping down the wall.

Hollow By Name.

Blake stared at the words, dread crawling up her throat.

"It doesn't mean it's me," she whispered.

"It's possible it's a coincidence, but it seems unlikely," Turner said. "Are you a member of the church congregation?"

"No, but my mother is."

"And Judy Moon is a friend?"

"One of my oldest. Ever since school." Blake stared at the words again, her head spinning.

Hollow by name. 'Hollow by nature' was the insinuation.

Turner clasped his hands together. "I need to ask you again, have you made any recent enemies other than the Trezises?"

Her heart was racing now. The image on the screen before her seemed to waver, the blood sliding down the walls. She pushed the tablet away and crossed her arms over her stomach.

"No one sick enough to do something like this," she said.

"Then talk to me about the Trezise family."

Blake told him what she knew—that they lived an isolated existence, hidden away from the world at Saltwater House, with the Bodilys and a tragic legacy of death as their only companions.

"It can't be them," she said. "They never leave their home."

"People with power and money rarely do their dirty work themselves," said Turner.

"True. But I recently learned their money is running out."

"What about the Bodilys?"

"They're retirement age. Besides, I'm investigating a family suicide. I hardly think that would drive the Trezises to commit murder just to warn me off, do you?"

Unless, of course, it wasn't a suicide, she thought. The toxicology results were highly suspicious. And then there was the occult symbology used in the Wheal Marow attacks.

Blake sat up. "My mother is alone at home. I need to call her."

Turner glanced at Collins. "Speak to uniform, see what they have on the church and the attack at Judy Moon's. And while you're at it, see if there have been any other reported incidents with similar traits." The detective constable nodded, shut her notebook, and left the room. Turner stared at Blake. "Until we have more to go on, it would be a sensible idea for us to keep a watchful eye over your family. Is your father at home?"

Blake shook her head. "My parents are still separated."

"Then we'll need his address. Anyone else we need to be concerned about?"

"My cousin Kenver, maybe." Nausea had gripped Blake and was refusing to let go.

"As for the Trezise case," Turner continued. "It might be a wise idea to press pause for now."

"I can't do that. Time isn't on my side right now and I'm *very* close to an answer. Besides, I can take care of myself. I took down a serial killer last year, remember?"

"And you almost lost an arm in the process. Anyway, it's not you I'm worried about. If these attacks *are* linked to you, then whoever is behind them is going for the people you care about. They've just proved that they're capable of taking a life. Let's not provoke them any further until forensics have come through."

36

OUTSIDE THE POLICE STATION, the cold, damp air chilled Blake's bones. She had told DS Turner that she was stepping outside to make a call, but now she was hurrying away from the station on foot, instinct sending her in the direction of Old Bridge Street. As she walked, she took out her phone and called her mother.

"Did you find out about Faith?" Mary asked.

Blake caught her breath. "She's gone, Mum. Someone killed her."

"Oh, dear Lord. The poor woman! Who would do such a terrible thing?"

"I don't know." Cars shot by on the busy street, toxic exhaust fumes throttling the atmosphere. "What are your plans for today?"

It took Mary a moment to compose herself. "Well, I was supposed to be meeting your Aunt Hester for a coffee in town."

"I need you to cancel that and stay at home. A police officer is coming over very soon."

"What? Why are they coming here?"

"It's just a precaution."

"I don't understand, Blake. What's going on?"

Blake bit down on her lip. She didn't want to frighten her mother, but she didn't know any other way to explain. "They think whoever killed Faith might be targeting me. Which means I need you to stay home, lock the door, and wait for the police to come."

There was a long silence. A motorbike raced by, deafening Blake's ears.

"Where are you now?" Mary said.

"Truro. There's something I need to do."

"Oh Blake, if you're in danger you should come straight here."

Blake sucked in another breath as she forced out the words she didn't want to say. "Call Ed. Explain the situation and tell him to come over right away."

"Your father? But he'll be working."

"He won't care about that when you tell him what's happening. Call him, Mum."

She stepped off the road and cut through the pedestrianised Pydar Street. Truro Cathedral loomed over her, its Gothic Revival architecture intimidating against the slate sky.

"When will you be home?" Mary asked.

"Soon. I'm sorry Mum, but I have to go."

"But Blake —"

"The police will be there any minute. Call Dad."

She hung up. Pydar Street merged with High Cross. Blake swung left, stopping in front of the cathedral to call Kenver. The line connected and began to ring. After a few seconds, the automated voicemail kicked in. He was still sleeping off last night's beer, she told herself. That was all. Leaving a message, she told him to call her as soon as he woke up. She turned into Old Bridge Street and stopped outside Campbell Green's front door. She pressed the buzzer and he let her in.

The front door of his flat was ajar when she arrived on the top floor, and Campbell was in the kitchen area, pouring black coffee into two mugs.

"If I'd known you were coming, I would have tidied up," he said without looking up.

Blake looked around. The place was immaculate.

Campbell walked over and handed her a mug. He frowned. "Are you okay? You look terrible."

The crime scene photographs flashed in Blake's mind, followed by flickering memories of Faith Penrose.

"I'm fine." Her tone suggested he didn't probe further.

Campbell shrugged. "You have some news for me?"

"Actually, I need to ask you some questions, and I need you to answer me honestly."

"Of course. Why wouldn't I?" He perched himself on the edge of a kitchen stool and stared at her.

"Did Kerenza have a drug habit?" Blake asked. There was no point in being subtle now.

Campbell's jaw swung open. He smiled in astonishment then grew deadly serious. "No, of course not! Kerenza hated the idea of drugs. She didn't even drink alcohol. Why are you asking me that?"

Blake let out a breath. "I wasn't going to tell you until I had more answers, but the toxicology report from Kerenza's post-mortem showed dangerous levels of tropane alkaloids in her blood from a plant known for its psychoactive properties. It's called *Datura stramonium*. Indigenous tribes used to ingest it during spiritual ceremonies, believing it heightened their visions.

Used in the wrong doses, it causes terrifying hallucinations and extreme paranoia. It can kill you."

Campbell's complexion had paled. "This is a joke, isn't it?"

"Believe me, I wish it was."

"So you're saying that Kerenza didn't kill herself? That, what? She ate this stuff, had a bad trip, and accidentally jumped to her death?"

"It looks that way, yes."

"I don't believe it." Campbell shook his head, over and over. "She would never have taken something like that. Especially not on our wedding day, for Christ's sake."

He got up from the kitchen stool and began pacing in front of the window, arms wrapped around his rib cage.

"Can you say that for certain, Campbell?" Blake said. "You've already learned things about Kerenza that you didn't know about before. Like her paintings, for example."

"There's no way. She would never have taken it." His face was red now, his eyes shining in the winter light. "It was meant to be the happiest day of our lives. She loved me, and I loved her. I'm telling you, she wouldn't have taken something like that —or anything else—on our fucking wedding day!"

Blake set her coffee down, untouched, on a side table. "The coroner is considering further investigation. If you're positive that Kerenza didn't take *Datura* willingly, it means someone else somehow made her ingest it. So the next questions are 'who?' and 'why?'"

Campbell stopped pacing. "This can't be happening."

"I'm afraid it is." Blake tried to sound sympathetic but the numbness she felt made it difficult. "And if it's true, if a crime has been committed here, we need to inform the police."

"Well, it can't be anyone from her family," Campbell said. "I mean yes, they all had their squabbles and disagreements, but they loved Kerenza. She was a good person. None of them would ever dream of hurting her like that."

The bruises on Tegen's arm flashed in Blake's mind. "Which brings me to my second question. You told me the Trezise family were running out of money. Why?"

Shrugging, Campbell avoided her probing gaze.

"You need to tell me. What if it's connected to Kerenza's death?"

"It's not. It can't be."

"Then tell me so I can scratch it off the list."

He padded over to the sofa and sat down heavily. Blake sat opposite him, suddenly feeling exhausted.

"Most of the Trezise fortune is gone," Campbell said. "Much of it was frittered away years ago, on whatever rich people spend their money on. The rest of it was lost, some through bad investments made by Griffin Trezise, the rest by him trusting the wrong people. Overzealous hedge fund managers who lost billions of other people's money due to derivative bets, around the time of the Financial Crisis. I guess things like that happen if you're an arrogant prick with accounts full of Old Money and no head for business." Campbell leaned forward, his eyes filling with unease. "But there's something else. Not long after Griffin hired me to manage the accounts, I noticed some discrepancies."

"What kind?" Blake asked.

"The numbers didn't add up. So I did some digging and I discovered that fifty thousand a month was being deposited across three different offshore bank accounts. It looked like it had been going on for the past few years with no explanation as to why. When I questioned Griffin about it, he became extremely agitated. He told me my job was to balance the books, not to worry about what he did with his money. I was instructed to keep records and to never ask about it again."

Blake heaved her shoulders. She'd never had an interest in the financial world. All she cared about was how much went into her bank account and how much went out. "So what was it? Offshore accounts for tax evasion purposes?"

Campbell shook his head. "I've managed the accounts of several wealthy people. That kind of thing happens all the time, and I'm expected to turn a blind eye. But this was different. I would assume, judging by Griffin's reaction and the anonymity of the bank accounts, that he's either involved in criminal activity, which I highly doubt, or he's the victim of someone else's."

"Blackmail," Blake said.

Campbell nodded in agreement. "You think it's about the slavery?"

"What else could it be?"

"Behind every great fortune there is a great crime."

Blake had thought the same thing days ago. "Did Kerenza know?"

"I thought about telling her but decided against it. I was scared she would confront Griffin and he would ruin the wedding." He paused to let out a sad sigh. "I was going to tell her after we were married."

"What about the offshore accounts?" Blake said. "Did you find out who they belonged to?"

"That's way beyond my skill set and resources. All I know is those monthly deposits were still being made when Griffin fired me. Which means they're probably still being made now."

Blake sucked in a breath. Campbell's explanation accounted for the state of Saltwater House: there wasn't enough money left to pay for its upkeep.

"That's all I know," he said. "But I still don't believe it's connected to Kerenza's death."

"Unless," Blake said, "Kerenza found out who was blackmailing her father."

"How? She didn't know anyone, only her family. And I doubt it was one of them because they all benefit from their dirty little secret. Even Kerenza did. If it got out, every one of them would be exposed."

Getting to her feet, Blake crossed the room and stared out the window. What did she do? Her mother was expecting her home. Turner had warned her to drop the Trezise case so as not to further endanger her family. But if she let it all go now, she would forfeit any chance of finally solving Kerenza's death. She only had until the end of the afternoon before the gates of Saltwater House shut on her forever, and it was already eleven-thirty.

"What are you thinking?" Campbell asked from the sofa.

Blake walked to the front door and opened it.

"I'll call you tonight," she said. "Hopefully with answers."

She took the stairs down to the street. Below her the muddy waters of Truro River ran by. Five minutes later, she was entering the police station car park and climbing into her car. Then Blake was driving away, her heart hammering in her chest as she headed back towards Saltwater House one last time.

37

THE SKY GREW dark as Blake drove along the country lane that led to Saltwater House. Through the brush on her right, Helford River was the colour of charcoal. The lane turned and plunged into the trees. The gates of Saltwater House stood up ahead. To Blake's surprise, they were unlocked and slightly ajar. She pulled up in front of them and hit the brakes, just as her phone started buzzing in the cup holder. Blake snatched it up and saw Kenver was calling. Relief surged through her body.

"What's the problem?" he said, his voice full of sand. "You sounded unhinged in your voicemail."

Blake peered through the windscreen at the gates. She hadn't called ahead to let Saul Bodily know she was coming, so why were they open?

"Hello?" Kenver said.

Clearing her throat, Blake told him that Faith Penrose was dead and that one of her family might be next, so it was a good idea if he went over to Mary's house, where a police officer would be waiting. Kenver was silent for a long time. She asked if he was still there.

"For fuck's sake, Blake," he said. "I'm hungover as hell. I don't want to go anywhere today."

"So you'd rather risk getting murdered?"

"I feel like I'm dying, anyway."

"That's not even funny." Sometimes Kenver had no tact. "Look, just go over there, okay? I could do without someone else I care about ending up on a mortician's slab right now."

He sighed in her ear. "Fine. I'll head over once I've had a vat of coffee."

"Good. Text me when you get there." Blake was unnerved by how calmly Kenver seemed to be reacting to the situation. Maybe it was a blessing he was so hungover.

"I'm sorry about Faith," he said. "I didn't really know her, but from what you've told me she was dealt a shitty hand. She didn't deserve to die like that."

"No, she didn't."

She said goodbye and hung up. Getting out of the car, she pushed the gates open wider then froze, staring into the trees. The feeling that she was being watched had returned. She hurried back to the car and drove on to the house, leaving the gates open.

Saltwater House was still and quiet. Blake heard no voices, no birdsong, no creaking branches. She walked her usual route, around the side of the house and into the kitchen. Violet Bodily wasn't there. There were no pans simmering on the stove, and no sliced vegetables on the chopping board. It was cold, the hearth unlit and full of ashes.

Of course. It was the Bodilys' day off. Blake had been so caught up in everything that she hadn't even realised it was the weekend.

Leaving the kitchen, Blake walked through corridors and

passageways, checking each room for signs of the family. The classroom was empty and so was Jack's gym room, the weights all neatly stacked in a pyramid. A trace of sweat hung in the air, suggesting the room had been recently used.

She retraced her steps and headed towards the rear of the house, until she reached the orangery. Inside, the furnace was alight, the room sweltering as usual. Grey daylight filtered through the glass roof. Below on the lawn, a fine shroud of mist still lingered. Abigail was nowhere in sight.

As Blake walked through the aisles of exotic shrubs and plants, her unease grew. At the workbench, she examined the pots and tools scattered on top, then turned back to face the room.

Removing her phone, she found the images of *Datura stramonium* that she'd saved from the internet. Standing up to a metre tall, the plant had broad, toothy leaves and long funnel-shaped flowers, usually white but sometimes lilac, that flowered in the summer and early autumn. Its most distinguishing feature was its bulbous and spiny seed pods, which gave the plant its common name of 'thorn apple'. Despite its alien appearance, the plant was considered a weed in Britain, usually found growing on roadsides and in wastelands. But perhaps it could also be found growing right here in the orangery.

Blake began a slow walk around the room, moving up and down the rows of tables, looking for a match. When she couldn't find one, she turned her attention to the trays of seedlings and young plants. None resembled *Datura* in shape or colour.

She returned to the workbench and chewed the inside of her mouth. Her eye caught the shelves on her right, where Abigail kept tubs of dried flowers, seeds, and home-made ointments. Blake searched through them, unscrewing jar lids, then peering inside and sniffing the contents. Some of the ointments had labels, others didn't, and Blake had no idea what she was looking for. Frustrated, she put her phone away.

What now?

Leaving the orangery, she made her way to the central hall and the foot of the stairs, staring up into the gloom. Surely they couldn't all still be asleep; it was almost one in the afternoon. Or perhaps that was exactly what the Trezise family did when the Bodilys weren't here waiting on them hand and foot.

Blake turned a half-circle, spying Griffin Trezise's office door in the north corridor. She walked towards it in quick strides, then knocked three times.

Silence answered her.

Glancing both ways, Blake turned the handle and pushed the door open. She caught her breath.

Griffin Trezise was sitting in a leather chair behind his desk, a large glass of amber liquid in his hand. His eyes flicked up from the heavy-looking book he was reading, ready to admonish whoever had disturbed him.

"Sorry for the intrusion," Blake said, hovering on the threshold. "I did knock."

Trezise eyed her but said nothing.

"It's my last day here," she continued. "Which means it's time for your interview."

"I'm extremely busy right now. Go and bother someone else."

Blake arched an eyebrow as Griffin returned his gaze to the book. She entered the room and closed the door behind her, then pulled the book across the desk and flipped it shut, revealing the cover. *The Metamorphoses* by Ovid.

"You're not that busy," she said. The office reeked of alcohol.

It was on the man's breath, seeping from his pores. "Besides, I think you'll want to hear what I have to say."

They locked eyes, both refusing to look away. At last, Griffin Trezise heaved his shoulders, picked up his glass and took a drink.

"Well then," he said. "I suppose you better sit down."

38

BLAKE SANK into the leather chair, feeling it mould around her body. Griffin nodded to the whiskey decanter on the table, which would soon need topping up.

"Drink?" he said.

"Thanks, but it's a little early in the day for me."

"Suit yourself." He shrugged and leaned back in his chair. "So, please enlighten me. What is it that you know?"

The arrogance emanating from the man was only fuelling Blake's dislike of him.

"The house is very quiet today," she said. "Where are the children?"

"My dear girl, I neither know nor care. Now stop wasting my time and tell me what you've found."

Blake was silent as she debated how much to tell him. "Has anyone been in touch with you from the coroner's office?"

Trezise shook his head then looked at the pile of unopened letters sitting on his desk. "Violet collects the post from Helston once a week. I haven't had the opportunity to look through it yet."

Too busy drinking, Blake thought. "No one has telephoned?"

"Violet takes care of any incoming calls. If someone from the coroner's office had been in touch, I'm certain I'd already know about it." He cocked his head slightly. "Why?"

"Because I know the results of the coroner's report. I know why Kerenza died."

Trezise grew still.

"I imagine it was the impact from hitting the steps," he said, then quickly drained his glass.

"I mean *why* she jumped."

Blake told him what she'd learned from Jason Harris but omitted that the coroner was suggesting further investigation into Kerenza's death. As she talked, Trezise listened, his face an emotionless mask. When she'd finished, he got up from his desk on unsteady feet and moved over to the window, where he stood for a long time, staring out at the grounds.

"Campbell is adamant that Kerenza wasn't into drugs," Blake said. "Would you agree? Or do you think it's possible she could have willingly taken a psychoactive drug?"

"Kerenza was a sensible girl who took her responsibilities to this family seriously," Trezise said. "Until Campbell Green came along, filling her head with false hopes and fanciful ideas, convincing her that she didn't need her family, that there was happiness and freedom waiting for her outside these walls. It was a lie, of course. All that's out there is selfishness and misery, no different to what's in here. But that's the human condition, don't you think? To look out for oneself and be damned with everyone else. It's why the world is in such a dire state. And it's why Kerenza was a fool to ever think she could find happiness in the first place."

Blake had anticipated cynicism from a man who hid in his study every day, drinking himself to death while his house crumbled around him, but his words still unnerved her.

"And the drugs?" she said.

"I told you my daughter was a fool. I didn't say she was reckless. No, I don't believe she would have taken such a drug, nor any other."

"Then if Kerenza didn't willingly take it," Blake said, "it means someone else poisoned her."

"Why would anyone want to harm my daughter?"

"To sabotage her wedding day, perhaps. To stop her from leaving."

She stared pointedly at Griffin, who stared right back, a sneer on his lips.

"Exactly what are you suggesting?"

"Abigail keeps a lot of exotic plants here in the orangery. Perhaps even *Datura stramonium.*"

Returning to the desk, Griffin sat down and stared at Blake. He was smiling now, but there was no joy in it. "Are you suggesting Abigail deliberately poisoned her sister? That's a bold and slanderous accusation, especially when you haven't presented a single shred of evidence."

"I'm not pointing fingers just yet," she said. "But anyone could have entered the orangery that morning. And anyone could have poisoned Kerenza's breakfast without her even knowing."

"Preposterous!" Trezise laughed, then picked up the decanter and refilled his glass.

Blake leaned forward. "It may sound preposterous, but the toxicology report is hard evidence. Those alkaloids didn't appear in Kerenza's bloodstream by magic." She paused, observing him. "What were your movements on the morning of the wedding?"

Trezise's expression changed in an instant. "Are you suggesting I killed my daughter?"

"I'm merely asking where you were."

Violence flashed in his eyes. For a second, Blake thought the old man would launch himself across the desk and grab her by the throat. But he didn't. "On the morning of the wedding, I went to visit my wives in the family cemetery while I waited for the guests to arrive. When they did, I spent the rest of the morning entertaining them while we waited for the ceremony to begin."

"Were you alone in the cemetery?" Trezise hadn't mentioned his son's grave.

"Yes. Is it a crime to seek solace in the dead?"

"When did you last see Kerenza?"

"The night before the wedding. We had a rare family dinner together. It was full of tension and squabbling of course, sibling rivalry at its finest."

"And in the morning?"

"I only saw her alive one last time, when she emerged on the balcony." He froze, his bloodshot eyes staring into space.

"Tell me about the other guests," Blake said. "Who else was there?"

"Campbell's parents. A few old family friends. No one who would harm my daughter. And why would they? She was hardly a threat to anyone. Now, is that it? I'd very much like to get back to my book."

Blake clenched her fists in her lap, the last few threads of her patience finally unravelling. "Was Kerenza aware of the financial troubles you're facing?"

Trezise froze, the whiskey glass hovering beneath his lips. "Who told you . . ." He put the glass down. His eyes narrowed. "Of course. Well, when you run back to Mr Green, you can inform him that he's in breach of his confidentiality agreement, and he can now expect a letter from my solicitor and a date in court, where I'll be seeking extensive damages."

Blake smiled. "From what I hear, hiring a solicitor might be out of your budget. Does Campbell's replacement know about the blackmail?"

Griffin flinched as if she'd slapped him. His face turned red again, then scarlet, until Blake was convinced he was about to have a heart attack. She watched him shrink in on himself, like a dying weed captured by a time-lapse camera. He was silent for a long time, until at last he heaved his shoulders and let out a trembling breath.

"There is no replacement," he said. "Kerenza didn't know about the blackmail or the financial problems. None of my children do. Unless Campbell has told them, too."

"He hasn't. And he never told Kerenza because he was scared it would interfere with the wedding."

Griffin drained his glass. He reached for the decanter with a trembling hand and found it empty. He smiled in surprise, as if its contents had vanished into thin air.

"My children are expecting to inherit the Trezise family fortune," he said. "They'll be lucky to even have a roof over their heads once I'm dead."

He was broken now, his hardened exterior cracked wide open.

Blake stared at him. "Who's blackmailing you?"

"My dear girl, if I knew the answer the blackmailer would be dead and I would have my money back."

Faith Penrose's kind face flashed in Blake's mind. She pushed it aside. "What were you being blackmailed about? The origins of the family wealth? The slavery?"

Trezise threw his head back and laughed. "You honestly believe I'd pay hundreds of thousands of pounds to hide something my ancestors were guilty of, something that I had nothing to do with? Yes, I benefited from their supposedly abhorrent behaviour, but so what? This entire world is built on exploitation. Always has been and always will be. Another facet of the human condition: to take what we want and to hell with everyone else. That money belongs to my family, no matter where it came from. It's ours to do with what we will."

"Except that money is gone now," Blake said. "And now you have nothing except a house that's falling down around your ears, and a family that's either dead or can't stand the sight of you."

She watched the anger in the man's eyes flicker and die, the reality of her words like nails in his coffin.

"So if it's not the slavery, what is it?" she said.

"You think I would tell you? So you could blackmail me, too?"

"That's not my style."

"Really? Because wasn't it blackmail that helped you worm your way into my house in the first place?"

Blake glared at him. "If you're not going to tell me, then I have no choice but to inform the police. Because a crime has been committed, Mr Trezise. Whether they meant to or not, someone killed your daughter. She deserves justice. And if you won't help her get it, then I will."

Griffin leaned forward, a cruel smile twisting his lips. "You? But you didn't even know her."

"Clearly, neither did you."

"Touché!" He picked up his empty glass then put it down again. "So, perhaps I'm wrong. Perhaps Kerenza was a drug user. Or she was insane, just like her mother. You see, these children of mine, they're all tainted. We have the exiled fool with the morals of a snake; the bitter shrew who prefers weeds to people; the genetic aberration with a Neanderthal brain and a head full of rage; the blonde-haired imbecile who cannot distinguish fantasy from reality; and last but not least, Kerenza, the only one I was ever proud of. The one who was set to abandon this family for a man who was nothing more than a half-rate employee." He leaned back, triumphant in his downfall. "Every one of them is a bitter disappointment. But it's my own fault for breeding with inferior stock. Regardless, I'm glad there's no money, because not one of them deserves a single penny."

Blake got to her feet, the stench of alcohol and lack of air making her nauseous. She looked down at Griffin Trezise. She had no pity for him, only disgust.

"Did you ever think your children might have turned out differently if you'd shown them even an ounce of love?" she said. "I'm done with this place. And I'm done with you. Thank you for your time, Mr Trezise. It's clear to me that Kerenza's death was no accident, so you can expect a visit from the police."

Griffin stared at her, his expression blank. "Perhaps the curse is true after all. Perhaps we Trezises are destined to never leave this place alive."

"I don't believe in curses," Blake said. "But I do believe we reap what we sow."

She threw the door open.

And saw Tegen jump back.

For a moment, the teenager stood frozen, her face wet with tears and her eyes round with horror. Then she bolted, an anguished wail escaping from her lips as she vanished from view. "Shit," Blake said. And took off after her.

39

BLAKE RAN THROUGH THE CORRIDOR. She had already lost sight of Tegen, but she could hear her hurrying in the direction of the kitchen. She staggered around the corner, almost slamming into the wall, then ploughed forward until she reached the kitchen door and threw it open. The room was empty, the back door shut. But another stood wide open.

The door to the old servants' quarters was shorter than the other doors, as if specifically designed to make the servants stoop as they went back and forth, a reminder of their place and purpose within the household. Blake stood on the threshold, staring at the rickety wooden steps that led up to the attic. She listened for a moment, but all she heard was blood rushing in her ears.

"Tegen? Are you up there?"

She began to climb, her boots clumping on the steps, her hand gripping the railing as daylight quickly faded. Reaching the landing, she stopped still.

"Tegen?" She called into the gloom. "It's Blake. I just want to talk."

She felt along the wall, searching for a light switch. Finding one, she flicked it on. There was a burst of light, then a loud pop, followed by the sound of shattering glass. Blake flinched and instinctively covered her head as she was plunged into darkness once more. Shards of glass bounced off her hair and landed on the bare floorboards.

The stench of rotting wood was overpowering, tasting sharp and bitter on her tongue.

Blake called out again. "Come on, let's talk downstairs. It doesn't feel safe up here."

Pulling her phone from her pocket, she activated the light and held it up before her. She was standing in the mouth of a long corridor that stretched out into the distance before the darkness swallowed it up again. Doorways stood on both sides. Blake stepped forward, glass crunching beneath her boots. She swung the light to her left and peered into the first room. It was small and box-shaped. A single mattress covered in black mildew was slumped against the wall, and the floor was covered in a thick carpet of dust that looked like it had been undisturbed for years.

The room on her right was in the same condition, only with a pile of rotting cardboard boxes in the corner and what looked like an old ball gown draped over them. It was hard to imagine the servants from two hundred years ago living in such claustrophobic conditions, the rooms just big enough to fit a single bed and a chest of drawers. Blake was reminded of the cramped battery cages that were used to house chickens before the law changed.

She continued shuffling forward in the darkness, checking each room and finding only decay.

An anguished sob came from somewhere up ahead. Reaching the last room on the left, Blake pushed the door open.

"Tegen?" she said softly. "Is that you?"

She stepped inside. Tegen was crouched in the corner, her knees pulled up and her face buried in them as she wept. Candles had been lit all around the room, and their flames danced and flickered on the walls. A framed photograph of Kerenza was propped up on a silk covered box, one taken from happier times. Dried flowers and coloured stones were scattered around it, and a stick of earthy-smelling incense burned in a small holder. A shrine to the dead.

Blake deactivated the light and slipped her phone into her jacket pocket.

"Leave me alone," Tegen moaned, her shoulders trembling.

Blake took a small step forward and crouched in front of her. "I just want to help, that's all."

She reached a hand towards Tegen, who immediately flinched. Her hair fell away from her neck, revealing angry red marks.

Blake stared at them in horror. First the bruises on Tegen's arm. Now this.

"Who hurt you?" she asked.

Tegen pulled away from her. "I said leave me alone! I don't want to talk to you."

"Please," Blake said. "Let me help you."

"You can't."

"I can try. Tell me who hurt you. I'll make sure they never do it again."

Tegen looked up, her eyes red and raw. "I heard what you told my father. I heard what he said about us, too. You're going to tell the police, aren't you? You're going to tell them what really happened to Kerenza."

"I have to," Blake said. "Your sister didn't kill herself. She didn't want to die. She was happy and in love. Someone took that away from her."

"You're not wanted here!" Tegen wailed. "All my family wants is to be left alone. And now everyone is blaming me. They say everything would have been fine if I hadn't let you in. But all I was trying to do was help my sister."

Blake stared at her. "You know who did it, don't you? That's why you're covered in bruises. Someone's been hurting you, to frighten you off from telling the truth."

The teenager choked back more tears then laughed hysterically, sounding half mad. "You're so stupid! Even now, when it's all right in front of your face, you still don't get it!"

"Then tell me. Tell me who —"

Blake froze. Something in the corner of her eye had caught her attention.

Propped up against the wall was a stack of three large picture frames. Blake shot a glance at Tegen, who had balled her hands into fists and was pressing them into her face, the bruises on her wrists turning black in the candlelight.

Leaving her, she got up and flipped the first one over. Just like 'The Red Serpent', it had a dark and foreboding atmosphere. It was an oil painting of a lone tree standing on a hill at night. On closer inspection, she saw the tree was made of bones. Bloody sap seeped from its trunk to feed the worms that waited below, their hungry mouths wide open. Except they weren't worms, Blake realised. They were human foetuses.

The second painting was a depiction of Mother Crow's cottage. It was even more unsettling than the real thing. Bone talismans hung from the trees, while animal skulls littered the garden and a hideously deformed figure stood at an illuminated window, peering out into the night.

"These are Kerenza's," Blake said. "You told me she burned her paintings."

Tegen lowered her hands. "She did. Except for these. I found them one day, hidden away up here."

Blake turned over the last painting.

A naked woman with a swollen belly was lying on her back, her legs spread wide apart. A red snake was birthing from her vagina, coiling around her thigh and sinking its fangs into her left breast. Blake shivered, right down to her core. The woman looked exactly like Abigail Trezise.

She stared in horror at Tegen, who was as pale as a death shroud in the candlelight.

"I was only trying to help," Tegen whispered.

She started wailing again. She reached up and pinched the skin of her neck, twisting it sharply between her fingers, causing more red welts.

"Tegen, stop." Blake lunged forward and grabbed her hands, pulling them away. Tegen tried to wrench free, then shrieked and slammed the back of her head against the wall. "Please, stop! Why are you hurting yourself like this?"

"Because it's my fault!"

Realisation hit Blake like a punch to the gut. She tried to breathe and found she couldn't. Words raced through her mind, conversations, voices rushing together. Suddenly they fell away, until all Blake could hear was Violet Bodily:

'She's just a child playing games with herbs and berries, thinking she can heal this family of its pain.'

"It was you, wasn't it?" Blake said. "You did it."

Tegen emitted a gut-wrenching howl. "I didn't mean to kill her! I was trying to help. I don't understand what happened. Oh, Kerenza, I'm so sorry!"

A tremor ran through her body as she collapsed against Blake, who held her like a crying baby in her arms, gently rocking back and forth. And as she comforted Tegen, Blake felt her own grief for Faith Penrose seeping through the cracks and threatening to drown her.

40

THEY WERE in Tegen's bedroom now, with the door shut. Tegen was sitting in bed with her legs crossed beneath the sheets and her back propped up with pillows. All the threads of dried leaves and berries had been torn down, her incense and candles thrown into a waste bin. Blake sat in an armchair next to the bed, worrying about the young woman's mental state. She was terribly pale, and her eyes couldn't seem to focus on one place for more than a few seconds. The welts on her neck, self-inflicted it seemed, looked raw and angry.

"Tell me everything," Blake said.

Tegen's voice was slow and unsteady, the words unsure of themselves after being hidden away for so long. "Kerenza was nervous. I was in her room like I told you before, helping to fix her hair and makeup. She looked so beautiful, all done up. But at the same time, I could tell something was wrong. I asked her what it was, and she told me she felt sad. I said, 'You're not allowed to feel sad on your wedding day. It's the happiest day of your life.' Then she started crying. She said that she was scared about leaving Saltwater House, but at the same time she knew she had to. Because she couldn't breathe here. None of us can."

Tegen paused, swallowing back tears. "She kept on crying, and I was annoyed because she was ruining her makeup, and I'd spent hours putting it on. And I shouldn't have said this, but I told her I was worried about Mother Crow's curse. That if she left the house for good, terrible things would happen. But Kerenza just smiled and dried her eyes, and she told me not to be so silly. 'It's just a story,' she said. 'And I'll prove it to you by leaving Saltwater House and living a happy new life with Campbell.'"

Blake heaved her shoulders, saddened by the irony.

Tegen continued: "I wanted to help her. To heal her pain. She looked so miserable, so I told her I'd make something special, something that would calm her nerves and make her happy. I left her alone and went down to the orangery. Abigail wasn't there, so I helped myself to some dried herbs and flowers from her jars on the shelf. I took what I thought was chamomile, lavender, and St John's wort. Then I went into the kitchen. Violet was there, along with some of the catering staff Father had hired for the day. She was making a fuss, telling them all off and then getting annoyed with me for being in the way. So I quickly fetched some hot water and took it back to Kerenza's room."

"Violet told me that Kerenza had come down to the kitchen that morning," Blake said. "She'd torn a hole in the sleeve of her wedding dress."

"Yes, that's true. It was earlier on. She'd tried to attach her wedding corsage with a pin. She'd been so nervous that she'd torn right through the lace."

"What happened when you went back upstairs with the drink?"

"Kerenza was still at the dressing table. She'd been crying again and her eyeliner had run. I fixed it for her and then she grabbed my hand. I don't know why but I started crying, too. I didn't want her to leave. She was the only good thing about this place. The only one who ever loved me for me, who didn't look at me with pity or hate or shame. I loved her more than anything else. She was my sister." Tegen's lower lip trembled as she stared pleadingly at Blake. "We hugged, then we laughed about how miserable we were being. And then Kerenza said she needed to be alone, just for a little while. I kissed her on the cheek and told her to drink her tea. Then I left and went downstairs."

Tegen slipped a hand under the sheets and Blake could tell she was pinching herself again.

"Stop," she said gently, leaning forward to take the teenager's hand and hold it in her own.

Tears splashed down Tegen's face and soaked into the bedsheets. "I wasn't even trying to use magic that day. I was just making her a cup of tea, that's all. Something to relax her. But I killed her instead. I didn't mean to. I loved her. Now Kerenza is dead, and it's all my fault."

She buried her face in her hands and wept.

Blake was unsure of what to do. Kerenza's death had been an unfortunate accident, the wrong dried leaves picked up in a hurry and brewed into a deadly tea. And yet Blake had a duty to inform the police. But what would happen to Tegen? She was technically still a minor, and there was no proof of malicious intent. There would be an inquest, possibly a court case. Kerenza's death might still be ruled an accident. Or Tegen might be charged and tried for involuntary manslaughter, which rarely went unpunished.

Yet, there was still one element that puzzled Blake.

Tegen didn't know about the coroner's report or the presence of *Datura stramonium*. So how could she be so sure that she was responsible for Kerenza's death?

"Did you tell anyone else about what you think you did?" Blake asked.

Tegen continued to cry into her hands. "Father was right. I can't tell the difference between fantasy and reality. Stupid magic and stupid spells. Stupid, stupid! You're almost eighteen, Father says, but you behave like a baby. Well, it's not my fault! It's because of who I am. How I was born. They told us we almost died. Did you know that? Crushed together in our mother's womb, our brains starved of oxygen. Jack said they were going to cut my head off if I died first, so they could pull him out to safety. The doctors do that, you know, if one of the twins dies and their heads become locked together. Sometimes Jack says they should have done it anyway. And he's right! He's right!"

Blake squeezed Tegen's hand. The teenager was unravelling before her eyes and it felt like there was nothing she could do to stop it.

"Jack is wrong," she said. "I've only known you for a few days, but I can see that you're good and kind. You loved your sister. What happened wasn't your fault. It was an accident. You can't even be sure it was the tea."

"It was!" Tegen cried. "Abigail told me I'd taken from the wrong jar. She said she found the mess I'd made, that I hadn't put the lids back on. I poisoned Kerenza. She went mad and jumped off the balcony."

Blake leaned forward. "Then why on earth did you let me in? Did you want to get caught? Maybe go to prison?"

"No, no, I don't want that!"

"Then what? If you knew you were guilty, why risk everything by bringing a private investigator into your home?"

"Because —" Tegen clamped her jaw shut.

Exasperated, Blake shook her head. "Because what?"

"Because I want you to stop them!"

They stared at each other, Tegen wild and manic, Blake filled with confusion.

"Stop who from doing what?" she said.

"It's my own fault," Tegen said. "I should never have looked inside Mother Crow's cottage."

She fell back against the pillow and refused to speak another word.

41

MOTHER CROW'S cottage stood on the bank of Frenchman's Creek, a fetid, rotting thing that was heaving its last breaths and ready to return to the earth. Blake stared at the animal skull that was staked in the rear garden. Its eyeless sockets stared back at her, daring her to come closer. She could not allow herself to believe in witchcraft, or supernatural beings such as Bucca Gwidder and Bucca Dhu, the two faces of the old Horned One that Tegen both feared and revered. But Blake did believe in evil, in the wickedness that people could do.

I want you to stop them.

Stop who from doing what?

The answer lay inside Mother Crow's cottage, Blake was certain. It was the one place Tegen had been too terrified to enter. The place that she had been warned to stay away from because it was derelict and dangerous, a home to evil, cursed by the very witch responsible for the deaths of half her family. The only trouble was that once you told teenagers they couldn't do something, they would make it their mission to defy you.

Reaching for the rusty bar she'd found just a few days ago, Blake approached the cottage. She could hear the nearby song of the creek. All around her, the trees were still.

The board that covered the end window was still loose. Using the bar, it came away easily. Blake propped it up against the wall. The window it had been covering was broken, the glass removed.

Inside, she could see shapes and shadows, none of which were moving.

Feeding the rusty bar through the window, Blake let it drop with a clang, then she hoisted herself up and inside. Daylight filtered through the broken window, but it was not enough to illuminate the gloom. Retrieving the bar from the floor, Blake removed her phone from her pocket and activated the light.

She was standing in a living area. Mould covered the carpet. A battered and torn sofa sat in front of a stone fireplace, ash and charcoal lying in the hearth. Bookshelves were collapsed in a heap on one side. Mould spores clung to the damp air, making Blake cough. An old coal oven that had fallen into disrepair stood closed to the swollen front door.

But Blake wasn't looking at any of that. She was transfixed by the bone masks hanging from hooks on the walls.

All of them were animal in origin. Some had horns, others had sharp fangs. All of them were polished and gleaming in the torchlight. There were other horrors here, effigies and strange symbols made of sticks and bones that dangled from the ceiling from strands of thread, just like the ones hanging from the trees in Kerenza's painting of Mother Crow's cottage. Some swayed in the breeze coming through the broken window. Others spun in slow circles.

Her heart pounding in her chest, Blake turned away from them and pointed the light towards the far wall. Two doors stood on opposite sides. The first opened onto a small bathroom, containing a filthy toilet and a bathtub filled with decomposing leaves and the remains of a dead animal. Bone figures jangled together above the bath as Blake gasped and retreated from the room.

She pushed open the final door and stepped inside.

It was a bedroom, dark and shadowy, the window boarded up. A single bed was pushed up against one wall, the sheets crumpled and sodden from rain that had fallen through a small hole in the roof. Next to the bed was a side table, with a rusty storm lantern and a pile of old books that had yellowed and mildewed. Philip Pullman's *The Amber Spyglass*. Sarah Dessen's *Dreamland*. Novels written for teenagers. Blake leaned over and touched the lantern. The metal was cold against her skin.

She stepped back and cocked her head. There were no masks in here. No effigies or skeletal trinkets. But there was an old wooden trunk concealed beneath the bed.

Getting on her knees, Blake rested her phone on the floor with the light pointing upward, then dragged the trunk out. There was a clasp, with an old padlock that had rusted and was falling apart.

Blake looked around, found a chunk of wood and smashed the lock into two pieces. Holding her breath, she opened the lid and peered inside.

The trunk was full of old toys and childhood keepsakes: a battalion of wooden toy soldiers, their paintwork aged and cracked, a moth-eaten rag doll with a missing eye, and a teddy bear that had lost half of its fur. Blake laid them gently on the floor, then removed a small pile of clothing. At first, she thought they were dresses for the doll. Then she held up a garment to the light. It was a cardigan for a new-born baby, lovingly knitted with pearly blue buttons. She placed it on the bed and sifted through the rest of the clothes. They were all hand-knitted, all for a baby.

The one remaining item in the chest now was an old shoe box. Fishing it out, Blake removed the lid.

The box contained a handful of photographs. She carefully took them out, one after the other. The first was of Olivia Trezise, the older children's mother. She was perched on a wicker chair in the orangery, looking radiant and beautiful, as she bounced baby Abigail on her knee, while toddlers Aidan and Kerenza stood to the side, their faces wrinkled with envy.

The second photograph was taken just a few years later. Abigail and Aidan lay together on a blanket on the lawn. They were both staring at each other, big smiles lighting up their faces. In the background, Kerenza wandered through the garden maze, her head bowed with concentration.

Time skipped a year or two. Now Aidan and Abigail were on their stomachs in front of an open fire, legs and feet tangled together as they read a children's storybook, while Kerenza sat alone at a table drawing a picture with crayons.

Time shifted again, and now the trio were all adolescents and no longer smiling. Just like the previous photographs, Kerenza was segregated from her siblings, while Aidan and Abigail held hands and stared angrily at the camera. It was an unsettling picture, one presumably taken after their mother's death.

Blake reached for the next photograph. Abigail was a blossoming teenager now, fourteen or fifteen years old, with a radiant smile and eyes that glittered as she lay back on the carpet. She wore shorts that came to mid-thigh and a sleeveless vest, and her long dark hair had been swept to one side. She looked up into the camera as if it held all her joy. Two sets of toes could be seen in the lower portion of the image, the photographer accidentally capturing his feet as he stood over his subject. Blake stared at the image, shocked by the difference between this younger, happier Abigail and the stony-faced woman she had come to know.

She reached for the next photo, then wrinkled her brow.

A young baby, fat and rosy with a thick shock of hair, lay in a Moses basket. The baby was yawning, its eyes squeezed shut and its tiny hands curled into loose fists.

And there the infant was again in the next photograph, cradled in Abigail's arms. She was slightly older than she'd appeared in the previous picture, perhaps now sixteen, and she was sitting up in bed, the sheets pulled up to her waist. Blake could see the joy was already fading from her eyes. She was pale and exhausted, much too thin, as if the baby was weighing her down. Was it one of the twins she was holding? Jack or Tegen?

She picked up the final photograph and found herself staring at Aidan Trezise. He had grown into a handsome young man. He was shirtless in the picture, healthy and strong with defined muscles, his dark eyes staring confidently at the camera. The same baby rested in his arms, content and peaceful as it slept.

Blake's stomach fluttered. She spread the photographs out on the bed, her gaze moving from left to right, then over to the baby clothes and children's toys.

She froze. Griffin Trezise's words filled her head.

Picking up the image of Abigail and the baby, she held it up to the phone light and peered into Abigail's haunted eyes. She looked up, then twisted around as a chill slipped beneath her clothes.

Blake got to her feet, feeling sick and dizzy. The photograph had been taken right here in this room. On this bed. In Mother Crow's cottage, which was now a tomb for the darkest Trezise family secret of all.

42

ABIGAIL WAS PERCHED on the edge of the chaise longue, one leg crossed over the other, a cup and saucer in her hands, perfectly posed and prepared as Blake entered.

"You're still here," she said, as Blake came closer. "Would you care to sit down? Perhaps you'd like a soothing cup of herbal tea?"

Blake remained on her feet, leaning against a table filled with plant pots.

"No, thank you." She made a mental note to stick to coffee for the duration of her life.

Abigail smiled. "I've just been speaking to Tegen. She's terribly upset."

"She told me the truth about what happened to Kerenza," Blake said. "Or at least her version of events."

Abigail gave a slight nod. "It's not a version. It's the truth."

"How can you be so sure?"

"Because after Kerenza died, I came in here to hide away. It was the shock, I suppose. It's not every day you see your sister fall to her death. It's an image that will never leave me. I sat right here in this exact spot for the longest time, trying to make sense of it all. Of course, I couldn't. To distract myself I decided to tend to the seedlings. That was when I noticed the mess on my workbench. Jars from the shelf had been left open, dried herbs and seeds scattered everywhere. I knew it was Tegen immediately. She's always coming in here, borrowing ingredients for her silly spells and never tidying up. But I didn't make the real connection until I saw what had been taken in error. Until Tegen came to me, a nervous wreck, and confessed what she'd done."

Blake studied her closely. "What had she taken?"

"*Datura stramonium*," Abigail said. "It was next to the chamomile flowers, listed alphabetically. It's a member of the nightshade family and originates from —"

"I know what it is," Blake said. "I've done my research. What I don't understand is why you would keep something so dangerous in a place where Tegen could easily pick it up by mistake."

Abigail sipped her tea, then set the cup and saucer down on a side table. "Tegen is seventeen years old, almost an adult and quite capable of reading labels."

"Yet in her haste she still picked up the wrong one." Blake folded her arms over her stomach. "And you still didn't answer my question."

"*Datura stramonium* is well-known for being psychotropic and highly toxic, but it also has many medicinal benefits," Abigail said. "Its seeds contain analgesic and anti-inflammatory properties, which in Eastern medicine are used to treat a range of ailments: ulcers, wounds, fever, asthma, bronchitis. My mother used *Datura* to treat her toothache. Perhaps a little too often." She smiled knowingly. "If you look around the grounds, you'll find it growing in places, just a rather exotic looking weed. I collect the seeds from time to time and replenish my mother's jar on the shelf. It may seem ridiculous to you, even reckless. But it's how I like to honour her, and a way to keep her spirit alive."

"Except now one of your sisters is dead," Blake said quietly. "And the other could go to prison."

"But it was an accident."

"She'd still have to prove it in court. The prosecution could say it was negligence and try her for involuntary manslaughter."

"My father wouldn't let that happen. He knows people."

Except her father's money was all gone, Blake thought. Without it, he had no more influence than she did. "So, Tegen accidentally makes a highly poisonous and hallucinogenic tea, offers it to Kerenza to help calm her wedding jitters. She drinks it, and is plagued by terrifying hallucinations and paranoia, then loses her mind and jumps to her death."

Abigail let out a faltering breath and stared at the floor. "It seems that way, yes."

"I took magic mushrooms once in my misspent youth," said Blake. "It was an interesting few hours, but I didn't conjure up anything that would drive me to take my own life."

"Then perhaps your research didn't go far enough. *Datura stramonium* is the only psychedelic that is a true hallucinogen. All the rest, they're just changes in colour, perception, and suggestion. After thirty minutes of ingesting *Datura*, your pupils begin to dilate and your mouth goes dry. Your heart rate increases. You begin to experience feelings of weightlessness, like your body is a feather in the wind and you have no control over where gravity might take you.

"When the hallucinations begin, they are so vivid, so real that it's almost impossible to distinguish what is reality and what is not. Inanimate objects may start talking to you, like something out of a Disney film, except it will feel normal and everyday. You may peer into a mirror and see a completely different reflection peering back. Or suddenly absent friends and family will materialise. They may just stand there, watching you in silence, or they may engage you in conversation, until you turn around and they disappear. But even then, you won't realise you've been talking to yourself for hours on end.

"Some people have been known to see terrifying apparitions. Ghosts. Demons. Monsters. The dead brought back to life, so corporeal that they could reach out and grip you by the throat." She paused, staring at Blake. "I can't imagine what Kerenza saw, but it must have been so terrifying, so real, that her only way to flee from it was to climb over the balcony balustrade. Perhaps, at that moment, she didn't even know where she was or what she was doing, only that she had to escape."

Blake was silent, recalling how Saul Bodily had seen Kerenza in a frightened state, peering at something behind her bedroom door. What an awful death, she thought. The woman's brain so poisoned that no matter where she looked, all she saw was horror.

"Kerenza's death was an accident," she said, testing the words out. Seeing if they tasted of the truth.

Abigail clasped her hands together. "No one in this family would ever willingly harm Kerenza."

"And the staff?"

"Everyone loved her. Even my father, who loves only himself, was fond of her." She let out a small sigh. "Kerenza's death was a terrible accident, nothing more. One that Tegen will have to carry on her shoulders for the rest of her life. But I will be there, walking right beside her, helping her to bear the weight, as only a sister can do."

"Nevertheless," Blake said, "the coroner's report will likely lead to further police investigation. Hiding the truth is only going to make matters worse for Tegen."

"Which is for her family to worry about." Abigail leaned forward, pressing her lips together. "Campbell hired you to find out the truth about Kerenza. Now you have. You can choose to tell him what you've learned, that Tegen killed his fiancée. Or you can simply tell him nothing and walk away. Whatever you decide, your business here is over and it's time for you to leave." She stood up and brushed the creases from her dress. "Come along. I'll show you to the door."

But Blake remained where she was. "Actually, I'm not finished yet. Because during my time at Saltwater House, I've had the distinct impression that something is very wrong here. I sensed it from the moment I arrived, and I'm not just talking about the hostility I've been met with or the ardent attempts to sabotage my investigation."

Uncertainty rippled across Abigail's face. "If your family was under threat, wouldn't you do the same?"

"My family *is* under threat," Blake said. "Right now there's a police officer watching over my parents because two nights ago, someone broke into my close friend's home and almost harmed her seven-year-old daughter. Before that, they desecrated the church my mother attends every Sunday. And last night, they murdered someone I cared for deeply, someone I've known since I was a child." Her body trembled with anger and grief. "And the strange thing is none of it happened until I started investigating your family."

The muscles in Abigail's face seemed to paralyse. She tried to smile but only managed a slight grimace. "I have no idea what you're talking about."

"Oh, but I think you do," said Blake. "Because I saw something just now, in Mother Crow's cottage. A room with a bed and a trunk filled with secrets."

Beads of sweat had broken out on Abigail's forehead. The half-grimace remained frozen on her lips.

Blake stepped closer. "I also found some of Kerenza's paintings. They're very dark in tone. Disturbing, even. The one of you is particularly unflattering."

Abigail's knees buckled and she sank back onto the chaise longue, her skin the colour of bone.

It all made sense now, all the pieces finally fitting together. The baby. Mother Crow's cottage. The painting of the snake feeding from Abigail's breast. The argument between father and son. Griffin Trezise's disgust for his own children. The news article image of Genevieve Trezise, her pregnant belly half the size of someone who was meant to be carrying twins.

Blake pulled the photographs from her back pocket. She held them out in a fan. Abigail stared at them, her mouth half open. Then, one by one, she took them between her trembling hands.

"How old were you at the time?" Blake asked. "Fifteen? Sixteen? No more than a child yourself. But they kept you hidden away out there in the cottage, like a dirty secret, until the baby was born. Because the twins aren't twins, are they, Abigail? One of them belongs to you."

A single tear coursed down Abigail's cheek.

"You need to leave," she said through gritted teeth, her eyes fixed on the photographs.

"I can't. Not yet. Because Tegen didn't invite me in to find out why Kerenza died. She said, 'I want you to stop them.' Who was she talking about? What does she want me to stop?"

Abigail placed the photographs next to her as more tears spilled down her face. They were not tears of sorrow, Blake noted, but tears of rage.

"Get out," she said.

"No. I'm sorry, but I can't. Someone is threatening my family, and I won't leave until I know who and why."

Abigail leapt to her feet. "Who do you think you are? Coming into our home, waltzing around like you own the place, when you have no idea what you're talking about. No idea at all!"

"Except I do," Blake said.

Because suddenly it all made sense now. What could be worse in Griffin Trezise's eyes than the shame of living off a family fortune made from the slave trade? Something so terrible that he would willingly pay his blackmailer thousands of pounds every month to stop it from getting out?

"Aidan wasn't sent away because of a bad attitude, was he? That was why you were shut away out there. Why Aidan got himself discharged from the army and came back. And why your father finally banished him for good. Because brother and sister fell in love and had a child together."

Abigail dug her fingers into her palms, a look of pure hatred in her eyes.

"Was it the plan all along for Genevieve to take on your child once hers was born?" Blake said. "To keep your baby hidden away from prying eyes while they waited for the unexpected miracle of twins? Genevieve didn't even want children. Was her pregnancy an accident? Or was it by design to cover up yours? Either way it didn't matter in the end because Genevieve died, and suddenly you had the opportunity to raise your own child along with the other. But your father wouldn't allow it, would he? He forced Kerenza to return home to care for the babies instead. And you had to go along with it. No choice but to pretend your own child was merely your sibling."

"Ridiculous," Abigail hissed. "You're making it up as you go along."

But Blake knew she was right. "Jack and Tegen, they've both had to bear the guilt of Genevieve's death their entire lives. It's shaped who they are. Turned Jack into an angry, spiteful young man. Tegen into a ball of anxious guilt, seeking solace in witch-craft and nature. And you, you've been forced to live a lie, shut away from the world. Only able to grieve Aidan's death as his sister, not as his lover."

"Stop it!" Abigail stepped forwards and stabbed a finger at Blake. "You don't know what you're talking about."

Blake stood her ground.

"They must have all known," she said. "Your father, Genevieve, Violet and Saul. Creating the lie of twins would have only been possible with everyone involved. But what about Kerenza? She was away for a year, studying at Oxford, free for the first time in her life. Until Genevieve died and she was called home. She gave up everything for those babies, while everyone else lied to her. But she found out, didn't she? Somehow, some-time later, she learned the truth. She must have felt so betrayed. So bitter that she'd sacrificed her hopes and dreams for her siblings' incestuous relationship. Look at the portrait she painted of you!"

Blake snapped her head up, a memory suddenly returning. "That's why you didn't say anything that morning, when you found Tegen had taken the *Datura* by mistake."

Abigail shook her head. Her mouth opened and closed. "I don't know what you mean."

"Violet saw you," Blake said, recalling her interview with the housekeeper. "She told me that on the morning of the wedding, Tegen came into the kitchen and got in the way of the catering staff, presumably when she was fetching hot water for Kerenza's tea. Then you came in not long after, looking for her. Violet would have told you what she was doing and where she was going, but you didn't stop Tegen, did you? You knew she'd taken the *Datura*, and you didn't warn her. Because you hated that Kerenza was leaving. You hated that she got to have the one thing you always craved. The one thing that was taken away from you. The ability to love and be loved out in the open."

Abigail's face twisted. Her teeth mashed together.

"Maybe you didn't mean to kill Kerenza. But you certainly meant to ruin her day. As for Tegen . . ." Blake shook her head. "Jack is your child, isn't he? Because if it was Tegen, you wouldn't be letting her take the blame, or helping her to bear the weight of Kerenza's death. You'd be doing everything in your power to prove her innocence."

Abigail shut her eyes for a moment and let out a shuddering breath. When she opened them again, they glittered with fury.

"You have no idea what it feels like to stand by and watch your child grow up not knowing who you really are," she said. "Or who his father is. Knowing that he'll never feel the love I was forbidden to give him. Why should Kerenza get to be happy, or anyone else, when all I've ever been made to do is suffer in silence?"

Blake watched Abigail coming undone, feeling sick to her stomach, unsure whether it was because of pity or disgust. Perhaps a little of both.

She stared at her. "What are you planning to do that Tegen wants me to stop?"

Abigail stared across the orangery, then back at Blake, her chin lifting, her smile suddenly emboldened. "You really want to know? Fine, I'll tell you. Why not? I saw my father's will. I went searching for it a long time ago in his office, but I still remember every word. It said he was going to leave everything to Kerenza and Tegen. Every single penny. There's nothing for me. Or for Jack." She smiled bitterly. "Actually, that's not true. There's an instruction for the lawyer to announce Jack's true parentage at the reading of the will. Just like that. No warning, no preparation. Just one shocking revelation that will tear my son's life apart."

The smile on her face grew tighter, her lips turning white.

"Do you know how it feels to be raised without love? Without kindness or empathy? Do you know how it feels for your father to deem you so worthless, so deviant, that he would rather see you and your child destitute than receive your fair share? Well, I won't stand for it. We can't choose our blood family, just as we can't help who we fall in love with, or that sometimes they happen to be one and the same. But we can choose to stop our father from ruining us completely."

Blake stared at her. "How?"

"With Kerenza gone, Tegen is now the sole beneficiary. She doesn't know that yet, but once our father is dead, I'm confident she'll share her fortune with us."

"It's a sound plan, so long as Tegen doesn't find out you're responsible for Kerenza's death."

"She won't. There are a lot of things that Tegen has yet to find out."

"I wouldn't be so sure about that. How do you think I knew

to look in the cottage?" Blake watched shock sweep over Abigail's face. "And what about your father? He could live for another twenty years. Twenty long years in which you'd have to keep up the pretence. What would that do to you? To Jack?"

Abigail stepped towards her. "Oh, my father will be dead soon. I can guarantee that. As for Tegen, if she doesn't want to share then I expect she'll end up taking her own life, just like her poor, dear sister. And when she does, the law says that without a surviving spouse or children, her estate must be passed on in its entirety to her siblings."

"You can't do that," Blake said. "I won't let you."

"You won't be here to stop me."

As Abigail moved closer, Blake saw the madness in her eyes, the anguish and bitterness that had been festering for almost two decades finally poisoning her sense and reason.

"Abigail, stop. Don't make things worse."

She took another step forward.

Blake reached behind her back, searching the table for something to defend herself. She felt plant pots and seed trays, then the three sharp prongs of a weeding fork. Abigail was almost upon her now, her pupils dilated, her mouth pulled into a frozen smile.

"There's something you need to know," Blake said. "Something your father doesn't want you finding out."

Abigail stopped moving. The smile remained but now there was uncertainty in her eyes.

Blake gripped the handle of the weeding fork. "Your father's will is null and void. The money's gone, Abigail. He frittered half of it away. The rest he's given to his blackmailer, to stop them from telling the truth about you, Aidan, and Jack. When he's dead, all that will be left is Saltwater House. No one's going to buy this place when it would cost more than it's worth to repair. You'll be stuck with it, trapped here while it falls around your ears. Until it buries you, along with all of your secrets."

"You're lying." Abigail shook her head, but the uncertainty remained.

"It's true. He told me not even two hours ago. He called your son a genetic aberration. I didn't understand then, but I do now."

"No, that's not true. Of course there's money!"

"There isn't. Not even for Tegen."

Abigail had turned deathly pale. When she spoke it was through clenched teeth. "Who is blackmailing my father?"

"You tell me," Blake said. "Half the people who knew your secret are dead. That leaves you, Violet, and Saul. If your father suspected the Bodilys he would have already confronted them. Which means unless you're lying, someone else knows."

"Stop it!" Abigail cried. "You're the one who's lying."

"Then go and ask your father right now. He's getting drunk in his study."

"No. You're just making it all up, so you don't get hurt."

"But I'm already hurt. My friend is dead. You killed her."

"I told you, that wasn't me!"

She was just two feet away now, her eyes bulging with rage.

Blake dropped her hand to her side. The weeding fork pressed against her thigh. "Then who was it?"

Abigail froze, her eyes lingering over Blake's shoulder. She smiled. "You'll have to ask him."

A powerful arm wrapped around Blake's neck and squeezed.

Her feet swung through the air as she was lifted from the ground. She kicked out, thrashing her legs. She brought up the weeding fork, but a hand gripped her wrist and wrenched it viciously to the right. Pain shot up her forearm. The fork fell from her fingers and clattered to the ground.

Abigail backed away, her wide eyes blinking in disbelief.

"You're lying," she mouthed, over and over.

Blake sank her nails into her attacker's arms, who squeezed tighter, crushing her windpipe. Then he swung her by her throat to the left. She crashed painfully into the table, knocking trays of tiny seedlings to the floor.

The room turned red. Her eyes rolled back in their sockets. Her arms fell limp and her feet stopped kicking.

Blake was laid gently on the ground. A face appeared above her. At first, she thought it was Jack. But then, as she slipped into unconsciousness, she realised she was staring into the eyes of a dead man.

43

A VOICE, muffled and panicked, flitted around the darkness like a colony of bats. She felt hands on her body, shaking her.

"Wake up! You have to wake up!"

Blake snapped her eyes open. She was lying on her back in the orangery, surrounded by spilled soil and crushed plastic pots. Tegen's terrified face peered down at her.

"Thank God," she said. "I thought you were dead."

Blake tried to sit up but was gripped by dizziness. She lay back down, her eyelids fluttering. Her throat was on fire. She tried to swallow and tears of pain stung her eyes.

"Let me help you."

Tegen wrapped an arm around her shoulders and pushed her up into a sitting position. The room swam around Blake as she took in the destruction. Tables lay in broken pieces. Seedlings lay crushed on the floor. Larger plants had been torn apart and stamped on, their leaves scattered like confetti.

Patting down Blake's hair, Tegen gave her a brief hug and then helped her to her feet and guided her over to the chaise longue.

"Where —" Blake began, her voice cracked and raspy. She swallowed again, wincing at the pain. She touched the sides of the neck, felt the bruising. "Where are they?"

Tegen paced up and down. "I should get you some water. You don't sound right."

"Where are Abigail and Aidan?"

The teenager froze, staring at Blake before quickly looking away. "We have to stop them. They've taken Father to the cemetery."

"You knew Aidan was alive, didn't you? All this time, you knew and you didn't say anything."

"We all knew," Tegen said. "All of us except for Father. Abigail said it was the only way that Aidan could be with his family, because Father hated him so much that he would rather die than let him come back home."

Saul Bodily's words came back to Blake. 'It's not just misery that haunts Saltwater House. It's full of ghosts. Some more real than others.'

Aidan Trezise had been here the whole time, alive and well, hiding from the eyes of his father. It would have been easy with everyone involved. Aidan could come and go freely if he avoided certain areas of the house and the Bodilys kept their mouths shut and didn't intervene. But then Blake had shown up and ruined everything, forcing Aidan back into hiding.

"How long has he been here?" Pain punctuated her every word.

"I don't know. I really thought he was dead. I watched them bury his coffin. I cried and cried for days. Until one morning Abigail came to me and told me she had a surprise. When Aidan walked into my room, I thought I'd gone mad. But he was real. He was alive."

"He killed Faith," Blake said, the grief rushing back. "How did he even know about her? That I was close to her?"

Tegen wrung her hands. "We don't have time for this now. Because they're angry with Father. Aidan hurt him and Abbie was screaming about there being no money. Now they've taken him to the cemetery. I think they're going to kill him."

Of course they are, Blake thought. It had been the plan all along. Aidan would hide away until their father's sudden death, then he would finally come out of hiding and they would all share the family fortune together. Except Abigail had found the will and discovered that she had been cut off, along with her son, and that Jack's parentage was to be announced to the world. Would Tegen and Kerenza have readily shared the money anyway? Or would they have been repelled by their siblings' incestuous affair and refuse to give them a penny?

None of that mattered now because Kerenza was dead, and the family had destroyed itself over an inheritance that no longer existed.

Tegen went to help Blake to her feet, but Blake shook her off.

"Did you know they were planning to kill him?"

Tegen shook her head. "No! I didn't, I swear. I thought they would just wait, or that one day Father would finally forgive them for what they'd done."

Blake stared at her. "You know about Jack? Of course you do. You went inside the cottage."

Tears splashed down Tegen's face. "I went in there a few months ago. I know I shouldn't have. But sometimes I'd see Aidan and Abbie sneaking in through the window, and I was cross because everyone was always telling me, 'You mustn't go into the cottage. You'll anger Mother Crow.' But they all lied.

So, one day I climbed through the window. I found the trunk. One of them had left it unlocked, so I looked inside." Her fingers scratched at her wrist and pinched her skin. "I shouldn't have gone in there. Poor Jack! He has no idea."

Blake staggered to her feet. She swayed from side to side, still feeling woozy. She tapped her pockets until she found her phone.

Tegen froze. "What are you doing?"

"Calling the police."

"Oh no, please don't. You can't. They'll take me away for what I did to Kerenza!"

She sobbed loudly.

Blake lowered the phone. "Tegen. It's not your fault."

"But it is. It is!"

"No. Abigail knew what you'd done. She found the mess you left."

"I know that. She told me. She's never let me forget it."

"She lied to you. She discovered your mistake on the morning of the wedding, just minutes after you'd left the orangery. She found you'd taken *Datura* and she didn't tell you because she wanted to ruin Kerenza's wedding out of spite."

Tegen was staring at her with wide, unblinking eyes. "No. That can't be true."

"I'm sorry," Blake said. "But it is."

She lurched forward, finding the weeding fork among the debris. She picked it up then headed for the French doors that led to the lawn. She stopped, turned back to Tegen, who was deathly white, her fingers twitching by her sides.

"Come on," she said. "I'll call the police on the way. But right now we have to stop Aidan and Abigail from hurting your father."

44

As BLAKE STAGGERED across the misty lawn, she heard Griffin Trezise's frightened sobs coming from the cemetery. She shot an alarmed glance at Tegen, who was hurrying alongside and staring straight ahead with a coldness in her eyes that Blake hadn't seen before. They passed the maze and the mist parted slightly, revealing the cemetery gate. The stench of kerosene flooded Blake's senses as she took in the scene before her.

Griffin was on his knees at the foot of Olivia Trezise's grave. His hands were tied behind his back with twine and his head was bowed. His shoulders trembled as he wept. Blood oozed down the side of his face, mingling with the fuel that drenched his body.

Aidan Trezise paced up and down in front of his father, fists clenched and bloody. He was tall and powerful, his wild black eyes ablaze with fury. Abigail stood to one side, quietly seething. A fuel can rested at her feet. In her hand was a box of matches.

Jack was also here, huddled by Kerenza's grave with his knees pulled up to his chest. He was no longer the angry young man Blake had encountered. Now he was a child, confused and terrified, his bravado snuffed out like a candle flame.

Tegen stormed ahead of Blake, her face so twisted with anger that she was unrecognisable. She threw open the gate and slid to a halt.

"Stop it!" she shrieked. "Let Father go!"

Aidan Trezise stopped pacing. He had clearly spent much of his time in hiding strengthening his body. His forearms bulged with veins, his shoulders and biceps were toned and powerful. Blake did not want to get into a fight with him.

Kneeling on the ground, Griffin started whimpering like a baby. "Call the police, Tegen! Tell them what your brother and sister are doing!"

Aidan smashed a fist into his father's face, snapping his nose. Griffin crumpled to the ground.

Jack covered his hands over his ears and squeezed his eyes shut.

"Go back to the house," Abigail hissed, narrowing her eyes at Tegen. "Take your little friend with you. You don't need to watch this."

But Tegen refused to move.

Blake entered the cemetery and came to a stop just a few feet away from the Trezises. She glared at Aidan, recalling the bloody crime scene photograph and her name scrawled on the wall in Faith Penrose's bed. Rage bubbled inside her, making her tremble. But she had to reel it in, lock it away in a box, or more people were going to die.

"The police are already on their way," Blake said, shifting her gaze to Abigail. "If you kill Griffin now, you'll only make things worse for yourself."

Abigail threw her head back and laughed, sounding nowhere

close to sane. "Worse? How could things get worse? This man took away everything I loved. He destroyed us, and now he's going to leave us with nothing."

"I get it," Blake said. "Sometimes parents don't deserve to have children. But if you kill him now, you'll spend the rest of your life in prison. Do you really want that? You'll be separated from the ones you love. From the one you never had a *chance* to love."

Abigail shot her a warning look then involuntarily stared at Jack.

Blake stepped forward. Aidan shot her a warning look.

"This is your one chance to make things right," she said. "Not everyone's life has to be ruined. Let your father go."

"You," Aidan said, his voice deep and dark, dripping with menace. "If anyone is at fault for what's happening here, it's you. You don't even belong here. You're no one to us. Meaningless. You came into our home, so arrogant and self-assured, thinking you could solve a riddle and save a stupid little girl like Tegen. But all you did was interfere and cause chaos. I should have followed you more closely. I should have realised what a stubborn, egotistical whore you are, who doesn't know her place. Now this family is in ruins and my father's going to die, all because you didn't give a moment's thought to the suffering you might cause."

The clasp on Blake's anger snapped open and out it came, spurting like a volcanic eruption. She turned towards him, the weeding fork gripped in her hand.

"Suffering?" she said. "You allowed your siblings to believe you were dead. You watched as they were torn apart by grief while you selfishly hid, waiting for the right time to reveal yourself. You made them lie for you and lie to each other. Worse than that, you're a murderer. You killed my friend, terrorised my hometown. And for what? To scare me off so I wouldn't find out your little plan to bump off Daddy? News flash: it didn't work."

Aidan's eyes burned into hers.

"Too bad," he said.

Blake tightened her grip on the fork. "I should gouge out your eyes from your skull. It's the least you deserve. But I won't do it. Because I want to see your face behind bars. I want to see the suffering in your eyes when you're taken away from your loved ones, just like you saw the suffering in Faith's eyes before you stabbed her to death."

Aidan smiled coldly. "I didn't see suffering. I saw gratitude. Then peace."

"You're lying." The urge to hurt him was almost overwhelming, but Blake forced her body to remain still.

He laughed. "Look around you. You're surrounded by liars. An entire houseful of tricksters. Even Tegen has pulled the wool over your eyes."

"It's not true," Tegen said, and shot a worried look at Blake.

Aidan's smile grew wider. "How do you think I knew where your mother went to church, or how poor old Faith had lost her daughter and had no reason left to live? Your little friend over there told me. You thought she was the one person you could trust. How wrong you were."

"That's not fair!" Tegen cried. "He made me tell. It's not my fault!"

Blake tried to draw in a breath but found she couldn't. She stared into Tegen's pleading eyes, recalling the conversation they'd had that first morning in this very cemetery.

"Please." Tegen begged her. "Don't hate me."

Blake turned back to Aidan and Abigail. "Let your father go."

Griffin's weak and pain-filled voice floated up from the ground. "Listen to her, Abbie. You don't want to go to prison. You don't want Jack to find out that —"

Aidan drove his foot into his father's gut.

Jack looked up. "You don't want me to find out what?"

"Stop!" Tegen shrieked. She tried to go to her father, but Aidan pushed her back with a powerful sweep of his arm. She stumbled and fell onto the grass.

Jack stood up, his eyes moving from Abigail, to Aidan, to Griffin. "You don't want me to find out *what?*"

"It's nothing," Abigail said.

"They're not —" Griffin began.

Aidan went to kick him again. Tegen sprang up and blocked his path.

"Get away from them, Jack!" she yelled. "You have no idea what's going on. Who they really are. What they've been planning to do."

"I told you." Abigail looked worried now. "Go back to the house!"

Tegen shook her head. "I'm not listening to you anymore. You're nothing but a liar."

"Tegen don't." Blake placed a hand on her shoulder, but she shrugged it away and stabbed a finger at her sister.

"You knew! You knew and you didn't try to stop me."

All eyes were on Abigail now, who smiled nervously and shrugged her shoulders. "I don't know what you're talking about."

"You're *lying* again!" Tegen marched forward, until their noses were almost touching. "*You* killed Kerenza. *You* did it. You could have stopped me from giving her the tea, but you didn't. Because you're selfish and bitter. Because you wanted what she had. To be normal. To be in love with someone that wasn't your brother!"

The crack of Abigail's hand against Tegen's face echoed through the cemetery. She staggered backwards and fell into Blake's arms. She straightened up again then wiped blood from her mouth.

"Do you want to know the truth, Jack?" Tegen was staring at Abigail, a terrible smile on her face.

Jack stared uncertainly. "What truth?"

"Not now," Blake said. "Not here."

But Tegen wasn't listening. Griffin stirred on the ground, barely conscious. Aidan and Abigail looked at each other, panic in their eyes.

"Please," Abigail whispered. "Don't."

But Tegen wasn't listening to her either. "It's all a lie, Jack. Everything you know is a made-up story, just like Mother Crow."

"Don't listen to her," Abigail said. "She's trying to confuse you."

But now Jack was staring intently at Tegen, his dark eyes round and wide. "What are you talking about? What's a lie?"

"All this." Tegen swept a hand around the cemetery. "Them. Your so-called brother and sister."

Aidan moved toward her, his powerful hands open and ready. "I'm warning you, Tegen. Keep your mouth shut."

"Please," Blake whispered in her ear. "Think about what you're doing. Your father needs an ambulance. This is not the time."

Tegen looked down at Griffin, who was reaching out a hand, his fingertips grazing her shoe. She shook him off.

Then stared directly at Jack.

"We're not twins," she said. "Genevieve was my mother. But Abbie is yours. And Aidan is your fath—"

Aidan grabbed her by the throat and hoisted her from the ground.

Blake lunged forward and sank the teeth of the weeding fork into Aidan's thigh. He screamed and released his grip on Tegen, who fell to the ground next to her father. The tines of the fork had gone in deep. Aidan swung around wildly. His elbow struck Blake in the temple. She staggered to the side, reaching for the cemetery railings to stop herself from falling.

Jack was paralysed, his skin the colour of sour milk.

"It's not true," he whispered. "It's not true."

Abigail was sobbing loudly, nodding her head.

"It is!" she cried. "You're my beautiful baby boy."

Aidan howled and clenched his teeth as he tore the fork from his leg. Blood spurted from the puncture wounds in wide arterial arcs, splattering Abigail and his father. He clapped a hand over his thigh, but the blood kept on coming, oozing between his fingers and running down his leg.

Jack was on his haunches, rocking back and forth, hitting himself in the side of the head. Oblivious to Aidan's wounds, Abigail went to her son and wrapped her arms around him.

"It's true," she whispered. "You're mine. You always were."

"Get off me!" Jack shoved her hard, knocking her onto her back and punching the air from her lungs. He scrambled away on his elbows, climbing over Kerenza's grave and disturbing the loose soil.

Aidan fell on one knee, blood flowing all around him.

Paralysed, Blake stared in horror. She had severed the femoral artery, the main vessel that supplied blood to the lower body.

"Abbie," Aidan gasped.

He reached for her. She stared in horror at all the blood, then back at Jack, who was gurgling like an infant as he continued to crawl away.

Aidan slumped on the ground, losing consciousness. His hand fell away from the wounds and blood began to spray in arcs again, but weaker now.

"No!" Abbie went to him, pressing her hand over the puncture wounds, watching his blood leak between her fingers. "Oh, God. Please, someone help!"

No one moved.

Aidan sucked in a shuddering death rattle. He released it, then his body went still. The cemetery fell silent.

Abbie raised her bloody hands and stared at them. She threw her head back and shrieked. Tears fell. Her shoulders trembled.

"This is your fault," she said. "All of it."

But she wasn't staring at Blake. She was staring at her father.

She bent down and reached for the box of matches that had fallen on the ground.

"Abbie, don't!" Blake cried.

Abigail laughed. "I'm so tired of that word. I've heard it my entire life. Don't fall in love. Don't dare to dream. Don't care for your child. Don't ever imagine a world in which you deserve to be happy."

She struck the match and covered the flame with her hand.

Blake plunged forward, reaching for Tegen, who sat numbly by her father in the grip of shock.

Abigail sighed and flicked the match.

There was a terrible *whoosh*. Fuel ignited and Griffin Trezise went up in a ball of flames.

Jack stopped crawling. He peered over his shoulder, his eyes growing impossibly wide.

Blake continued to drag Tegen away, the heat of the fire searing her skin, the smell of charred flesh making her sick.

Griffin did not scream or try to escape. He lay on the ground, flesh and muscle peeling and bubbling, as he burned quietly to death.

Flames danced on Abigail's skin and flickered in her eyes. She stared at Aidan's lifeless body, which had started to catch fire, then across at her son.

"All I ever wanted to do was love you," she said. "That was all."

She picked up the fuel can, emptied it over her head, and walked calmly into the fire. Then she was burning, too. Burning and screaming.

Leaving Tegen at a safe distance, Blake raced across the cemetery and took Jack gently by the arm. She covered his face and turned him around, guiding him towards Tegen and the cemetery gate. And as their family burned behind them, as Abigail's horrible shrieks were suddenly cut short, Blake dragged the teenagers across the lawn like lifeless puppets, back towards Saltwater House.

45

THE TEMPERATURE HAD DROPPED OVERNIGHT, leaving frost on the ground and a promise of snow in the clouds. It was 6:57 AM. Blake hadn't slept. Her body was weighed down by exhaustion, yet her mind was caught in a maelstrom of thoughts. She had spent hours at the police station with DS Turner and DC Collins, going over and over the events leading up to the deaths in the family cemetery. Now, in the burgeoning daylight, it all seemed unreal, like Saltwater House and the Trezise family were remnants of a strange and disturbing dream.

There were still questions hanging over Blake's head regarding Aidan Trezise's death. Why had she felt the need to attack him with the weeding fork? Could there have been another, less violent way to prevent him from causing more harm?

The truth was that rage had ignited Blake's veins, burning out of control, until she had no choice but to unleash it. She hadn't meant to kill Aidan, although she had wanted to. She had only tried to injure him so that he would release his grip on Tegen's throat. Puncturing his femoral artery had been an accident. He had bled out so quickly there hadn't been time to save him.

But had she *wanted* to save him? Her memory there was hazy at best, so she told Turner what she had told Aidan: that she wanted to see him spend the rest of his life behind bars. Turner had remained quiet, scepticism in his eyes, but at last he'd given her a slight nod. With Aidan and Abigail hellbent on vengeance, Blake's priority had been to protect the children. Even so, there was still a possibility of criminal charges if Tegen and Jack failed to corroborate her story.

Blake tried not to worry about it now as she stood on the wintry, grey street and pressed the buzzer to Campbell Green's flat. After a long wait, the intercom crackled to life.

"Blake? It's early. What are you doing here?"

"I need to see you," she said. "It's urgent."

He buzzed her in. Blake hurried up the stairs, grateful to be out of the cold. Campbell's front door was already open. She found him in the kitchen area, pulling a vest over his bare chest. He glanced at her with tired eyes and an irritable expression that suggested he hadn't slept either. The room was warm and airless.

"You want something to drink?" he asked, reaching for the coffee pot.

Blake shut the door and stood motionless in front of it. "No thank you. This won't take long."

"What's so urgent that you had to get me out of bed?"

Blake stared at him, shell shocked.

"They're all dead," she said. "Only Tegen and Jack survived."

The colour drained from Campbell's face. His gaze drifted down to the bruising on Blake's neck. "What?"

They sat down on the sofas, facing each other. Blake told him about the terrible business in the cemetery. About Aidan

Trezise faking his own death, and how everyone except Griffin knew about it. That it was Aidan who had desecrated the church in Wheal Marow, who had broken into Judy Moon's house, and who had brutally murdered Faith Penrose.

"Ever since I set foot in Saltwater House, he must have been watching me come and go, following me home, using the family four-by-four to get around. I found animal skull masks inside the groundskeeper's cottage, along with some other seriously disturbing things. Aidan was deranged. A psychopath. It looks like he'd spent all his time in exile learning about the occult, obsessing over it in the same way Tegen obsesses over witchcraft. I didn't get a chance to ask her, but I wouldn't be shocked to learn that Aidan was the one who introduced her to it. But where he only wanted to cause harm, Tegen only ever wanted to do good."

"Jesus." Campbell stared at her in disbelief.

Blake continued. "Aidan and Abigail had been planning to murder their father ever since learning Abigail and Jack had been cut out of the will. When they found out there was no money left at all, they snapped." She paused and stared at the floor. "That's on me. If I hadn't told Abigail about the missing money, Griffin would still be alive. They all would."

Campbell was quiet, his hands clasped together on his knees. "Maybe. But for how much longer? It sounds like they were going to kill him anyway. Jesus, I can't believe that Aidan was alive all this time! Why would he fake his own death?" He leaned forward a little, peering into Blake's eyes. "What about the twins? Are they safe?"

With a heave of her shoulders, Blake revealed the one family secret that had ruled them all. Campbell's eyes grew wide with shock as he slumped back on the sofa.

"Jack and Tegen were still being held at the police station when I left. Social services were there, but I don't know how much they'll be able to do for them. They're both nearly eighteen. Adults. Who knows, Jack may even be eighteen already." She gently touched her swollen throat. It hurt to speak. "I suppose Violet and Saul Bodily might look out for them. But when this is all over, Saltwater House will be Tegen's cross to bear, and I have a feeling she'll be carrying it on her back for a long time."

"Poor Jack," Campbell said. "How do you come to terms with the fact your brother and sister are also your mother and father? That everything you knew was a lie?"

"Everyone knew Abigail and Aidan were Jack's parents, and everyone played their part in covering it up. Except Kerenza. She was in Oxford when Abigail became pregnant. When she returned to take care of the children after Genevieve's death, she honestly believed they were twins. But then she found out about Jack's parentage. I don't know how. Maybe she went looking in Mother Crow's cottage, too. But she must have felt so cheated, so betrayed, knowing that her own family was working hard to keep her in the dark." Blake stared at Campbell. "You were going to be her way out. Her chance to start over, free and in love. Until her wedding day."

"You know, don't you?" Campbell leaned forward on the sofa. "You know what happened to Kerenza."

She told him the truth. About Tegen's fatal mistake made in haste. About Abigail's decision to do nothing about it.

Campbell clenched his jaw. "Abigail killed her."

"I don't think she wanted Kerenza to die," Blake said. "She just wanted to ruin her day. Why should Kerenza get everything that Abigail ever wanted? That's what she told me. Now Abigail is dead, too. She felt remorse in the end. I think that's why she walked into the fire."

Tiredness pressed down on Blake's shoulders. She knew that if she leaned back on the sofa right now, she would close her eyes and sleep for twelve hours. But she couldn't. Not yet. Not here.

Campbell was staring at her. He was close to tears.

"Thank you, Blake. For finding out the truth. I'm sorry you had to go through hell to do it. And I'm sorry your friend is dead. Had I known Aidan was still alive and a homicidal maniac, I would never have hired you in the first place." He smiled sadly, then reached for his phone and tapped the screen. "I'm transferring the rest of your fee right now, and of course I'll recommend you to anyone needing an accomplished private investigator."

With the transfer made, Campbell placed his phone on the coffee table and stood up. Blake thanked him then followed him to the door. He opened it. But she wasn't quite ready to leave.

Campbell frowned. "Is there something else?"

"Actually there is," she said. "One more unanswered question. Who was blackmailing Griffin Trezise?"

"Of course. I'd completely forgotten," Campbell said. "I assume it was the Bodilys?"

"I thought so too, at first. But then the Bodilys don't seem like the kind of people who would know anything about offshore bank accounts. And unless they're award-winning actors their loyalty to the Trezise siblings seems genuine enough that I can't imagine they'd leave them with nothing."

Campbell shrugged and glanced at the open door. "I suppose, but some people can pull the wool over your eyes without you even knowing."

"True," said Blake. "But the Trezises cut themselves off from the world because their secrets were so terrible they couldn't risk letting them get out. Which means whoever was blackmailing Griffin Trezise had to be hiding within their inner circle, because no one else was allowed in."

"So one of the siblings was blackmailing their own father?" Campbell said.

"That was my second thought. But Jack didn't know the truth, and Tegen is, well, just a child. It makes no sense that it was Aidan and Abigail, not when they were already plotting their father's death so they could share their siblings' wealth."

Campbell's jaw dropped open. "Which leaves Kerenza."

Blake nodded. "Kerenza had found out that everyone had been lying to her. That she'd given up everything for her family only to be betrayed by them. Why would she want to share her fortune with her siblings when they'd not only committed incest and exploited her for their own gain, but also treated her like a fool? Why would she give them anything when she'd already given them years of her life?" She paused. "But that didn't make sense to me either, because everything I've learned about Kerenza tells me that she was good and kind, and she'd fallen in love and had a way out. Besides, whether she knew it or not, her father was going to leave the estate to her and Tegen anyway."

"But that's everyone," Campbell said, shaking his head. "So, are you saying Griffin Trezise blackmailed himself?"

"No," said Blake. She reached for the intercom and pressed the buzzer, unlocking the downstairs front door. "I'm saying you did."

There was a beat of silence. Campbell paled, then let out a peal of nervous laughter.

"Me?" he said. "That's preposterous!"

Blake smiled. "I thought so, too. Which is why I ran a background check on you and your predecessor. It turns out that, until his death, you used to work with him. And when he died you took over managing his clients. You must have noticed the discrepancies, little bits of money shaved off from all the various accounts, including the Trezise family's. You could have told the police about his theft, but you didn't. Because you saw an opportunity, one you could benefit from yourself."

Blake stepped towards him. Campbell backed away, his eyes fixed on hers.

"Your old colleague was a crook," she said. "But his little operation was already set up and running smoothly. It would have been easy to create your own offshore accounts and redirect the money. When you took over the accounts, you introduced yourself to the clients, face to face, which included a trip to Saltwater House. That's where you met Kerenza. She fell in love with you, and when she began to trust you, she told you her family's dirty little secrets. You comforted her, you told her you loved her, that you would take care of her and give her a chance at freedom. Except your greed got in the way. You saw another opportunity, to blackmail Griffin Trezise, anonymously of course, and threaten to expose the truth about Abigail, Aidan, and Jack. You've been draining the Trezise family fortune ever since."

Footsteps echoed on the stairwell. Campbell retreated further into the living room.

"That's quite the tall tale," he said, staring at the door. "And bloody ridiculous, if you ask me."

"Maybe. But there's no one else left who could have known. You tried to hide the truth from me about the Trezise family fortune. I kept asking you and you kept putting me off. But then Griffin told me about the blackmail, and suddenly you didn't have a choice anymore. But you still lied to me about when the blackmail started. And it was easy because Griffin was a drunk who didn't know what day it was half the time. You could have told me it started ten years ago, and he would have been none the wiser."

The footsteps were louder now, mingling with radio crackles and murmured voices. Campbell took another step back. Blake matched him with a step forward.

"You can stand there, telling more lies and smiling that smug little smile of yours," she said. "But it doesn't matter. Because as soon the police get hold of Griffin's financial records and your own, they'll be able to confirm the truth."

Four uniformed police officers appeared in the doorway and rushed in. They looked at Blake, then fixed their eyes on Campbell who was pressed against the window.

He whimpered and shook his head, then tried to open the window to escape. The officers rushed him. Two pinned him to the ground, while one read him his rights and another handcuffed his hands behind his back.

Another figure appeared from the stairwell. Detective Constable Rory Angove. He entered the flat and stood next to Blake, taking in the scene.

"Are you okay?" he asked.

She nodded. "I've been better."

Now on his feet, Campbell was escorted towards the door by two of the officers. He was crying and his eyes were glazed with fear.

Blake stepped in front of him. "Why did you hire me?" she asked. "Were you arrogant enough to think I wouldn't find out the truth? Or did you think a woman would easily be sucked in by your grief?"

Campbell choked on his tears.

"In spite of everything," he said, "I loved Kerenza. I didn't want to, but we can't help who we fall in love with. When she died, I had to know why. I had to know it wasn't because of what I'd done."

"Well, now you know," Blake said. "I hope your ego is satisfied."

The officers escorted Campbell out of his home, while two others stayed behind to search the place.

Blake stared at Rory, who was watching her closely.

"How did you know it was him?" he said.

She shrugged. "Educated guess. Besides, there was no one else left."

"What about evidence?"

"I'm sure you boys in blue will come up with something."

She turned to leave.

"Do you need a lift home?" Rory asked.

"No. My car's still back at the police station."

"Then I'll walk with you." There was something about him that seemed different to Blake. She didn't know what. Or if it was she who had in fact changed.

"Don't you need to be here, overseeing the search?"

Rory grinned. "It's not *my* case. I just wanted to check in on you."

Blake took one last look at the room. Her father's favourite saying echoed in her head: *Better to be rich with love than poor with money.*

She brushed past Rory, her elbow grazing his. "In that case, I'll let you buy me a coffee. But not from the station. That crap tastes like shit."

46

FAITH PENROSE'S funeral was held on a bitterly cold Friday morning. The small congregation kept their coats on despite the heating panels placed around the interior of the church. There were no relatives in attendance, even though Blake knew Faith had a brother somewhere, and nephews and nieces. Reverend Thompson, who was now fully recovered from her injury, gave a warm, emotional service that celebrated Faith's life and contributions to the community, without forgetting the tragedy and loss that she had endured.

Now in the church graveyard, which was covered in a light dusting of snow with more on the way, they all gathered around the six-foot hole in the ground as Faith's casket was gently lowered towards her final resting place. Blake stood with Kenver, who looked uncomfortable in his suit, and Judy, who had left the girls at home with Charlie, after deciding they'd already suffered enough trauma without subjecting them to a funeral. Rory Angove stood among the mourners on the other side of the grave, occasionally flicking glances in Blake's direction, while

Mary and Ed Hollow held hands and solemnly bowed their heads.

Reverend Thompson said a closing prayer, then a few of the townsfolk dropped flowers onto the casket below. Blake was frozen, a single red rose held gently in her hand. A deep sadness weighed her down, along with an inescapable feeling of guilt. She peered into the hole. Judy gave her a gentle squeeze.

"It's not your fault," she whispered

Blake turned to her. "Isn't it?"

"Of course not. Aidan Trezise did this. Not you."

"I was meant to see her two days before she died. I cancelled because of that damn family."

Judy gave her another squeeze.

The service ended and the mourners dispersed, quietly heading home or to work; Faith's will had specifically stated there was to be no wake. Even if there had been, Blake didn't think many would come, not when Faith Penrose would forever be associated with the horrific crimes of her serial killer ex-husband. It was cruel and unfair, a stab in the back to someone who had only ever shown Blake kindness, and continued to even in death.

In a final benevolent act, Faith had left Blake a generous sum of money in her will. It would come in useful now that Campbell Green's assets had been frozen and Blake's payment had been reversed.

Kenver pulled at his tie, loosening it then sucking in a dramatic gasp of air. He was paler than normal, which Blake didn't think was possible, and there was an unsettled look in his eyes. A thirst. There had been more drinking incidents lately. Blake was doing her best to help him. She supposed it was the least she could do, since she had been the one to put him in temptation's way.

"Hey," Judy said softly, nudging her arm. "What's on your mind?"

Blake shrugged. The small crowd had thinned, leaving them alone at the graveside. "Aidan told me that when he killed Faith, he saw gratitude in her eyes. Peace. Do you think he was telling the truth?"

"I doubt it," Judy said. "Who would be thankful for such a violent death?"

"Well, I hope he was right about seeing peace. Faith had suffered so much already."

Blake looked over at her parents, who lingered on the church path. Her father glanced in her direction then quickly looked away.

Judy pulled the folds of her coat around her neck and shivered. "How's the new place? You need help with decorating?"

"Kenver is coming over at the weekend to help. You're welcome to join."

Kenver stared at her, his teeth chattering. "I am? Since when?"

"Since I need to keep a closer eye on you."

He blew plumes of frozen breath into the air then muttered to himself.

Blake's eyes returned to the hole in the ground, and she was unable to peel them away.

"Have you heard any more about Tegen and Jack Trezise?" Judy asked.

"I talked to Violet Bodily a few days ago. The children are staying with them for now. Jack still isn't saying much, and

Tegen is struggling with nightmares. Violet is confident they'll be okay, eventually. I'm not so sure."

"Time heals all wounds," Kenver said.

Blake scoffed.

"It must be a step down from that big old mansion," he continued. "Living in a normal little house like the rest of us."

"True. But unlike the empty rooms of Saltwater House, the Bodilys' home will be filled with love, which is exactly what Tegen and Jack need right now."

"It's freezing," Judy said, rubbing her arms. "I'm going to the Honeybee for a hot chocolate. Are you coming?"

Blake's parents were still hovering, her father still glancing in her direction.

"You two go ahead. I'll be there in a minute."

She watched Judy and Kenver say hello to her parents, then exit the graveyard. When they were gone, she walked along the snow-covered path to where Ed and Mary were still waiting.

Mary pulled her in for a hug. "It was a lovely service, wasn't it, bird?"

Blake was silent, staring at the ground.

"You coming around for your tea later?"

"I can't. I need to get back to the office."

Mary frowned. Ed shifted uncomfortably beside her.

"Well, stop by in the week then. I miss you being around." She drew Blake in again and kissed her cheek, then shot a nervous glance at Ed. "I'll wait in the car."

Saying goodbye to Blake, she circled the church and disappeared out of sight.

Blake stood motionless, the red rose still clasped in her gloved hand. She peered up at her father, who had aged terribly in the last year and lost more weight than was healthy.

Ed stared back at her, but only for a moment.

"How's the new place?" he said. "Heard it's out in the sticks."

"It's not too far, just outside Falmouth," Blake said. "There's a nice view of the reservoir."

"Need any help fixing it up?"

"Kenver and Judy are on it. We'll be fine."

More quiet. More discomfort. Ed shoved his hands in his pockets and nodded at the open grave. "The vicar did a good job with the service."

"I suppose." Blake scuffed her foot through the snow, revealing the coarse gravel beneath. "So, you and Mum are back together, then?"

Her father nodded. "We're trying. To be honest, I never expected her to take me back."

"Then you're a damn fool," Blake said, the words coming out sharper than she'd intended.

Ed shrugged and looked away. An icy gust of wind sprayed them with loose snow from the gravestones.

He turned back to her. "Blake, I —"

Blake held up a hand.

"Listen," she said. "The last year has been horrendous. For both of us. And I'm still struggling with what you did and all the lies you told. If I'm honest, I don't know if I'll ever get over it. Or if I can ever forgive you."

"Right. I see."

She glanced at him, saw the defeat in his eyes. The despair. She heaved her shoulders and let out a trembling breath. "But I'm willing to try."

Her father seemed to freeze. His eyes met hers, and they were filled with tears.

"I'm not saying it will be easy. Or it will happen overnight, or that things will ever be the same again. But I'm tired of people suffering. Of losing people I care about. So let's just take one day at a time. And if that's too much, we'll slow it down even further."

Ed turned away to wipe his eyes. When he looked back, he said, "Whatever it takes, bird. Whatever it takes."

They stood in more silence, the snow swirling around them. Blake felt the urge to embrace her father but found that she couldn't. Not yet. She could tell he felt the same.

"You better go," she said. "Mum will be getting cold."

Ed nodded. "Make sure you come over one day this week, or she'll be disappointed."

"I will."

She watched her father leave. She was alone now, a dark smudge on a blanket of white. Walking slowly back to the open grave, Blake peered inside. She held out the red rose above the chasm for a few moments, then let it slip from her fingers. It sailed through the air to land gently among the other flowers that had been laid to rest with Faith Penrose.

Her eyes shifted to the grave on the left, where Demelza's recovered remains had been buried last year. Now mother and daughter lay side by side, finally reunited.

"I'm sorry," Blake whispered. "I wish you'd both had easier lives. Maybe death will be better."

Pulling her coat around her body, she walked away from the dead, through the snow and out of the churchyard, heading into town and towards the living.

ACKNOWLEDGEMENTS

Thank you to my editor, Natasha Vickery-Orme; Isabel Doverty and Marty Confray for help with proofreading; Patrick O'Donnel and *Cops and Writers*; and the Museum of Witchcraft and Magic in Boscastle, Cornwall—I highly recommend a visit if you're at all interested in the history of the occult.

Thank you to my family and friends, with special thanks to Xander for all your encouragement and support; and to my fantastic readers, including my Read & Review team.

As well as visiting the Museum of Witchcraft and Magic, I used a number of books to help with my research on all things occult. These included: *A New History of Witchcraft* by Jeffrey B. Russell & Brooks Alexander, *Between the Realms: Cornish Myth & Magic* by Cheryl Straffon, and *Traditional Witchcraft: A Cornish Book of Ways* by Gemma Gary. As always, any factual errors made in *Down in the Blood* are my own.